"EMILY BRIGHTWELL . . . knows how to write a mystery that will keep you under its spell."
                                                          —*Rendezvous*

INSPECTOR WITHERSPOON ALWAYS TRIUMPHS . . . HOW DOES HE DO IT?

Even the inspector himself doesn't know—because his secret weapon is as ladylike as she is clever. She's Mrs. Jeffries—the determined, delightful detective who stars in this unique Victorian mystery series! Be sure to read them all . . .

The Inspector and Mrs. Jeffries
A doctor is found dead in his own office—and Mrs. Jeffries must scour the premises to find the prescription for murder!

Mrs. Jeffries Dusts for Clues
One case is closed and another is opened when the inspector finds a missing brooch—pinned to a dead woman's gown. But Mrs. Jeffries never cleans a room without dusting under the bed—and never gives up on a case before every loose end is tightly tied . . .

Continued on next page . . .

The Ghost and Mrs. Jeffries
Death is unpredictable . . . but the murder of Mrs. Hodges
was foreseen at a spooky séance. The practical-minded housekeeper may not be able to see the future—but she can look
into the past and put things in order to solve this haunting
crime!

Mrs. Jeffries Takes Stock
A businessman has been murdered—and it could be because
he cheated his stockholders. The housekeeper's interest is
piqued . . . and when it comes to catching killers, the smart
money's on Mrs. Jeffries!

Mrs. Jeffries on the Ball
A festive jubilee ball turns into a fatal affair—and Mrs. Jeffries must find the guilty party . . .

MRS. JEFFRIES
TAKES THE STAGE

Emily Brightwell

BERKLEY PRIME CRIME, NEW YORK

To a wonderful friend and a wonderful writer, Maureen Child

MRS. JEFFRIES TAKES THE STAGE

A Berkley Prime Crime Book / published by arrangement with the author

PRINTING HISTORY
Berkley Prime Crime edition / March 1997

The Putnam Berkley World Wide Web site address is
http://www.berkley.com/berkley

ISBN: 0-425-15724-5

Berkley Prime Crime Books are published
by The Berkley Publishing Group,
200 Madison Avenue, New York, NY 10016.
The name BERKLEY PRIME CRIME and the BERKLEY PRIME CRIME
design are trademarks belonging to Berkley Publishing Corporation.

PRINTED IN THE UNITED STATES OF AMERICA

10 9 8 7 6 5 4 3 2 1

MRS. JEFFRIES
TAKES THE STAGE

CHAPTER 1

———◦◦◦———

"What's that blackguard doing here?" Albert Parks muttered under his breath as he watched the small man in elegant black evening dress march down the center aisle of the Hayden Theatre.

Parks's heartbeat raced, beads of sweat popped out on his forehead and his hands started to shake. He dropped the velvet curtain, letting the material close so he wouldn't have to look at that hated face. What in the name of God was he going to do? The bastard wasn't even supposed to be in England. The last Parks had heard, Hinchley was in New York savaging careers and giving the theatre people of London a well-earned rest from his vicious pen.

Now oblivious to the hustle and bustle going on around and behind him on the stage, Parks peeked through the curtain again. He spotted the critic taking a seat in the third row center. Damn. His eyes hadn't been playing tricks on him. It was Hinchley all right.

"Mr. Parks," the wardrobe mistress called from the

back of the stage. "Mr. Swinton wants a word with you before the show starts."

Parks nodded dully and stepped away from the side curtain. "All right, Agnes. Tell him I'll be right there."

He wondered if Tally Drummond still kept a bottle of whiskey in the bottom of the prop box. With Hinchley here, they'd probably all need a drink by the end of the evening.

Trevor Remington, the leading man, saw Albert Parks wander off the stage. Parks's shoulders were slumped and his face was pale. Remington, always curious, dashed over to the spot Parks had just vacated and inched the curtain apart. The house was full. Remington couldn't see an empty seat, so what was wrong with dear old Albert? Fellow was a bit on the high strung side, but then again, most good directors were, Remington thought.

He started to step back when a man in the third row suddenly stood up. Remington's breath left him in a rush, his ears rang and he felt his face flush with remembered shame. What was he doing here? Remington leapt back from the curtain so fast he almost tripped over his feet. Dear God in heaven, what was he going to do? Ogden Hinchley was in the audience. Ogden-the-ugly wasn't in America; he was sitting right out front! Swearing softly, Remington stalked off the stage, brushing rudely past Edmund Delaney without so much as a word.

Edmund Delaney watched the actor stomp towards the back of the theatre. Must have a bad case of opening-night nerves, Delaney thought, then dismissed the man in favor of curiosity. He stepped up to the curtain on stage left, pulled it apart and peeked out. He smiled. Not an empty seat in the house. Quickly, he scanned the first few rows, wondering which critics had bothered to come. He hoped the *Gazette* and the *Strand* were here. Both papers were quite sympathetic to new playwrights. Then he spotted the man in the third row. Delaney stared hard for a few moments, hoping his eyes were playing tricks on him. But they weren't. The devil. In the flesh. Delaney's hands clenched into fists, a red mist of rage floated in front of his face and for a brief moment, he thought he might be sick.

"Five minutes, everyone." Delaney heard Eddie Garvey, the stage manager, call the warning.

Delaney, his face set like a stone, turned and walked stiffly off the stage without so much as a glance at the stage manager or the wardrobe mistress. He was too sunk in his own misery to notice anyone.

"Well, what's got into him?" Garvey asked. But Agnes had already hustled off to make sure the first scene changes were ready, so he ended up talking to himself.

"What's got into who?" Willard Swinton, the owner of the Hayden Theatre, said from behind Garvey.

"Mr. Delaney." Garvey nodded toward the curtain. "He was having a peek at the house and then he walked off like he'd seen a ghost."

Swinton, a balding man with a huge mustache and an infectious grin, laughed. "He probably saw one of his former mistresses in the front row. No doubt that would give a man pause." Swinton wandered over to the curtain, eased it apart and looked out. "I wonder which of his former lovelies has turned up to torment the poor man . . ." His voice trailed off as he saw a familiar figure sitting in the third row. "Blast and thunder," he cursed softly under his breath.

"What'd you say, Mr. Swinton?" Garvey asked curiously. "Who's out there?"

Swinton quickly dropped the curtain and leapt back. "No one," he said hastily. "No one at all. Go on, Garvey,

get about your business. We've a play to put on and I
don't want any mistakes tonight.''

''Yes, sir.'' Garvey hustled off. But he wondered just
who was sitting out front. This was the fourth person now
who'd looked like they'd seen the devil himself out front.
The director, the playwright, the leading man and now
Mr. Swinton had turned pale as curdled milk when they'd
peeked through that curtain. Eddie Garvey decided he'd
take a gander himself as soon as he got Mr. Swinton out
of his way.

''What time's the inspector's train due in?'' asked Wiggins, the footman. He settled himself in his usual spot at
the kitchen table and reached for one of the apple turnovers Mrs. Goodge had baked early that morning. Wiggins,
with his round, innocent face, fair skin and chestnut
brown hair that no amount of pomade could keep plas-
tered to his head, was the youngest in the household of
Inspector Gerald Witherspoon of Scotland Yard.

''Half eight,'' Smythe, the coachman, answered. ''But
he said he'd take a hansom home. He doesn't want me to
bother gettin' the carriage out to collect him from the
station.''

Smythe was a big, muscular man with dark hair, heavy,
almost brutal features and brown eyes that generally twinkled with good humor. Unless, of course, he was annoyed,
as he was now. He turned his head and frowned at Betsy,
the pretty, blonde maid. The lass could get his dander up
quicker than anyone, but by the same token, one smile
from her could brighten his whole day.

But Betsy wasn't in the least intimidated by the coachman's glare. She knew him too well ever to be afraid of
him.

''It's no good you giving me those dark looks,'' she

said tartly. "My mind's made up. Tomorrow I'm going to Whitechapel whether you or anyone else likes it."

"Then I'm goin' with you," Smythe shot back. "I'll not have you over there on your own. It's too ruddy dangerous."

"That woman was murdered in the middle of the night," Betsy said irritably. The last thing she wanted was Smythe tagging along with her. Not that she didn't like his company—she did. Lately they'd been keeping quite a bit of company together. But this time, she had a special errand to do. She didn't want to be explaining herself to anyone else from the household. "I'm going to be there in broad daylight. Besides, murders happen all the time in the East End. I don't know why everyone's makin' such a fuss over this one."

"'Cause this one's different," Wiggins chimed in. "This lady were out and out butchered. I know, I over-'eard Constable Barnes talkin' to Constable Griffith when they brought the inspector's reports round this mornin'." He was glad he'd had the good sense to dally about the hall when the constables had come by that morning. You could pick up quite a bit of news if you kept yourself quiet and took plenty of time polishing a banister.

"What'd he say?" Mrs. Goodge, the cook, asked eagerly.

Wiggins's eyes grew as big as egg yolks. "Constable Barnes 'eard that the constable that found that woman's body was so sickened 'e lost his stomach. And it's not just one person that's been done in, accordin' to today's *Penny Illustrated*. The police think there might 'ave been two more ladies killed as well."

"Two others?" Mrs. Goodge exclaimed. "What nonsense."

"It's what was in the paper," Wiggins argued.

''Since when have you taken to reading that rubbish?''
the cook scoffed. ''Radical nonsense, if you ask me. And
where did you get a copy? We don't have it here.''

''I buy it,'' Wiggins replied. ''It's not radical, it just
prints the truth. Not like the borin' ole *Times*. They don't
even 'ave pictures.''

''I like the *Illustrated* too,'' Betsy said hastily. She'd
much rather talk about newspapers than her proposed trip
to the East End. ''The drawings are ever so clever.''

''Goin' over to Whitechapel isn't bein' very clever,''
Smythe snapped. He wasn't about to be sidetracked by a
discussion of the literary merits of London's daily newspapers. He narrowed his eyes and gave Betsy his most
intimidating frown. It had no effect whatsoever.

''You got an itch on your face,'' Betsy asked bluntly,
''or are you just glaring at me?''

For a few moments, they had a silent contest of wills.
Smythe capitulated first. Though he was twice her size
and outweighed her by two stone, he knew he was help-
less against that stubborn set to her chin and that determined glint in her blue eyes.

''You're daft, girl.'' Smythe slumped back in his seat
and looked at the woman sitting at the head of the table.
Keeping Betsy safe was worth appealing to a higher authority. The housekeeper. ''You tell her, Mrs. Jeffries.
Tell her it's not safe to be runnin' about that part of London now.''

Hepzibah Jeffries, a plump, middle-aged woman with
dark auburn hair liberally streaked with gray, a kind face
and sharp eyes that seemed to see everything, only smiled.
She'd deliberately stayed out of this particular debate.
Though she could see Smythe's point, she rather thought
he was being a bit overprotective. Betsy had a right to
both her privacy and her time. ''It is Betsy's day out,

Smythe," she said gently. "If she wishes to go to White-chapel, it really isn't any of my concern. Though I do understand your trepidation and to some extent, I share it. This murder was particularly brutal. But I'm sure Betsy will be very careful." She smiled at the maid. "Won't you?"

"Of course I'll be careful. I'm not stupid. I know there's a killer about," Betsy replied eagerly. "I'll not be gone long. Just a couple of hours in the morning. Do you think the inspector will get that awful murder case?"

"I sincerely hope not," Mrs. Jeffries said soberly.

"But why don't you want him to get it?" Mrs. Goodge exclaimed. "We haven't had us a murder in months. I mean, it's not a very nice murder, but still, it's better than just sitting here doing nothing."

Mrs. Jeffries tapped her finger against the handle of the tea cup. She needed to explain things carefully. It wouldn't do to have the others thinking she didn't believe the inspector was capable of solving the crime.

"I have an awful feeling about this one," Mrs. Jeffries replied slowly. "It's going to be very political. The radicals won't hesitate to use the poor Nicholls woman's murder for their own purposes. They want to call public attention to the conditions in the East End and this murder is a good way of doing that."

"And about time, too," Betsy muttered.

"I agree," Mrs. Jeffries said quickly. "It's shocking the way the government has conveniently ignored the plight of those poor unfortunates living in abject poverty and misery."

"Then 'ow come you don't want the inspector to get this one?" Wiggins asked. "A man as kindhearted as our inspector would do his best to see this poor lady's killer brought to justice."

To give herself a moment to think of exactly how to say what she thought ought to be said, Mrs. Jeffries reached for her teacup and took a sip. "Please don't misunderstand. You're right, Wiggins, Inspector Witherspoon would do his best. But I've a feeling in this case, it wouldn't be enough. He is a wonderful man and an excellent detective, but in many ways, he's very, very naive."

"Innocent like," Smythe added with a nod. He understood what the housekeeper was saying.

"This murder, with the radical press following it and using it, is going to be mired in politics from top to bottom," Mrs. Jeffries continued. "I'd hate to see the inspector subjected to that. He's far too honorable a person to know how to protect himself in those kinds of situations. They always get terribly complicated. Furthermore, it's not the kind of case he'd be much good at, I'm afraid."

"Why not?" Betsy demanded. "He solved our last case all on his own." That was still a sore point with the staff, but in all honesty, she had to give credit where credit was due.

Mrs. Jeffries held up her hand. "Don't mistake my meaning, Betsy. But frankly, I'll be surprised if anyone solves this murder. There was something so savage, so awful about it, that I rather suspect the murderer is more like a mad dog than a human being. I've a feeling there won't be any clues or any connections or threads for the police to follow. It was an act of madness as well as murder." She shivered. "The inspector is well out of this one. It's fortunate that he had to pay a duty visit to his cousin. Otherwise, considering his record of success at the Yard, no doubt he'd have been dragged into it."

"I don't reckon any of us could suss this one out,"

Wiggins said. "None of us would 'ave the stomach for it."

"Speak for yourself," Betsy said. "I'd like to get my hands on the animal that did it."

"That's why I don't want you anywhere near Whitechapel," Smythe exclaimed. "You don't need to be pokin' into this one, girl. It's too dangerous."

"I'm not goin' to be pokin' into anything," she snapped. "I've got a personal errand. But that don't mean I'd lose my stomach for catching the killer. Just because the Nicholls woman was a prostitute don't mean she doesn't deserve justice."

"No one said that," Mrs. Jeffries said softly. "Of course she deserves justice. But Smythe is correct. Whoever killed that woman is dangerous. Very dangerous. I hope none of us gets involved. Something like this could scar one for life."

"Seems to me that we're not likely to get involved in any murder." Mrs. Goodge snorted delicately. "Not with the way the inspector was carrying on before he left to visit that wretched cousin of his."

Everyone stared at the cook in shocked silence. She'd said what all the others had been thinking, but hadn't wanted to actually say.

Mrs. Goodge folded her arms across her ample bosom. "Well, I'm right, aren't I? Just because Inspector Witherspoon solved that last case all on his own, he's been strutting about like the cock of the walk. It's not like him. Maybe the next time there's a murder, I'll just not help at all. Then see how he likes it."

Mrs. Jeffries's heart sank. This situation had been brewing since June. Since Gerald Witherspoon had solved their last murder completely on his own. Oh, they'd helped as they always did. But they'd been completely wrong. They hadn't even come close to figuring out who the real killer was. "I wouldn't say he's been strutting about," she said. "But I will admit he's been quite proud of himself and justifiably so."

"I know, I know." The cook waved her arms impatiently. "But if I have to listen to him go on and on about how he solved the whole thing from one little clue . . ." She broke off and sighed. "Well, it's enough to drive a person mad."

"He does rather go on about it," Betsy agreed.

"Of course he does," Mrs. Jeffries said. "He's very proud of that particular case. But it's not as if he realizes what he's doing. Remember, the inspector has no idea we've ever helped out on his investigations. So it isn't as if he's . . ."

"Lording it over us," Wiggins suggested. "I read that in a book. Good, huh?"

"Excellent, Wiggins." Mrs. Jeffries always took the time to encourage education. But she also wanted to get this problem aired out too. "Furthermore," she continued, "the inspector's behaviour hasn't been objectionable." She wasn't so sure that was a correct assessment at all. There had been several times in the weeks following their last case in which she'd definitely heard a very patronizing tone in his voice when she and the inspector were having one of their chats over a glass of sherry. But really, she mustn't be silly about it. Inspector Gerald Witherspoon was the best of men. Truly one of nature's gentlemen.

He'd spent years in the Records room at the Yard. It was only after he had inherited this house and a fortune from his late Aunt Euphemia that his skills as a detective had really blossomed. Of course the fact that he'd also hired Mrs. Jeffries had much to do with that blossoming.

As a policeman's widow, Mrs. Jeffries had a keen interest in justice. She'd taken one look at the others in the household of Upper Edmonton Gardens and realized that all of them were intelligent, loyal and utterly dedicated to Gerald Witherspoon. Naturally, they'd taken to helping him surreptitiously with his cases. They took great pains not to let him know they were helping him.

"He's not been objectionable," Betsy agreed, "but I agree with Mrs. Goodge—he has been a bit full of himself. I'm not so sure I want to help him anymore either. Not after all those nasty things he said about the idea of women police constables."

"He were only sayin' he didn't think it was a safe thing for a woman to be doin'." Smythe defended his employer. "Catchin' killers is dangerous work. He's a gentleman, is the inspector, wouldn't want to see a woman in 'arms way, that's all."

"He was full of himself," Mrs. Goodge said firmly. "And whether he knows it or not, he needs us. But if he don't change his attitude a bit, the next time round, I just might tend to my cookin' and leave him to it."

Two days later, Inspector Gerald Witherspoon came down the stairs and into the dining room. "Good morning, Mrs. Jeffries," he said brightly. "Is breakfast ready yet? I'm in a bit of a rush this morning."

Mrs. Jeffries put the pot of tea she'd just brought up from the kitchen on the table. "Betsy's just bringing it, sir. Shall I pour your tea?"

"Thank you." He sat down and laid his serviette on his lap. "That would be most kind."

As she poured his tea, she could feel him watching her expectantly. Silently, Mrs. Jeffries sighed. She knew he wanted her to ask why he was in a rush this morning. But before she could get the question formed, Betsy, carrying a covered silver tray, came in with his breakfast.

"Thank you, Betsy," Witherspoon said. "It's very good of you to be so prompt; I'm in a bit of a hurry this morning."

"Something interesting going on at the Yard?" Mrs. Jeffries asked. She glanced at Betsy, who rolled her eyes heavenward. The staff already knew what was going on at the Yard. The inspector had told them at least a dozen times.

"Why, yes, now that you ask." Witherspoon picked up his fork. "Ever since I solved that last murder, the Chief Inspector has kept me dreadfully busy. I've another one of those lectures to give this morning. You know what I mean, a group of police constables get bundled in and I tell them about my methods."

"Do you tell 'em about your inner voice, sir?" Betsy asked, her voice seemingly innocent.

Mrs. Jeffries gave her a sharp look. But Witherspoon hadn't heard the laughter in the girl's tone.

"Well, not precisely," the inspector said. "That's a difficult idea to get across."

"Do you tell them about . . ." She broke off as they heard the pounding of the brass knocker. Betsy smiled apologetically and went to answer the front door.

They heard voices in the hall, and a moment later Betsy came back followed by a tall, gray-haired man in a police constable's uniform. "Constable Barnes is here to see you, sir," she announced.

"Good morning, Inspector. Mrs. Jeffries." Barnes smiled and took off his helmet. "Sorry to interrupt your breakfast, sir."

"That's quite all right," Witherspoon said. "Do have a seat. Have you eaten?"

"I've had breakfast, sir." Barnes pulled out the chair next to him and sat down. "But I wouldn't say no to a cup of tea."

"I'm already pouring it, Constable." Mrs. Jeffries handed him a cup.

"Ta." Barnes's craggy face relaxed a little as he took a long, slow sip. Then he put the cup down. "There's been a murder, sir."

Betsy, who'd been on her way toward the door, stopped dead.

Mrs. Jeffries sat down at the end of the table.

"Oh, dear," Witherspoon replied. "Not another one of those poor women in Whitechapel, I hope."

"No, sir. Nothing as grisly as that." He grimaced. "But bad enough. This one's a man. They found him floating in the Regents Canal late last night. Fully dressed, too. It looked like an accidental drowning, except that Dr. Bosworth happened to be at the mortuary when they brought the body in. Sharp fellow, that Bosworth. He noticed there was lavender soap under the victim's fingernails."

"Lavender soap?" Witherspoon looked puzzled.

"Yes, sir." Barnes took another sip of tea. "That got the doctor curious so he had a good look at the man. There's indications he didn't drown in the canal at all. Bosworth thinks his head was held under in a bathtub. There's marks around the fellow's ankles."

"Marks around the ankles?" the inspector repeated. "Gracious, how could that indicate someone had drowned in a bathtub?"

As puzzled as the inspector, Barnes shrugged. "I don't know, sir. Dr. Bosworth said he'd explain it to you when you get to the mortuary."

"Perhaps the marks were caused by the fall into the

canal?'' Witherspoon suggested. He really didn't believe in going about looking for a murderer when there was a chance that the man's death had been accidental.

"Bosworth doesn't think so."

Witherspoon tapped his fingers against the tablecloth. He had a great deal of respect for Dr. Bosworth's opinion. "Has the victim been identified?"

"That was the easy part, sir." Barnes grinned. "Dr. Potter identified him."

"Potter?" Witherspoon's eyebrows rose. "But I thought you said that young Dr. Bosworth examined the corpse."

"He did." Barnes chuckled. "But you know what an old busybody Potter is. He stuck his nose in to see what Bosworth was up to. Seems the victim was one of Potter's acquaintances. Fellow was a theatre critic. According to Potter, he's quite well known. Name of Hinchley, sir. Ogden Hinchley."

"How dreadful," Witherspoon murmured.

"Gave Potter a bit of shock, sir. Especially as Hinchley was supposed to be out of the country, not dead and floating in the Regents Canal."

"Did Bosworth have an estimate on how long the body's been in the canal?"

"He said he'd know better after he finished the post-mortem, but his best guess is about forty-eight hours."

"How can he tell?" Betsy asked. "Oh, excuse me, sir." She smiled apologetically at her employer. "It's just, you know how we all like hearin' about your cases."

"That's quite all right, Betsy." Witherspoon smiled kindly at the girl. He was such a lucky man; his staff was so very devoted. "I'm curious myself."

Barnes picked up his helmet. "I'm not sure. Potter asked the same thing. Bosworth said somethin' about water temperature and fluid in the lungs, sir, and some new tests he'd read about. I really couldn't follow it all that well. Frankly, I don't think old Potter could either, but he pretended he knew what Bosworth was talkin' about. Didn't seem to believe it though; you know how Potter is, scoffs at anything he don't understand.'' He grinned again. ''Finally, after they'd argued for a few minutes, Potter stomped off in a huff. I told Dr. Bosworth to go ahead and do whatever tests he needed to do. I hope that's all right, sir?''

''Of course it is,'' Witherspoon said. ''Even if Dr. Bosworth's ideas aren't readily accepted by the courts or the medical establishment, I've found his insights to be quite useful in the past. If he thinks it's approximately forty-eight hours since the man was killed . . .'' He broke off and frowned in concentration. ''That would make it . . .''

''Saturday night, sir,'' Mrs. Jeffries finished.

''Right. Was he reported missing from his home?'' Witherspoon asked Barnes.

''I don't know, sir. There hasn't been much time to check. Dr. Bosworth had a word with the Chief Inspector and he sent me along here to fetch you.''

''So I'm getting this one,'' Witherspoon said thoughtfully.

''Probably, sir. If it turns out that Bosworth is right and Hinchley's death wasn't an accident. The Chief didn't say much, only to fetch you along to the hospital mortuary and get the inquiry started. Just between you and me, sir, with the papers full of that awful murder in Whitechapel, I expect the Chief isn't taking any chances. He'll want an investigation whether Hinchley was really murdered or not.''

''Do we have an address for the victim?'' Witherspoon asked.

Barnes dug his notebook out of his pocket and flipped it open. "Number fourteen, Avenue Road. St. John's Wood."

The inspector absently popped a bit of toast into his mouth.

"I haven't been round there, sir," Barnes continued. "I came here straight away."

"Not to worry, Constable. We'll call round Mr. Hinchley's residence as soon as we've been to the mortuary. Which hospital is it?"

"St. Thomas's, sir. That's why Bosworth was on hand."

Witherspoon tossed down his serviette and stood up. "Right then. Let's get cracking."

"Will you be home for lunch, sir?" Mrs. Jeffries asked.

"No, I don't think so. If young Dr. Bosworth is correct, we've a murder to solve."

Mrs. Jeffries walked her employer and Barnes to the door. As they reached the front door, she glanced back down the hall and saw Betsy dart out of the dining room, walk casually to the top of the back stairs and then disappear in the blink of an eye. Good girl, the housekeeper thought. She had no doubt that Betsy had gone to tell the others. They had a murder to solve. Thank goodness.

And this time, she was going to make very sure that they solved it properly.

"Good day, Mrs. Jeffries," Witherspoon called over his shoulder as he closed the front door. "Don't be alarmed if I'm home later than usual."

"Yes, sir. I'll have Mrs. Goodge do a cold supper, sir." She smiled broadly. With any luck, he wouldn't be home for hours.

She closed the door, took a deep breath and then ran for the back stairs. Coming into the kitchen she wasn't surprised to see Mrs. Goodge hurriedly clearing up the last of the breakfast dishes and Betsy heading for the back door.

"I'm just off to get Smythe," Betsy said. "He's at Howard's playing about with those ruddy horses. I've sent Wiggins for Luty Belle and Hatchet. I hope that's all right."

"That's fine, Betsy," Mrs. Jeffries replied. "I'll help Mrs. Goodge clear up, and by the time everyone's returned we'll have tea ready. But do hurry."

The two women worked quickly and efficiently. By the time they'd washed up and brewed a large pot of tea, Smythe and Betsy were back.

"Betsy says we've got a murder," the coachman said.

"I said we *might* have one," the maid replied with a grin. She looked at the housekeeper. "How much longer do you think the others will be?"

"Not long now," Mrs. Jeffries replied. She was glad to see that Smythe and Betsy seemed to be speaking civilly. Ever since the girl's mysterious errand to the East End they hadn't been comfortable with one another. Mrs. Jeffries was fairly certain that the coachman wasn't annoyed that Betsy had disobeyed him. Smythe wasn't stupid enough to think that just because he was paying court to the maid, his word was law. Rather, she thought Smythe was hurt because Betsy hadn't confided in him. Now that they had a murder to solve, perhaps the two of them could iron out their difficulties. If, indeed, Dr. Bosworth was correct and they did have a homicide and not a case of accidental drowning.

"I suppose we have to wait for them," Betsy said. "But perhaps . . ."

"No buts, Betsy," Mrs. Goodge said firmly. "We'll wait. It wouldn't be fair to start without them."

"You're right." Betsy laughed. "I'd be annoyed if you started without me."

From outside the back door, Mrs. Jeffries heard the sound of a carriage pulling up. "Let's get the tea poured, Mrs. Goodge," she said. "I think I hear them now."

A few moments later Wiggins came into the kitchen, followed by two others. "Good thing I got there when I did," he announced as he hurried to take his usual seat at the kitchen table. "They was fixin' to go out."

"Oh, dear." Mrs. Jeffries smiled apologetically at the newcomers. "I do hope our summons didn't interrupt something important."

Luty Belle Crookshank and her butler, Hatchet, had helped on several of the inspector's cases. They would have been most put out if they weren't immediately summoned when a murder was afoot. Co-conspirators, they were trustworthy, intelligent and extremely well connected.

Luty Belle, an elderly American woman, waved her parasol impatiently. "Don't be silly, Hepzibah," she said, using the housekeeper's given name. "Nothin's as important as our investigatin'."

Luty was dressed, as usual, in an outrageously bright day dress of buttercup yellow. A matching yellow hat decorated with plumes, lace and brilliant blue peacock feathers sat at a jaunty angle on her white hair. Beneath the wispy vail, her dark brown eyes glowed with enthusiasm. The wealthy widow of a self-made English millionaire, Luty had plenty of time on her hands and liked nothing better than spending it catching killers.

"Please don't concern yourself," Hatchet, Luty's tall, white-haired butler said. "We were only going for a drive. Madam was bored."

"Good. Let's get started then." Mrs. Jeffries took her place at the table.

"Who's the victim?" Hatchet asked. He sat his black top hat down on the empty chair next to him.

"A man named Ogden Hinchley . . ."

"The theatre critic?" Wiggins exclaimed.

Everyone turned to gape at him.

"How'd you know he was a critic?" Betsy asked.

"Gracious, Wiggins, you do surprise one," Mrs. Jeffries said.

"I like to read," Wiggins said, somewhat defensively. "And he's famous. I've read some of his reviews in the papers. Funny, but nasty, too. Says the most awful things about people when 'e don't like a play."

"That's very good, Wiggins." Mrs. Jeffries smiled proudly at the footman. "How clever of you to recognize the name. Obviously, then, if he's as nasty in print as you say he is, he probably has plenty of enemies."

"How was he killed?" Smythe asked.

"I'll tell you everything I know." Mrs. Jeffries launched into the tale. "Therefore, I expect the first place to start is where we usually do, with the victim."

Mrs. Goodge cleared her throat. "Excuse me, Mrs. Jeffries. But that's what we did the last time and look what happened then."

"The inspector solved it!" Betsy cried.

"We was completely wrong on that one," Smythe muttered.

"Perhaps it would be best to take a different approach this time," Hatchet suggested.

"Fiddlesticks," Luty cried. "What's wrong with you people? Just because the inspector got lucky the last time don't mean our methods are wrong. Seems to me you all are forgettin' all them other cases we solved."

"Thank you, Luty," Mrs. Jeffries said primly. "I couldn't have said it better myself."

"I still think we ought to do like 'atchet says and try something different," Wiggins muttered. "It couldn't 'urt."

"No one's stoppin' ya, boy," Luty said tartly. "But I'm goin' to do what I always do. One piddly loss out of a whole bunch of wins ain't goin' to dampen my spirits. Anyway, enough of this chest bleatin'. Let's get on with it. We've got us a killer to catch." She smiled eagerly at Mrs. Jeffries. "Well, come on, Hepzibah, time's a wastin'. Where do we start? What do you want us to do?"

Mrs. Jeffries thought for a moment. "Do you have any connections in the theatre?"

"I've gone to a lot of plays." Luty frowned. "But I don't really know any actors or people like that."

"I do," Hatchet said quickly. "I've several acquaintances who have some connection to the thespian world. Should I start making inquiries of them?"

"Who the dickens do you know?" Luty asked, irritated that her blasted butler had the jump on her.

Mrs. Jeffries hurried to nip any incipient rivalry between these two in the bud before it had a chance to flower. "That's a wonderful idea, Hatchet. Luty, dear, if you wouldn't mind, I'd like you to begin making inquiries about Hinchley's financial situation. You've more sources in the financial community than the rest of us."

"Humph," she snorted. "Hatchet gets to talk to actors and interestin' people and I get to talk to bankers. It ain't fair, but I'll do it." For good measure, she shot her butler a glare. But he only grinned wickedly in response.

Dismissing Luty's good-natured grumbling, Mrs. Jeffries turned to Betsy. "You know what to do, don't you?"

"I'll get right to it. If I'm lucky, maybe I'll be able to

get round to Hinchley's neighborhood before the Inspector does. It'd be nice to get the jump on him.''

"Take care the police don't see you," Mrs. Jeffries warned. Betsy would do as she always did when they were starting an investigation. She'd talk to all the tradespeople and shopkeepers and learn as much as she could about the victim's household.

"I'll do the hansoms and the pubs," Smythe said. "Maybe I'll get lucky and find out who came and went on Saturday night."

"Excellent, Smythe." Mrs. Jeffries nodded in satisfaction. They were falling back into their old routine very nicely.

"I'll get round there and see if I can find a servant," Wiggins said. "But I'll be careful, Mrs. Jeffries. Fred and I'll lie low until we sees that the inspector and the rest of the constables is gone."

"I have no doubt you will, Wiggins." She glanced down at the black and brown mongrel dog lying by the footman's chair. "If you take Fred with you, make sure he doesn't see the inspector." Fred, hearing his name, raised his head and thumped his tail on the floor.

"The last thing we need is for the inspector to catch us," Mrs. Jeffries continued. She glanced at the cook. "You know what to do."

The cook nodded. She had a veritable army of people she called upon when they were investigating a murder. Without ever leaving her kitchen Mrs. Goodge used her very own, very sophisticated network of street boys, fruit vendors, chimney sweeps, delivery people and former acquaintances to suss out every morsel of gossip about the victim.

Gossip, Mrs. Jeffries had always found, was immensely useful in a murder investigation.

CHAPTER 2

Inspector Witherspoon hated mortuaries. He hated looking at dead bodies too. But as it was an integral part of his job, he did it without complaint. He stared at the corpse lying beneath the gray sheet on the wooden table and braced himself. "Right, Dr. Bosworth. We might as well get on with it."

Dr. Bosworth, a tall young man with red hair and an earnest, intelligent face, gazed at the inspector sympathetically. "He's not as bad as many victims, Inspector. By my estimation, he'd only been in the canal a couple of days, not long enough for too much decomposition to have set in."

Witherspoon smiled weakly, reminded himself of his duty and stepped closer to the table.

"Actually, the water in the canal was quite cold for this time of year," Bosworth continued chattily. "Kept the fellow very well preserved, especially as he hadn't sunk."

The inspector made himself watch as Dr. Bosworth

pulled the sheet away. The body was fully dressed in formal evening clothes—white shirt, proper black tie, black and gray vest and black longcoat. But the face was ghastly white, the eyes open and staring lifelessly up at the ceiling. They were hazel and bulging wide, as though the poor fellow was surprised to find himself lying on a mortuary slab. His hair was brown and thinning on top, his lips thin and his nose long and aquiline.

"Excuse me, Dr. Bosworth," Witherspoon said hesitantly. "I'm not trying to tell you your business, but isn't it usual to conduct a postmortem with the clothes off?"

"I left them on for a reason," Bosworth said. "They could well be evidence."

"Evidence?"

"Yes. Have a good look at this, Inspector." The doctor leaned over and pointed at the vest. "The buttons are fastened incorrectly. See, the top button goes into the second hole, not the first. But that's not all." He quickly undid the vest and pulled it apart, exposing the shirt. "Have a look at this."

Witherspoon noticed the shirt hadn't been buttoned right either. But he didn't quite see what that had to do with anything. "It's not done up properly either," he said.

Bosworth nodded. "That's what I noticed when the fellow was brought in. I asked the constable who pulled the body out of the canal if anyone had tampered with the victim's clothes. They hadn't. You do see what this means, Inspector."

"It could mean the victim had been dressed after he was already dead," the inspector guessed, hoping his reasoning was along the same path as the doctor's.

"My thoughts exactly." Bosworth leaned down and pointed at the man's shoes. "And look here. Brown shoes. Day shoes. No one wears brown day shoes with evening dress. It looked most odd to me. So I had a good look at the chap's feet.''

Witherspoon gaped at Bosworth, who was busily working the victim's right shoe and sock off.

"See." The doctor pointed to a pronounced bluish imprint angled at the bottom of the man's shinbone. The discolored flesh was approximately the size and shape of a withered sausage. "Look at this mark here." He quickly grabbed the other leg and shoved the sock down. "And here, there's another one. Equally pronounced and lying in almost the same position, only reversed." Bosworth looked at him expectantly.

Baffled, Witherspoon could only mutter, "Yes, it's most odd."

"There's more," Bosworth said excitedly as he yanked the right foot up again and stuck it under Witherspoon's nose. "See, there's a bruise on this heel."

The inspector stumbled back, almost tripping over his own feet to get away from the hideous dead foot the doctor thrust at him. But he did see the bruise. "You're right, Doctor," he mumbled, "it's . . . it's very much a bruise."

"Of course it is," Bosworth agreed. "But there isn't one on the other foot. I checked. Well, naturally, as soon as I saw this, I immediately notified the authorities that this might very well be a homicide rather than an accidental death."

"I see." Witherspoon didn't really see at all. What on earth was Bosworth getting at? But he wouldn't for the world admit that he couldn't follow the man's reasoning. His inner voice told him that Bosworth might be on to something. "Would you mind explaining how you came to that conclusion? Just so I have it clear in my own mind."

"Not at all," Bosworth said enthusiastically. "It's quite

simple, really. From all indications, someone drowned this poor fellow in a bathtub, stuffed him back in his clothes and then dumped his body in the nearest body of water, which just happened to be the Regents Canal. Your killer, Inspector, was hoping to make it look like an accidental death.''

For a moment, the inspector couldn't think of what to say. "Er, why do you think those marks on his ankle proved he was drowned in a bathtub?''

Bosworth looked surprised by the question. "I think it's rather obvious, Inspector.''

"But wouldn't the killer have just shoved his head under?'' Barnes asked. "Shouldn't there be marks around the neck, not the ankles?''

Witherspoon nodded gratefully at the constable, relieved that Barnes apparently didn't get it either. "That's right, if he was drowned in the tub, there should be some kind of bruises about the poor chap's neck.''

Bosworth shook his head stubbornly. "Not necessarily, Inspector. If someone has his head shoved under, he might be thrown off balance for a second, but he could use his legs and arms to fight back against the hands holding him under. Unless, of course, he was in a such a huge tub his legs didn't reach the end. And neither of the victim's arms had any bruises or abrasions at all. If someone was holding the poor chap's head under, unless the hands were tied, he'd have been flopping about and fighting back for all he was worth.'' Bosworth suddenly scurried down to the end of the table and grabbed the dead man's ankles. "However, if you walk up to someone in a bath, reach in and quickly jerk their ankles straight up''—to Witherspoon's horror, he jerked the corpse's legs straight into the air—"the entire upper torso and head gets pulled under quickly and the legs cannot be used defensively,''

Bosworth explained eagerly. "The arms are almost use-less because in most of the new baths, the sides are so high it would be hard to grab them to lever yourself up. Plus, if the killer acted quickly, the victim's mouth and lungs would be filled with water so fast, they literally wouldn't have time to react." Bosworth put the poor chap's limbs down.

Witherspoon sighed in relief. For a moment there, he'd been afraid that in his enthusiasm, the good doctor was going to yank the fellow off the slab. He glanced at Barnes, who was staring thoughtfully at the body.

"Too bad we don't have a bathtub handy," Barnes mumbled. "It could easily have happened like that."

"That would be a rather interesting experiment," Bosworth said cheerfully. "Perhaps I'll try it at home."

Scandalized, the inspector gasped. "You're going to take the body home?"

"No, no." Bosworth grinned. "I wouldn't be that dis-respectful, Inspector. However, I'm sure my landlady's son will give me a hand with it. He's helped me conduct some other experiments. Of course I will promise not to drown the lad."

Witherspoon smiled weakly. He wasn't sure this theory made sense but he made a mental note to have a good, hard look at the victim's bathtub. "So you think the killer held him under by grabbing his ankles? Right?"

"Yes," Bosworth said. "That would explain these bruises." He leaned over and gripped the dead man's an-kles again. This time, he carefully placed his thumbs over the bruises at the bottom of the shins. They fit perfectly. "See. That could be what made these bruises. I'd have to hold tight to keep him under the water, but it could cer-tainly be done."

"What about the bruise on the heel?" Barnes asked.

"Probably from the top of the tub." Bosworth stepped back. "Even under water, the victim would have had some fight left in him. I expect the killer had a bit of a hard time hanging on to him. With all the other evidence, I think it's quite clear, don't you?"

"Other evidence?" Witherspoon wasn't sure he wanted to ask.

"The soap under his fingernails." Bosworth lifted one of the lifeless hands. "Here." He shoved the extremity toward Witherspoon's nose. "Take a sniff, you can still smell it. lavender soap. Luckily, whoever dumped the body didn't realize it landed on top of a carriage wheel someone had tossed in the canal. This hand wasn't in the water at all and the soap didn't get washed away. Believe me, Inspector. One doesn't find much lavender soap in the Regents Canal. From the way the soap's caked under the fingernails of the hand, I'm rather led to believe that the victim must have been washing when the killer grabbed him. Too bad he didn't have a better defensive weapon at hand. You can't do much damage with a bit of soap. More's the pity." Bosworth smiled sheepishly. "Mind you, Dr. Potter doesn't necessarily agree with my analysis of the situation. But considering the evidence, I'd wager the family silver, if I had any, that you've a murder on your hands."

Impressed, Witherspoon gazed at the young doctor. "Are you doing the postmortem?"

"Yes. Potter didn't think it would be fitting for him to do it." Bosworth grinned. "Slicing into an old friend, you know."

"So, Dr. Potter *was* a friend of the victim," Barnes said.

"Not really. More of an acquaintance, I'd say." Bosworth pulled the sheet back up. Witherspoon smothered

another sigh of relief. "But it did give the poor fellow a
shock when he came barging in here and saw who was
lying on the table. That's how we identified the victim so
quickly. Well, what do you think, Inspector?"

Witherspoon wasn't sure what to think, but he did have
a great deal of respect for the doctor. "You've made a
most compelling case. Most compelling, indeed. But isn't
it possible that the buttons got mangled from being in the
canal? Currents, that sort of thing?"

Bosworth shook his head. "No. The buttons on the vest
are extremely small and quite difficult to undo. The shirt
buttons are even tinier. I had a good look at the size of
the holes too. No current is strong enough to worry the
material out of shape so much that buttons could slip out
then slip themselves back in again in a different order.

"Besides, as I said, the body was actually caught on a
carriage wheel some fool had tossed under the canal
bridge. I should have loved to have had a go at the poor
chap before they fished him out. I've a theory you can
get an awful lot of information about the crime if you just
take the time and trouble to look at the body before people
start mucking about with it."

"Yes, yes, I'm sure." Actually, Witherspoon thought
that was a rather silly notion. Dead was dead. Furthermore, most police surgeons did have a look at the corpse
before it was moved. He didn't see what good it would
have done Dr. Bosworth to stare at this poor fellow while
he was flopped over a wheel in a canal. But there was no
point in being rude.

"There's the shoes as well," Barnes added. "I'd say
that's good evidence of a murder."

Witherspoon glanced at the feet again. "True. One
doesn't usually wear brown shoes with full, formal evening dress."

"And don't forget the soap, sir," Barnes persisted.

"Thank you for reminding me, Barnes," Witherspoon said. He looked at the doctor. "How sure are you about the time of death?"

Bosworth looked doubtful. "Not as positive as I'd like to be. I should have a better idea once I cut him open."

Witherspoon shuddered and glanced at the shrouded body. "Poor chap. I wonder where he'd been?"

"I know," Dr. Bosworth announced proudly. "At least, Dr. Potter knew where he'd been on Saturday evening. He saw him, you see."

"Saw him? Where?" Witherspoon hoped that didn't mean that old Potter was going to end up being a suspect. He didn't much like the doctor but he couldn't quite see him as a murderer.

"The Hayden Theatre. They were both there. Not together. Dr. Potter was with his wife. But he said he saw Hinchley there and actually spoke to the man. A new play was opening. Potter said that it was duller than a rusty scalpel."

"It were a right surprise, Mr. Hinchley coming back the way he did," said Maggie Malone, proprietress of Malone's, a grocer's shop at the end of Avenue Road. She flipped her duster over a row of tinned sausages. "Saw him Saturday afternoon when I was sweeping the stoop," she continued. "Told Mr. Malone he ought to go round to Hinchley's house right away and collect what's owed to us, but Mr. Malone said we'd wait until Monday. Had a bit of a row over it, we did. We're only a small shop, now, aren't we? Can't be waiting forever for our money. But Mr. Malone says Mr. Hinchley's a good customer, so he had his way. Blast, now the man's dead and who knows if we'll ever get paid?"

Betsy nodded sympathetically. She'd struck gold on her first try this morning. "Can't you talk to this Mr. Hinchley's solicitor and get them to pay it out of the estate?"

"That'll take forever." Maggie tossed the duster under the counter and began straightening a row of tinned ox tongue. She was a tall, rawboned middle-aged woman with frizzy brown hair and a ruddy complexion. "Once you get solicitors and such muckin' about, you're lucky if you get a tuppence for your trouble."

Betsy nodded in agreement. "How long had he been gone?"

"Almost three months." Maggie tugged at the tight bodice of her gray broadcloth dress. "He were supposed to stay gone for six."

"How come he went there?" Betsy asked.

Maggie shrugged. "Who knows? Took it into his head to go and so up he went. He was an odd duck, if you know what I mean. I think he might have been writin' for one of them American newspapers but I expect the Americans didn't like his nasty pieces any better than anyone over here does."

"Nasty pieces?" Betsy prodded gently. She wasn't worried about this one shutting up on her. The minute Betsy had mentioned Hinchley, the shopkeeper's tongue had taken off like a greyhound after a rabbit. "Was he a newspaper reporter, then?"

Maggie shook her head. "Not a reporter, a critic. For the theatre. He wrote reviews of plays and such for some of the newspapers. Seems a silly thing for a grown man to do, if you ask me. But he liked it well enough. Mind you, the people he wrote about didn't like him much. More than once Lilly's been round here telling tales about some actor or writer raising a ruckus with the man. Not that Mr. Hinchley cared what people thought of him.

Rather hard sort of man, if you get my meaning.''

Betsy thought it sounded like Lilly liked to talk as well. She made a mental note to try and find the girl. ''Some men are like that,'' she agreed. ''Don't care if half the world hates them.''

''Hinchley certainly didn't.'' Maggie broke off just as the shop door opened and a well-dressed woman stepped inside. ''Good morning, Mrs. Baker. I'll be right with you.'' All business now, Maggie looked inquiringly at Betsy. ''What was it you wanted, miss?''

''A tin of Le Page's Liquid Glue, please,'' she replied. Drat. If that woman hadn't come in, she'd probably have been able to get a lot more information out of the shop-keeper. But Mrs. Baker had a list in her hand and didn't appear to be in any hurry. So Betsy paid for her glue, which would make a nice gift for Wiggins, smiled at Maggie Malone and left. She could always come back.

The late Ogden Hinchley had resided in a large, beige brick townhouse at the very end of Avenue Road, only a few hundred feet from the canal where his body had been found. From the outside, nothing about it looked extraordinary. But the inside was quite another story.

Inspector Witherspoon gazed curiously around the drawing room. Voluminous sheer fabric had been draped artfully across the ceiling, giving one the effect of standing in a rather opulent tent. The floor was covered with a huge, intricate and boldly patterned oriental rug. Gigantic red and white pillows were tossed willy nilly around the room and several low tables, all draped in elegant red and gold fringed silk were ringed about in strategic places next to the pillows. The air smelled faintly of incense. Tapestries, mostly Indian in style, and bright brass plate completed the decorations on the wall. The far end of the room was dominated by a low day bed covered with a white silk spread and canopied in sheets of sheer cream. At the foot of the bed was a chair, ornately carved and covered with a deep maroon velvet.

"Place looks like the throne room of a heathen king," Barnes muttered, staring at the chair.

"It certainly does," Witherspoon agreed. "Do you think the whole house is like this?"

"No, sir," a low voice said from behind him. "Only this room and the master bedroom and bath. The rest of house is quite ordinary."

Witherspoon and Barnes both whirled around. A tall, dark-haired man with brown eyes, sculpted cheeks and exceptionally pale skin stood just inside the doorway. "I'm Rather, sir. Mr. Hinchley's butler. Lilly said you wanted a word with us."

"Yes, I'd like to speak to the entire staff, if I may," Witherspoon replied.

Rather smiled faintly. "There's only Lilly and myself, sir. Mr. Hinchley sacked everyone else when he left for New York."

"He wasn't planning on returning then?" Barnes asked.

"Yes, sir," Rather replied. "He was planning on coming back."

"You don't mean he expected a house this size to be managed by only two servants?" Witherspoon asked. Odd-looking room and all, it was still a big house.

Rather's lip curled. "I wasn't privy to Mr. Hinchley's expectations, sir. Perhaps he was planning on hiring new servants when he returned. I wouldn't know. I'd planned on leaving well before he got back."

"You didn't like Mr. Hinchley?" the inspector probed.

"It wasn't a matter of liking or disliking." The butler

shrugged negligently, as though the matter were of no consequence. "I simply felt I could better myself somewhat by seeking employment elsewhere. Lilly was planning on going as well. Ogden Hinchley wasn't the kind of employer to inspire loyalty amongst his staff."

Witherspoon thought that most interesting. "Is there somewhere else we can talk?" This room was getting on his nerves. Perhaps it was that sickly, cloying incense smell. But he didn't much like being in there.

Rather looked at him for a moment and a flash of amusement flitted over his face. "We can go into the butler's pantry."

The man led them down a long, wide hall toward the back of the silent house. Their footsteps echoed eerily on the polished wood floor. At the last door, the butler stopped. "In here, gentlemen. Should I call Lilly?"

The room was small and ordinary. A tiny fireplace, an overstuffed settee and two wing chairs.

"We'd like to speak with you first," Witherspoon said. "Do you mind if we sit down?"

"Please do." Rather nodded at the settee, but remained standing himself.

As soon as they were seated, Barnes whipped out his notebook while the inspector started the questioning. "You do know that your employer was found dead last night?"

"Yes. A police constable came round and told us this morning."

"Mr. Hinchley's body was found in the canal. Have you any idea how he got there?" Witherspoon asked.

"None, sir."

"When was the last time you saw your employer?" Barnes asked.

"Saturday evening," Rather replied. "He left for the

theatre at half six. He told me he was going to a new play that was opening at the Hayden Theatre.''

''He left at half six?'' Barnes asked.

''Yes.''

''Why so early?'' the constable persisted. ''The theatre usually starts at eight. Was he going to stop and have supper first?''

Rather shook his head. ''He ate a light supper before he left.''

''Then why did he leave so early?'' Witherspoon asked. ''Even in traffic it doesn't take an hour and a half to get to the Strand.''

''I've no idea,'' Rather said calmly. ''It wasn't my place to question the man.''

Witherspoon leaned forward. ''Weren't you concerned when he didn't return home that night?''

''I didn't know he hadn't come home, did I? I was asleep.''

''But when you saw he wasn't here on Sunday morning, weren't you alarmed?''

Rather hesitated. ''Not really. Sometimes he'd go off for a few days on his own. He'd done it before. As his clothes were still packed, when he didn't come down to breakfast, I thought he'd come home, grabbed a few things and gone off with a friend.''

''Did he have a lot of friends, then?'' Barnes asked softly.

The butler smiled slyly. ''Not really.''

''So the last time you saw Mr. Hinchley was early Saturday evening,'' Witherspoon mused. ''Tell me, how long would you expect him to be away without communicating with his household?''

''Lilly and I were thinking that if we didn't hear from him by tomorrow, we might go to the police. But I honestly thought he'd simply gone off with a friend.''

"And you didn't wait up for him on Saturday night, then?" Barnes asked.

"No. I was under my usual instructions. I left the side door unlocked and went to bed at my normal time."

"Mr. Hinchley had you leave the door unlocked?" Witherspoon pressed. This was most curious, most curious indeed.

"Yes. That's the way he liked things done," Rather said firmly.

Witherspoon drummed his fingers against the settee. "Did Mr. Hinchley have enemies?"

"If you're looking for people who wanted him dead, you'd best try the Hayden Theatre." Rather laughed nastily. "The last person any of that lot wanted to see in the audience that night was Ogden Hinchley."

"Took 'im to the Hayden, guv," the cabbie told Smythe. The big burly man whipped his hat off and wiped beads of sweat off his forehead. "That's a theatre over on the Strand."

"What time did ya pick 'im up?" Smythe asked and glanced up the road, keeping a wary eye on the corner. He didn't want the inspector or Constable Barnes to come barreling round and catch him chatting with a hansom driver. Finding the cabbie that had picked Ogden Hinchley up on Saturday had been a stroke of luck, but Smythe didn't believe in pushing good fortune too far. He wasn't one to take advantage of Lady Luck.

The man shrugged. "'Bout half six, I reckon. Might 'ave been a bit later. I wasn't watchin' the time. Why you so interested in this bloke, mate?"

"Doin' a bit of snoopin' for a lady," Smythe gave him a man-to-man grin. "She's sweet on 'im and she don't trust 'im much. Wants to make sure he minds himself, if you know what I mean.''

The cabbie's eyes glittered greedily. ''This lady pay good?''

Smythe wiped the smile off his face and replaced it with a scowl.

Unlike Betsy, the driver was immediately cowed. ''Don't get narked, now,'' he said quickly. ''I was only askin'. Can't blame a feller fer tryin' to pick up a bit of coin now and then. I'm round these parts lots. I wouldn't mind doin' a bit of watchin' if the pay was good. That's all I'm sayin'. Times is tough, you know. Hard to make a decent livin', what with fares bein' set by the bloomin' council and people stealin' lifts on the back instead of payin' properly.''

''I've already paid ya all you're going to get,'' Smythe snapped. He hated doing this. But sometimes, if you weren't careful, you'd get fleeced faster than a green boy at a racecourse. ''And I've paid ya well too.'' One thing the coachman didn't have to worry about was money. He had plenty of it. He felt just a bit guilty that he could buy his information when he needed to, while the others in the household had to dash about all over London to pick up clues. But it weren't his fault he had more money than he knew what to do with.

''Never said you didn't,'' the cabbie said quickly. ''Anyway, I took him to the Hayden and dropped him off. That's all there was to it. He were just a regular fare.''

''Did you see if he talked to anyone when he got out?''

''Didn't 'ang about to notice,'' the cabbie replied. He began to stroke the horse's nose. ''As soon as we pulled up, another fare got in.''

*   *   *

Witherspoon and Barnes walked slowly down the center aisle of the Hayden Theatre. The auditorium was horseshoe shaped. Boxes, stalls and galleries, each of them catering to a different class and different price level, layered themselves toward the large stage.

"What's that?" Barnes asked, pointing to the gilt-framed moulding flush with the front of the stage. "It looks like a giant picture frame."

"I think it's called a proscenium," Witherspoon replied. "I believe it's used to help stage the play. I say, do you think there's anyone about?"

He peered down toward the stage, but saw nothing in the poor light. However, he could see that the backing on the seats in this part of the theatre was aged and fading. On the boxes to his left, he noticed the paint was chipping.

"Can I help you gents?" someone called. Just then a head popped up from one of the front rows.

Witherspoon was so startled by the man's sudden appearance he didn't answer for a moment. "Uh, could we see someone in charge, please?"

"You coppers?"

"Yes, I'm Inspector Witherspoon and this is Constable Barnes."

"I'll get Mr. Swinton for you," the man said. "He's the guv."

"Odd sort of place, isn't it, sir?" Barnes commented as they waited. "For some reason, it makes you want to whisper. Like church."

A bald man with a huge mustache appeared at the front of the stage. He squinted at the two policemen. "I'm Willard Swinton. You want to see me?"

"If we could have a word, please," Witherspoon shouted. Swinton nodded and disappeared behind the proscenium. Witherspoon, alarmed that he'd lost his prey, hurried toward the stage. Constable Barnes was right on his heels.

By the time they reached the front, Willard Swinton had reappeared in front of a door tucked neatly to the left of the stage.

"This way, gentlemen," he called, waving them over. "We'd be more comfortable in my office." He led them through the door, down a long corridor and into a small room at the very end. Gaudy playbills decorated the walls. There was a huge rolltop desk in the center, a gas fire in the hearth and several overstuffed chairs. "Have a seat," Swinton invited, sitting down behind his desk. "Now, what can I do for her Majesty's boys in blue?"

It took a moment for Witherspoon to understand he meant the police. "Ah, we'd like to ask you a few questions if you don't mind. About Saturday evening."

"Great night it was, sir." Swinton beamed proudly. *Belvedere's Burden* was an absolute smash! We're sold out for the next three weeks."

"I take it that's the name of the current production?" Witherspoon asked.

"That's right. Saturday night was our opening. The house was sold out." Impossibly enough, Swinton's smile broadened even further.

Witherspoon asked, "Do you know a gentleman named Ogden Hinchley?"

Swinton's smile evaporated. "I know him," he sneered. "He was here Saturday night, sitting right in the third row."

"Did you speak to him?" Barnes asked.

"Not bloody likely," Swinton snapped. "I haven't spoken to that man for two years. The only reason I didn't throw him out when I spotted him was because I didn't want to create a fuss in front of the audience.''

''I take it you didn't like Mr. Hinchley?'' Witherspoon said.

Swinton's eyes narrowed suspiciously. ''What's this all about, then?''

Witherspoon realized he didn't have to break the news gently to the man. ''Mr. Hinchley's dead. His body was found in the Regents Canal. We've reason to believe the death wasn't an accident.''

Swinton's jaw gaped. ''Dead? Hinchley? That explains it then. We wondered why his review wasn't in the paper.''

The door flew open and a tall, fair-haired man came charging in. ''For God's sake, Willard,'' he cried, ''you promised you'd take care of those wretchedly old lime-lights . . .'' He broke off as he saw the two men, his deep-set eyes widening when he noticed Constable Barnes's uniform. ''Oh, excuse me. I didn't realize anyone else was here. Do forgive me for intruding.'' He started backing toward the door.

''Don't go, Edmund,'' Swinton said. ''These gentlemen are police. They've just given me the most shocking news. Ogden Hinchley's been murdered.''

He stopped. ''Murdered? My God, you are joking?''

Swinton shook his head.

Witherspoon quickly introduced himself and Barnes. ''And who are you, sir?''

''Sorry, Inspector.'' Swinton belatedly remembered his manners and introduced the newcomer. ''This is Edmund Delaney, the author of the play.''

''Did you know Mr. Hinchley, sir?'' Barnes asked quickly.

Delaney didn't speak for a moment. ''Yes,'' he finally replied so softly that Witherspoon had to strain to catch what he was saying. "I knew him. Everybody in the theatre knew him."

"Why don't you sit down, sir?" Witherspoon invited. He usually liked to interview people alone, but it might be interesting to try it a bit differently this time.

Delany sat down in a chair next to Swinton's desk. He clasped his hands together. "How was he killed?"

"He was drowned," Witherspoon said. It wouldn't do to give too much information away. From the reactions of both these men, it was obvious they had strong feelings about the victim. "And he was last seen alive right here at this theatre on Saturday night."

"What do you mean by that?" Swinton blustered. "Are you trying to imply this theatre had something to do with Hinchley's death?"

"I'm implying nothing, Mr. Swinton," Witherspoon replied calmly. He directed his attention to Delaney, noticing that the man's face had gone pale. "Did you know Mr. Hinchley well?"

"He was a professional acquaintance," Delaney muttered.

"Did you like him?" Barnes asked.

Delaney appeared surprised by the question, but he recovered quickly. "No one in the theatre liked him. He was a critic. Quite a nasty one too. Hinchley ruined a number of careers both here and in America." He laughed harshly. "I understand Americans are quite a violent people. Perhaps Hinchley's vitriolic pen didn't sit well with the New York theatre crowd. Maybe one of them followed him back and killed him."

Surprised by such a silly statement, Witherspoon's eyebrows shot up. "Are you suggesting he was murdered by an American?" he asked incredulously.

"Not really." Delaney smiled apologetically. "This is

a bit of a shock, Inspector. I'm just babbling nonsense.'' He stopped and took a deep breath. "Hinchley wasn't loved by any of us here in England, but he had been gone for rather a long time. None of us even knew he was back.''

"Mr. Swinton did," Barnes said.

"Here now, what are you saying?" Swinton snapped. "I wasn't the only one who knew he was back. Half of London saw him sitting big as a ruddy toad. And I wasn't the only one in the theatre who'd seen him either. Remington and Parks were both peeking out at the audience that night. They could've seen him too.''

"Please, Mr. Swinton, don't excite yourself." Gracious, the man's face had gone so red, Witherspoon was afraid he might burst something. "We're merely trying to ascertain Mr. Hinchley's movements on Saturday evening.''

Swinton seemed to calm down. "His movements have nothing to do with us. As far as I know, he watched the play and then left.''

"I see," the inspector replied. "And what time did the play end?''

"Around eleven o'clock.''

"It's three hours long?" Barnes exclaimed. Blimey, he thought, that would flatten your backside.

"Of course not," Delaney said. "But it was late starting and we had quite a long intermission." He tossed a quick frown at Swinton. "We had a bit of trouble with some of the limelights and that delayed us a good fifteen minutes.''

"So the play ended at approximately eleven," Witherspoon said.

"Closer to ten-fifty than eleven," Swinton interrupted.

"All right," the inspector said patiently, "ten-fifty.

What did you gentlemen do after the play was over?''

Both men appeared surprised by the question. Delaney answered first. ''I went for a walk, Inspector. By the Thames.''

''How long did you walk?''

''I'm not sure,'' Delaney replied. ''An hour, maybe more. Try and understand, Inspector, I was quite excited. This is my first play. I guess I was in a bit of a state. I knew I wouldn't sleep so I went down to the river and walked. Then I went home.''

''And you, Mr. Swinton?'' Barnes asked.

''I came in and counted the receipts,'' Swinton replied. ''Good take that night.''

''What time did you leave your office?'' Witherspoon glanced over to make sure the constable was getting this down in his notebook.

Swinton stroked his mustache. ''I wasn't watching the clock. It took a couple of hours to count out and do the books. By then it was late, so I went home.''

''Did anyone see you leave?'' Witherspoon asked.

''No. The place was empty when I locked up.''

The inspector turned to Delaney. ''Did anyone see you by the river?''

''Lots of people saw me, Inspector,'' Delaney replied sarcastically. ''But unfortunately, I doubt any of them knew who I was.''

Mrs. Jeffries spotted Dr. Bosworth the moment he left St. Thomas's Hospital through the side door. She darted forward and planted herself directly in front of his path. ''Good day, Dr. Bosworth,'' she said brightly.

Bosworth stopped and cocked his head to one side. ''Why am I not surprised to see you?''

''Because you're most intelligent.'' she smiled confidently. "And you know I'd want to hear every little detail of the postmortem on Ogden Hinchley." As one of her "secret sources," Dr. Bosworth had been most helpful on several of the other of the inspector's cases.

"Of course." He offered her his arm. "Let's stroll while we talk, Mrs. Jeffries. To be perfectly frank, I'm very tired. But I think I can manage to stay awake long enough to give you the essentials. Has the inspector got this one, then?"

"It seems so," she said as they walked toward the bridge. "I understand you don't think this is a case of accidental drowning."

"Absolutely not," Bosworth replied. He repeated everything he had already told Witherspoon. "And when I opened the fellow up, there wasn't any debris in the lungs."

"I'm sorry, I don't quite follow you."

Bosworth yawned. "If he'd drowned in the canal, there would have been dirt and filth from the canal in his lungs. Now, there was debris in his mouth, but not in the lungs, if you follow."

"So if he drowned in his bathtub, then someone would have had to move his body and take it to the canal," she said thoughtfully. "How big a man was he?"

"Quite small, really," Bosworth replied. "Very slender, with very poorly developed muscle. But even a small man would be quite difficult to move. Dead weight and all."

"Was there anything else, Doctor?" Mrs. Jeffries asked. Poor Dr. Bosworth did look very tired. She really mustn't keep him too long. "Anything else that might be useful to us?"

Bosworth thought for a moment. "I don't believe so, but honestly, I'm so tired I'm not thinking all that clearly.

Tell you what—if I remember anything else, I'll send you a note.''

''What about the time of death?''

Bosworth hesitated. ''It's only an educated guess, but my estimate is late Saturday night or the very early hours of Sunday morning.''

''But someone tried to make it look like he was murdered Saturday night as he walked along the canal?''

''That's how it appears to me,'' Bosworth yawned again. ''But I'm only a doctor, Mrs. Jeffries. I leave the real detecting to you.''

CHAPTER 3

Inspector Witherspoon arrived home for dinner that evening much earlier than expected. Luckily, as the weather was still quite warm, Mrs. Goodge had been able to whip up a cold, light supper, which the inspector ate quickly.

"I wish I had time to sit and talk with you, Mrs. Jeffries," he fretted, pushing the remains of his beef and cheese to one side. "Discussing the case does give me a better perspective on the whole matter. But Constable Barnes was quite tired this evening and as we couldn't interview any of the others involved in this theatre production until after this evening's performance, I told him to pop along home and take a rest. I'm meeting him at the theatre later. I only hope I can make sense out of what these people actually say. They are quite a dramatic lot, even the theatre owner. One would think he, at least, would be a businessman first and foremost."

"You always make sense of things, sir," she said kindly. She hoped Smythe and Wiggins would be back by the time Luty and Hatchet arrived. They had much to discuss. "So according to both Swinton and Delaney, a goodly number of people didn't like Hinchley."

"Yes. He certainly wasn't very popular. Even his servants didn't care for him. Both of them were planning on leaving before Hinchley got back from America. But"— he sighed—"we've no evidence that anyone at the theatre or his own household murdered him. Yet I can't help thinking that it must have been done by someone from the Hayden."

"Why, sir?" she asked curiously. This time, she promised herself silently, she wouldn't be so quick to ignore the inspector's ideas about the murder. After all, he had solved the last one. "Surely someone that unpopular would have many enemies."

"True. But he'd been out of the country, Mrs. Jeffries. According to what Lilly, his maid, told us, he'd arrived back only on Saturday afternoon." Witherspoon took a sip of beer. "He'd had no visitors, hadn't gone out and hadn't sent any messages. Regardless of how many people in London disliked the man, most of them wouldn't have known he was back. Besides, I've got a feeling about it. You know, my inner voice."

She cringed inwardly. Sometimes she wished he'd never mentioned that particular concept. "Yes, sir, your voice. It tells you that the killer is someone from the production of this play?"

"*Belvedere's Burden*," he said. "That's the name of the thing. I suppose I really ought to watch a performance. It's a melodrama. Something to do with murderous rages and all sorts of hidden emotions. Can't say that it's the kind of thing I much enjoy." He sighed. "But yes, in answer to your question, I do think it's someone involved in the production. Essentially, they were the only people in London who knew Hinchley had come back unexpectedly from America.''

"But wasn't he in the audience?" she asked. "Couldn't the killer have seen him there?"

"True." Witherspoon frowned thoughtfully. "But I've got to start somewhere, and just amongst the people involved with the play there's enough animosity toward Hinchley to warrant starting there. If it turns out that the killer isn't one of them, I'll look elsewhere."

"You obviously heard quite a bit today," she said pleasantly.

"Oh, I did," he said enthusiastically. He told her everything he'd learned, all about Bosworth's theory, the visit to the Hinchley house and how he'd gotten a good look at Hinchley's bath. "It was a jolly large tub," he concluded as he glanced at the clock. He got up. "I'd best be off, then. It's getting late."

"Surely the play isn't over this early," she said, getting to her feet and starting to clear the remains of his dinner.

"It's not. But I'm going to pop round to the Yard to do some background checking," he said, stifling a yawn. "By the time I've finished, it will be time to meet Constable Barnes. Don't wait up for me, Mrs. Jeffries. It'll be very late when I return."

Mrs. Jeffries and Betsy got the supper things cleaned up in record time. By the time the last plate was being put in the cupboard, the others had arrived.

Mrs. Jeffries took her usual seat at the head of the table. "Inspector Witherspoon's gone out," she began, "but we managed to have a nice chat before he went off. He had a number of things to report."

"Lucky for us, I had the rest of that beef joint left over from last night's dinner," Mrs. Goodge muttered. "Oth-

erwise, we'd have had some explaining to do. Tied up all
day with my sources, I didn't have time to cook a proper
meal.''

"Did ya find out anything?'' Wiggins asked the cook.

"Found out plenty,'' she replied. "Not that it's fit for
decent ears.''

"Would you like to start, then?'' Mrs. Jeffries said.

Mrs. Goodge shook her head. "Let's hear what you got
out of the inspector first. After our last muck-up, I don't
want to get sidetracked.''

"She's right,'' Betsy said quickly. "This time we've
got to keep right on top of what the inspector's doing.''

Faintly alarmed, Mrs. Jeffries frowned. "Do all of you
feel that way?''

"Yup,'' Luty said firmly.

"'Fraid so,'' Smythe agreed. "Don't want to waste my
time chasin' my tail instead of the killer.''

"Perhaps it would be in the best interests of justice if
we did pay proper attention to Inspector Witherspoon's
investigation,'' Hatchet said. "We certainly don't want a
repeat of our last performance.''

Mrs. Jeffries couldn't believe her ears. Had they all
completely lost confidence in themselves? "Nonsense,''
she said stoutly. "We've solved a number of cases and
just because we didn't solve the last one is no reason to
change our methods. I'm surprised at all of you. Have
you completely forgotten how many successes we've had
in the past? I'm not saying we ought to ignore the inspector's investigation; we don't do that in any case.
However, I won't have all of you sitting here on your
hands too frightened to tell what you've learned because
you're afraid you might be wrong. Is that clear?''

She spoke with the authority of a general addressing
his troops. For a moment, no one said anything.

Luty broke the silence. She laughed. "Turnin' my own words back on me—that's a good one, Hepzibah. You're right. We're all actin' like a bunch of greenhorns too scared to get back on a horse that's thrown us. Well, we're danged good at what we do and I'm glad you reminded me of it. Seein' as everyone else is still skittish, why don't I go first? I learned a bit today. To begin with, Ogden Hinchley's got plenty of money. Family money, all inherited."

"Who gets it now that 'e's dead?" Smythe asked.

"I don't know yet. Thistlebottom only handles his money, not his will. But I've got another source . . ."

She was interrupted by a loud, derisive snort from her butler. "Source. Why, that man's a senile old solicitor," Hatchet muttered. "You can't rely on a thing he says. Furthermore, the fellow's so indiscreet it's a wonder he's still allowed to practise."

"Stampton ain't senile," Luty snapped. "He's a drunk. There's a difference, ya know. But drunk or sober, the man knows his facts. Now, as I was sayin' before I was so rudely interrupted, Hinchley never had to worry about earnin' a living. He started out as an actor and a playwright, but couldn't get anyone to hire him or produce his plays so he started writin' pieces for some of the newspapers. That's how he become a critic."

"Was he ever paid for his writing?" Mrs. Jeffries asked curiously.

"Not at first," Luty said eagerly. "But after he got so mean and nasty, his reviews started to help sell papers. That's when they started payin' him."

"So he was a failure as an actor and a playwright, but not as a critic," Mrs. Jeffries mused. "That's quite interesting. Wealthy too. Excellent, Luty."

Luty shot Hatchet a smug smile. She was pretty sure he hadn't found out a danged thing.

Smythe said, "I'd like to go next if nobody cares. I found a hansom driver who picked Ogden Hinchley up on Saturday night. It was half past six and he took him to the Hayden Theatre. That's all I learned. Not much, I'm afraid."

"I think it's quite good, considerin'," Betsy said, giving the coachman a bright smile. It bothered her that things weren't right between the two of them yet and she was getting tired of walking on eggshells around the man. "We've only just got this case. It's still early yet."

But Smythe obviously didn't mind that they were still at odds because he simply stared at her with that closed-up expression he'd been wearing since she got back from the East End.

Flustered, she babbled on. "I didn't learn much either. Just that one of the shopkeepers saw Hinchley on Saturday and was surprised to see him back from America. He was supposed to be gone another three months. But he came back early. But I did find out that Hinchley's maid is a real chatterbox. She was always coming in to the grocer's and gossiping."

"Did you talk to the maid?" Mrs. Goodge asked eagerly.

Betsy shook her head. "I hung about Hinchley's house, but the only person who set foot out the door was a man. I think it was Hinchley's butler. He took himself off in a cab so I waited a bit, hoping the maid would come out, but she never did."

"Did you find out what the girl gossiped about?" Luty asked.

Betsy grinned. "The shopkeeper said she was always going on about the actors and theatre people comin' round to Hinchley's house and raising a ruckus over some of the nasty things he wrote about them in his reviews. I'm going to try and talk to the girl tomorrow.''

''Good idea, Betsy.'' Mrs. Jeffries looked at the footman. She rather suspected Wiggins hadn't had a good day. He hadn't asked one question since they'd sat down and he looked a bit down in the mouth. ''Did you learn anything?''

''Not a ruddy thing,'' he replied glumly. ''No one I talked to knew anything about Hinchley.''

''Don't take it so hard, lad,'' Mrs. Goodge said kindly. ''We all have our bad days. The only thing I found out was that Hinchley wasn't any better than he ought to be.'' Disgusted, she made a face.

''Go on,'' Mrs. Jeffries prompted.

''Give me a minute,'' the cook said. ''I'm tryin' to think of how to put it so it doesn't sound so . . . so . . . indecent . . .'' She waved her hands in the air. ''Oh, bother, I might as well just say it and get it over with. Hinchley frequented brothels.''

Betsy giggled. Luty laughed and Wiggins blushed a bright pink. Smythe looked down at the tabletop to hide a grin.

Mrs. Jeffries, who was trying not to smile herself, said, ''There's no need to be embarrassed, Mrs. Goodge. We all know that such places exist. Your information might become quite useful.'' Considering that probably a huge number of men in London frequented brothels, she didn't think this particular bit of information was noteworthy, but one never knew and she didn't want the cook to feel left out. ''Do keep on digging. Now, let me tell you what I got out of the inspector.'' She told them everything she'd learned and, more important, she shared Witherspoon's contention that the murder was related to the play at the Hayden Theatre. "I'm inclined to agree with the inspector," she concluded.

"Why?" Smythe asked. "Sounds to me like this 'inchley were the sort of man who prided 'imself on makin' enemies."

"Yes, but it would have been a very lucky enemy who spotted him in a crowded theatre that night," the housekeeper said. "And Swinton told the inspector that half the cast had seen Hinchley in the audience that night. Besides," she said honestly, taking another leaf from the inspector's book, "it's at least a place to start."

"Names, Hepzibah," Luty said eagerly. "Did ya get any names for us?"

"There's Willard Swinton, the producer and the owner of the Hayden," she said. "And the playwright, Edmund Delaney. The Inspector was quite certain both those men hated the victim. He also mentioned that tonight he'd be interviewing Albert Parks, the play's director, and the two leads, Trevor Remington and Theodora Vaughan. All of them knew Hinchley as well."

"That's a good start," Luty said. "I'll dig around and see what I can learn about Swinton. If he owns a theatre, some banker'll have the goods on him."

"I'll take Delaney," Hatchet said. "As I mentioned earlier today, I've a number of contacts in the theatrical world."

"Do you want me to take Remington?" Betsy asked. "It won't take long tomorrow to talk to Hinchley's housemaid."

"That'll be fine, Betsy," Mrs. Jeffries said.

"I'll go over to the theatre tomorrow and see what I can find out about all of 'em," Wiggins said enthusiastically. "I like theatres."

"I can do the pubs round there and see what I can pick

up,'' Smythe said. ''And maybe talk to a few more cabbies as well.'' He frowned. ''There's something botherin'
me about that cabbie who took Hinchley to the Hayden
on Saturday.''

''What?'' Betsy asked and then could have bitten her
tongue.

''Well, he picked Hinchley up at half six, but the theatre's no more than a couple of miles from Hinchley's
house. Why'd he take 'im so early?''

''I see what you mean, Smythe,'' Mrs. Jeffries said
slowly. ''The play wouldn't have started till eight o'clock.
If the cabbie picked Hinchley up at six thirty, they would
have been at the theatre by seven o'clock . . .''

''What if there was a lot of traffic?'' Wiggins interrupted excitedly.

''Even then they should have been there by seven-
fifteen, seven-twenty at the latest,'' Smythe said. ''That
means that Hinchley would have had a good half hour to
forty-five minutes to lark about and make himself known
to anyone who happened to be about.'' He looked at Mrs.
Jeffries. ''Which means that the killer isn't necessarily
someone from the play. Cor, Hinchley had time enough
to be seen by anyone at the ruddy theatre that night.''

''Dag blast it,'' Luty exclaimed. ''That means anyone
could've killed him.''

Smythe slumped back in his chair. ''It'll be like lookin'
for a needle in a 'aystack.''

''Not necessarily,'' Mrs. Jeffries said quickly. ''Before
we jump to any conclusions, I think Smythe ought to talk
to that cabbie again.''

''I'm thinkin' the same thing,'' the coachman muttered.
''I think I'd best ask the bloke what time they got to the
theatre. I never asked the cabbie if they stopped anywhere
along the way.''

''You mean you didn't ask him that when you had the chance?'' Betsy said.

Smythe kept a tight leash on his temper. The lass was just trying to rile him because he was still annoyed with her. He'd ignored her bright smiles and her overtures to make up because he was hurt. He gave her a cocky grin, the one he knew infuriated her. ''I know it's hard to believe, girl,'' he said slowly, relishing the way her eyes narrowed angrily, ''but even I can make a mistake. But not to worry, I'll hunt 'im up again tomorrow. This time, I'll make sure I ask the right questions.''

''Do sit down, Inspector.'' Theodora Vaughan, the star of *Belvedere's Burden* and the loveliest woman Witherspoon had ever seen, gestured gracefully at the overstuffed settee.

Witherspoon, staring like a schoolboy, tripped over his own feet, caught his balance before making a complete fool of himself and stumbled toward the settee. Constable Barnes, following at a more leisurely pace, couldn't quite hide his smile of amusement. ''Thank you,'' the inspector gushed. ''This is quite comfortable. Your dressing room is lovely, Miss Vaughan, absolutely lovely.''

Barnes gave the inspector a puzzled glance. The room was nice. Freshly painted cream walls, a colorful oriental dressing screen in one corner, long-stemmed roses on the vanity table and decent rugs on the floor, but it was hardly Buckingham Palace.

''That's very kind of you, Inspector,'' she replied. ''Willard wanted me to be comfortable. He insisted on redoing this room before we opened. Not that I cared one way or the other. But it is quite nice.''

''I'm awfully sorry to trouble you . . .'' he began.

"It's no trouble at all, Inspector," she interrupted, tilting her head to one side and giving him another dazzling smile. "I'm sorry you had to wait while I took off my makeup, but if I don't get it off right away, it does horrid things to one's complexion."

Witherspoon didn't see anything horrid about her complexion. In the soft light of the dressing room, her skin was creamy white and utterly flawless, as was the rest of her. Her hair was a deep auburn, reminding him of a blazing sunset on a summer's day. Her eyes were a dark sapphire color, set deep in a sculpted face beneath perfectly formed brows.

Awed by her beauty, Witherspoon gaped at her. Barnes cleared his throat. The inspector, still gawking, didn't seem to hear him. Barnes did it again, loudly this time.

"Oh." Witherspoon shook himself slightly. "Yes, yes, indeed. Now, where was I?"

"Apologizing for troubling me," she said with a laugh. "But as I said, it's really no trouble at all. Though I'm afraid I won't be of much help to you. I haven't seen or spoken to Ogden Hinchley in months. I didn't realize he was back in London until I heard of his death."

Witherspoon nodded. His mind seemed to have gone blank because he couldn't think of one single, solitary question to ask this lovely creature.

Barnes glanced at his superior, but the inspector was still staring at the actress with a rather glazed look on his face. "You didn't know that Mr. Hinchley was in the audience that night?" Barnes asked.

"No. I thought he was still in New York."

Witherspoon started. Really, he must concentrate on his duty. But gracious, it was difficult. Every time she looked his way his thoughts tended to muddle. "Er, I take it that neither Mr. Swinton nor any of the other cast members mentioned to you that they'd seen Hinchley in the audience?''

"Absolutely not," she said fervently. "It was opening night, you see."

"I'm afraid I don't quite follow."

"I'm an artist, Inspector." She emphasized the words with a graceful sweep of her arms. "I don't see or speak to anyone before a performance until the first curtain call. Naturally, I had to concentrate on my role before I went on. I'm afraid my dressing room is completely out of bounds for everyone. The entire cast knows that. I don't see anyone, not even the stage manager or the director. So even if someone had wanted to tell me that Hinchley was out front, they wouldn't have been able to."

"What about after the play?" Barnes asked.

"I left right after the performance," she said. "I was exhausted. I'm on stage for virtually every scene. As soon as the curtain went down, I had one of the crew call me a hansom and I went home."

"Hearing about Hinchley's death must have been a dreadful shock to you," Witherspoon said sympathetically.

She clasped her hands to her chest. "It was a terrible shock. Absolutely terrible."

"It's a wonder you were able to go on tonight," the inspector said earnestly. "You're obviously most sensitive. Otherwise you wouldn't be such a wonderful actress."

Barnes glanced at Witherspoon sharply. What was the inspector up to now? Was he trying to lull this woman into talking? He knew for a fact the inspector had never seen the woman perform.

"How very kind of you to say so, Inspector," Theodora

said, giving him another blazing smile. "I am sensitive. All great performers must be. But then you probably know that. From what I hear you're quite an artist in your own right. Scotland Yard's most successful detective."

Flattered, Witherspoon blushed. "Really, Miss Vaughan, there's nothing artistic about solving murders."

"Don't be so modest, Inspector." She leaned toward him and laid her hand on his arm. "I've heard about some of your cases. You were brilliant. Absolutely brilliant. In your own way, you have to be as creative as I am. And much braver."

"You're far too kind, Miss Vaughan," Witherspoon replied.

Again, Barnes waited for Witherspoon to ask a question. But the inspector only smiled at the woman like a smitten schoolboy. "Were you and Mr. Hinchley good friends?" Barnes finally asked.

"Friends? No, not really." She gave the constable the benefit of her smile.

But he, being older and a bit cranky at having to be out this late, wasn't in the least moved. Stone-faced, he stared back at her. "Then why was his death such a shock to you, ma'am?" he asked.

Theodora Vaughan's brilliant smile faded and was replaced by a look of offended dignity. "The London theatre world is a rather small community, Constable. Even though Mr. Hinchley and I weren't well acquainted, his death was still a terrible blow. One doesn't normally hear that one's acquaintance has been murdered. I was quite shocked when I heard the news."

"But of course you were, dear lady," Witherspoon said quickly. He flicked a disappointed look at his constable. "No doubt having to carry on and perform tonight has made you dreadfully tired."

"It has, Inspector. You must indeed be the most perceptive of men, for I pride myself on hiding my feelings well." She gazed at Witherspoon in admiration.

Barnes thought he just might be sick. He hoped Theodora Vaughan was a better actress on stage than she was tonight. This performance wouldn't fool a deaf mute. He glanced at his superior again, hoping to see a knowing gleam in the inspector's eyes. But instead, Witherspoon was getting to his feet.

"Then we shan't keep you, madam," Witherspoon said briskly. "You must have your rest. I'll call round tomorrow to ask the rest of my questions. Will that be all right?"

"Thank you, Inspector." She clasped her hands to her bosom again. "Rose, my maid, is right outside. She'll give you my address and I do thank you for being so astute. A performance exhausts me. It'll be far better for me to answer your questions tomorrow afternoon than tonight."

Barnes couldn't believe his ears. They'd come here at this god-awful hour of the night to question the rest of the cast and now the inspector was getting snookered by a pair of blue eyes and a few flashy smiles. Surely not? Barnes refused to believe the man he so admired for his detecting genius could be such a fool for a woman. The inspector must have a reason for what he was doing.

Witherspoon bowed formally. "Until tomorrow afternoon, madam. Good evening." With that, he turned on his heel and left.

As soon as the door of Theodora Vaughan's dressing room had closed behind them, Barnes said. "You think you'll get more out of her at her home, sir?"

"Oh, no, Barnes," Witherspoon said. "I just thought the poor lady looked tired. She's magnificient, isn't she?"

Barnes's jaw dropped in shock. But the inspector didn't notice as he charged for the dressing room down the hall.

"Let's go see what Mr. Remington has to say for himself. I believe his dressing room is here." He rapped sharply on the door.

"Who is it?" a man's voice shouted irritably.

"The police," Witherspoon yelled. "We'd like to speak with Mr. Remington."

"Just a moment, please."

They waited in the hall for quite a few moments. Barnes had just raised his fist to knock again when the door opened. A tall man, his hair mussed and his face shining with some greasy substance, stuck his head out. "Police? What do you want?" he asked rudely.

Witherspoon straightened his spine. "We would like to speak with you about the murder of Ogden Hinchley."

The man stared at them, then reluctantly opened the door. "Swinton told me you'd been here. But I honestly don't see why you're bothering me with this matter. I've nothing to do with it."

"Nevertheless, we'd like to ask you some questions," Witherspoon said.

Remington sighed dramatically, like a king condescending to speak to a stupid peasant. "Come in, then. But I don't know why you need to see me. I haven't talked to Hinchley in months. I didn't even know he was back from New York."

The room was identical in size to the one they'd just left. But size was the only thing the two rooms had in common. Remington's dressing room was dark and dingy, with bad lighting, ugly green walls, a bare floor and a scraggly hanging curtain on one end instead of a dressing screen. In place of a nice overstuffed settee, Remington had two disreputable balloon-backed chairs.

He sat down in front of his vanity table and gestured toward the other seats. "Sit down, please." He turned to his mirror, picked up a cotton cloth and began wiping his face.

Witherspoon took a moment to study the actor as he and Barnes sat down. The man's hair was dark but there were a few strands of gray sprouting at his temples. His nose was aquiline, his jawline firm and manly and his bone structure excellent. But there were more than a few age lines at the corners of his dark brown eyes, and the brackets around his mouth marked his years as numbering closer to forty than thirty.

"Mr. Remington," Witherspoon began, but the actor interrupted him.

"Is this going to take long?" he asked. "I've a supper engagement soon and I don't want to be late."

"We'll be as quick as possible," the inspector replied. "You were acquainted with Ogden Hinchley?"

"Everyone in the theatre knew Hinchley." Remington tossed the cloth down and turned to look at them. "What of it?"

"When was the last time you saw him?"

"Three months ago at the Drury Lane Theatre."

"Did you know that he was in the Hayden last night?" Barnes asked.

Remington shrugged. "I didn't know it at the time. Only after the play was over. Albert Parks told me he'd spotted him sitting down front."

"Albert Parks is the director of your play?" Witherspoon asked.

"That's right. Albert took a peek out the curtains before the lights went down and spotted Hinchley. But he didn't tell me until after the play was over."

"Was Hinchley here to review your play?" Barnes

asked. He didn't have a clue what the inspector was up to, so he decided to put his oar in the water as well. He could always shut up if need be.

Remington's mouth flattened into a grim line. "Probably. Not that I cared one way or the other. No one took Hinchley's reviews all that seriously anymore."

"Had he reviewed any of your earlier performances?" the inspector asked. "I mean, had he ever reviewed you in another play?" He'd no idea why he was asking the question, but it seemed to him that perhaps the victim's being a critic might have been important to his murder.

Remington lifted his chin. "I am rather well known, Inspector," he said stiffly. "Hinchley had reviewed me a number of times."

"Good reviews, sir?" Barnes asked.

Remington lifted his chin a notch higher. "Some were quite good, others weren't. He was a failed actor himself, you know. When he couldn't make it on the boards, he turned to writing reviews. And not writing them very well, I might add. Just read a few of his reviews and you'll see why there won't be many tears at his funeral."

"So you didn't know he was out in front until after the play was over," Witherspoon mused. He tried to remember exactly what it was that Swinton had told him. Surely the man had said that Remington and Parks had peeked out the curtain before the play. "What time did Mr. Parks tell you about seeing Mr. Hinchley in the audience?"

"It was quite late," Remington said. "Around eleven, I think, right before I left the theatre."

"Did you go straight home?" Barnes asked. They might as well start checking alibis.

"As a matter of fact, I did. Opening nights are always exhausting."

"Where do you live, sir?" Barnes continued.

"I've taken rooms in Sidwell Lane. I went straight there right after I left here."

"Did anyone see you?" Barnes persisted.

"No, I live alone."

"What about your servants?" Witherspoon asked.

Remington sighed loudly. "Really, Inspector, this is most tiresome. I don't have a house full of servants and if I did, I wouldn't keep them up that late to wait on me. My landlady doesn't keep late hours so she was already asleep when I got home. I saw no one and no one saw me."

"If the landlady was asleep," Barnes asked, "how did you get in?"

"She rents rooms to many in my profession. She gave me a key." He got up and began to pace the room. "This is most intolerable. I didn't even know Hinchley was back from America until late Saturday night and now I'm being questioned in the man's murder. It's absurd. Why would I want to kill him?"

"No one's accusing you of anything," Witherspoon said soothingly. "We're merely trying to eliminate as many people as possible. By the way, are you absolutely certain you didn't know that Hinchley was in the audience until Mr. Parks mentioned it?" He didn't know why that point seemed important, but it did.

"Of course I'm sure. Why do you ask?"

"Because you were seen looking out at the audience before the play began," Witherspoon said. "And I wondered if perhaps you'd spotted Hinchley. He was right in the third row center. I believe he would have been difficult to miss."

"I didn't see him," Remington snapped. "I may have glanced out but I didn't see Ogden Hinchley."

Witherspoon decided to try a different tactic. "Did Hinchley have any enemies that you know about?"

"He had dozens of them," Remington cried. "Virtually every actor in England hated him, and I dare say, by now most of the ones in New York loathed him as well. But egads, Inspector, if actors murdered every critic that had ever given them a bad review, there wouldn't be any left on either side of the ocean."

Smythe leaned against the doorjamb and watched Betsy put the teapot back in its proper place on the sideboard. She moved with the grace of a dancer and he sighed inwardly, wondering if he'd ever have the nerve to tell her his true feelings.

She turned and gasped, startled by his presence. "I wish you'd stop doing that," she snapped.

"Doin' what?" he asked innocently, knowing he shouldn't irritate her now that he was wanting to make peace. "I was just standin' 'ere."

"You come sneakin' up on a body like that and it's a wonder you don't scare them half to death," she fumed. She was embarrassed because she'd been thinking about him. "I thought you said you were going up to bed."

"I was." He walked to the table and pulled a chair out. "But Wiggins is still readin' all them wretched newspapers and I didn't 'ave the 'eart to make 'im turn out the lamps yet. Besides, I wanted to 'ave a word with you."

She gazed at him suspiciously. "About what?"

"About what you was doin' over at the East End the other day," he shot back.

"That's none of your concern," she replied.

Smythe opened his mouth and then clamped it shut again. Arguing with the lass would only put her back up.

He decided to take another tactic. "I thought we was friends, Betsy," he said gently. "I thought you trusted me."

Betsy felt her resolve melting. She didn't want to tell Smythe what she'd been doing. She didn't want to tell anyone. She was too ashamed. "I do. But sometimes people have things they'd rather keep private. I had some old business to take care of, that's all. But it's over and done with now."

Old business. The words sent a shiver up Smythe's spine. He'd run into some of Betsy's old business before and it liked to put the fear of God in him. On one of their other cases, they'd run into an old acquaintance of Betsy's from her days of struggling to survive in the East End. Raymond Skegit. Blast, Smythe thought, he hoped this latest trip over there didn't have anything to do with the likes of someone like him. Protecting Betsy was all he cared about. How could he protect her if she wouldn't talk? But pressing her wasn't going to get him any answers; that was certain. "All right, Betsy. I'll not bother you on the matter again. It's your secret."

"It's not a secret," she protested. "You're not always telling me what you're up to, either." She glanced over her shoulder at the clock. "It's getting late. I'm going up."

Smythe said goodnight and watched her leave. Her words had hit home. He too had a secret. But he fully intended to share it with her one of these days. When she was ready. When she could hear the truth without wanting to box his ears. He smiled wryly, thinking that the promise he'd made to the late Euphemia Witherspoon, the inspector's aunt, had caused him nothing but trouble.

Euphemia had known she was dying and she'd begged him to stay on at Upper Edmonton Gardens and keep an eye on her "naive nephew," at least until he'd settled in. Smythe, not wanting to upset his old friend, had agreed. One thing had led to another. Soon, Mrs. Jeffries and Betsy had arrived in the household and before you could say Bob's-Your-Uncle, they'd been investigating murders. Acting like a family.

Smythe turned and started for the stairs. But what would his "family" think if they knew that he was rich as sin and too scared to tell them? Would they think he'd lied to them all this time? Would they hate him? Smythe grimaced. The idea of Betsy or any of the others hating him was too awful to think about. One of these days he'd tell them the truth. One of these days. In the meantime he'd continue on the way he was and do his best to keep that silly banker of his from letting the cat out of the bag. Besides, he told himself as he started up the stairs, the fact that he was rich didn't change who he was. It wasn't as if he'd been born that way.

Mrs. Jeffries stared at the black night outside her window. She hadn't even tried to sleep. It would be pointless with her mind still so much on this case. Who had hated Ogden Hinchley enough to murder him? More important, who had gone to so much trouble to try to make it look like an accident? And why had they botched it so badly? Or maybe she was wrong.

If Dr. Bosworth hadn't been in the mortuary that night, they could well have gotten away with it being ruled an accidental death. It was Bosworth's sharp eye that had noted the buttons on the man's clothes and the fact that the shoes were all wrong. Of course the marks around the man's ankles should have been a signal to any physician doing the postmortem that it hadn't been an accidental death. But Mrs. Jeffries knew that there were many doctors who would have dismissed those bruises altogether, if they'd even noticed them at all. Or perhaps the killer hadn't realized he'd left those marks on the victim's body. Or perhaps the killer hadn't cared. Perhaps he was so arrogant that he felt absolutely sure he'd never get caught.

He? Mrs. Jeffries sighed. At least they knew one thing for certain. The killer was a man. No woman could haul a dead body even the short distance between Hinchley's house and the canal.

CHAPTER 4

"Miss Vaughan is a superb actress, Mrs. Jeffries," Witherspoon enthused. "She's so graceful, so accomplished. She fairly lights up the stage when she makes her entrance. It's no wonder the dear lady was so tired when I tried to interview her. Giving such a performance must be extremely taxing on one's strength."

"Excuse me, sir, but I didn't think you'd actually seen the play."

"Well, I didn't actually see her performance," he admitted, "but one could tell from just speaking with Miss Vaughan that she's a true artist."

"I'm sure she is, sir," Mrs. Jeffries said dryly. "No doubt Mr. Remington is an artist as well, yet he managed the interview."

"His part isn't nearly as complex or intense as Miss Vaughan's." Witherspoon waved his fork dismissively. "It's the sort of role a professional actor could do in his

sleep. Why, he was only offered the part because Miss
Vaughan interceded on his behalf.''

"Did he tell you that?" Mrs. Jeffries eyed her employer
suspiciously.

"Constable Barnes picked up that tidbit when he was
interviewing the stagehands," the inspector replied, fork-
ing up another bit of bacon. "Mind you, none of them
had any pertinent information to report, but all of them
knew who the victim was and they'd all heard about his
murder. But back to Miss Vaughan. I tell you, Mrs. Jeffries, I can't remember when I've ever met such a capti-
vating woman. She is utterly superb."

Mrs. Jeffries said nothing. Silently, she sipped her tea,
watching the inspector over the rim of her cup. He'd been
singing Theodora Vaughan's praises since he'd sat down
to eat his breakfast. That was fifteen minutes ago. Surely
the inspector wasn't getting hoodwinked by this actress?
Gracious, the woman was a suspect! But then she remembered the conclusion she herself had come to last night.
The killer was a man. Witherspoon, obviously, had come
to the same conclusion. Maybe well before she had.

Suddenly, her own high spirits plummeted. Mrs. Jeffries put her cup down and stared at the tablecloth. Perhaps the household wasn't as clever as they'd always
thought. Maybe the inspector *could* handle all his cases
on his own. He continued wittering on about Theodora
Vaughan as he finished his breakfast. Mrs. Jeffries, fighting off a sense of failure totally alien to her nature,
stopped listening.

Perhaps if they really worked hard, they could find
some useful information, she told herself. Surely they
weren't totally unnecessary to the investigation. Surely
there was something important they could contribute.

"I say, Mrs. Jeffries." Witherspoon raised his voice.

With a start, she looked up to see him staring at her curiously. "I'm sorry, sir. I was woolgathering. What did you say?"

"I asked you if you had any ideas," he repeated.

She stared at him blankly. "Ideas?"

He smiled kindly. "Why, yes. You've been ever so helpful in the past."

As she hadn't a clue whether he was talking about the household or about the case, she hesitated.

"Now, really, Mrs. Jeffries," Witherspoon encouraged, "you mustn't be so modest. You know very well that I rely on you for this sort of thing."

"Rely on me, sir?"

"But of course. Who else could I possibly ask to advise me on such a delicate matter?"

Now she really didn't know what he was talking about. "Yes, sir, it is a delicate matter."

"I mean, what is one supposed to do in a situation like this?" He drummed his fingers on the table. "Somehow, accepting the invitation seems a bit odd. After all, this is a murder investigation and even though I personally think the dear lady is probably quite innocent . . ."

"Probaby innocent," Mrs. Jeffries interrupted, her spirits lifting a bit. "But wouldn't the murder have had to have been committed by a man?"

Taken aback, he gazed at her. "Not necessarily. I don't see why a woman couldn't grab someone's ankles as easily as a man could. It might be a bit more difficult for a woman to hang onto the chap," he mused, "but certainly not impossible."

"But what about getting the body to the canal?" she asked. It was rare for her to be so confused, but that's exactly what she was. "Unless a woman had extraordinary strength, how could she possibly do it?"

"She probably couldn't." Witherspoon smiled slowly. "But she could have had help."

"Two people?" Blast. Why hadn't the idea occurred to her? Of course he was right. Conspiracies to commit murder were rare, but not impossible. From what little they knew of the victim, there were plenty of people who hated him. But did two of them hate him enough to conspire in murder? From her observation of life, if it were two people, why not more? Perhaps the whole lot of them had gotten together to kill him.

"It's highly unlikely that Miss Vaughan has anything to do with Hinchley's murder," Witherspoon continued. "But the possibility does exist. So you can see my quandry."

"No, sir, I'm afraid I don't."

He drew back, a puzzled frown on his face. "Really, Mrs. Jeffries, I'm surprised at you. Do you honestly think it's fitting to accept a social invitation from the lady when she's a suspect in a murder I'm investigating? Then, of course, there's Lady Cannonberry to consider. I realize there's nothing formal between us, no understandings or anything like that. But I shouldn't like to offend her." A slight blush crept over his cheeks. "She's become quite . . . er . . . important to me."

Mrs. Jeffries decided that she couldn't bluff her way out of this. She hadn't been listening and she might as well own up to it. "Inspector, please forgive me, but as I said a few moments ago, I wasn't listening properly when you were speaking. Precisely what invitation are you talking about?"

"Miss Vaughan's invited me to a dinner party next Monday evening," he said patiently. "She had her maid bring me a note before I left the theatre last night. But I feel I really must decline. Suspect or not, accepting the invitation seems a bit disloyal to Lady Cannonberry.''

Ruth Cannonberry, their neighbor and a very dear friend, was off in the country visiting relatives. She and the Inspector were becoming quite close.

''I understand.'' Mrs. Jeffries nodded in agreement. ''Well, sir, then if I were you, I'd politely decline Miss Vaughan's invitation. I'm sure she'll understand that under the circumstances it would hardly be appropriate.''

''Yes, well, I certainly hope so. I quite admire the lady, but I wouldn't hurt Lady Cannonberry''—he reached for his teacup—''for all the tea in China, as they say.''

''Did you discover anything else yesterday?'' Mrs. Jeffries prodded. She decided to worry about her own abilities as a detective later.

Witherspoon told her about the interviews he'd conducted at the theatre and the background information he'd gotten from the the police constables.

''What did you think of their alibis?'' she asked when he'd finished speaking.

He looked thoughtful. ''I don't really know what to think. The problem is, unless we know precisely when the man was killed, we've not much to investigate when it comes to alibis?''

''But you said you're fairly sure it was late Saturday night or in the very early hours of Sunday morning?''

''Yes, but we don't know for certain.'' He sighed. ''As most people are well asleep in their beds by the time Hinchley was probably murdered, it's difficult to break the alibis of our suspects. Unless we come up with a witness or a cabbie or someone like that, we've really very little hope.''

''I see your point, sir.'' She nodded in agreement.

"Then don't you think it might be useful to find the last person who did see the victim alive? But, of course, you've already thought of that."

As he hadn't, it sounded like a jolly good idea. Witherspoon smiled broadly. "Mrs. Jeffries, I do believe you ought to take to the stage yourself. Perhaps as one of those mind readers at the music hall. That's precisely what I'd decided to do. I'll get the uniformed lads working on it straight away. The man had to get home somehow. Someone must have seen him."

"Why, thank you, sir," she replied, genuinely pleased by his words. "And of course you're instructing the constables to ask about the neighborhood to see if any of them saw anything suspicious on Saturday evening?"

"We've already done that," Witherspoon said. "Yesterday. But no luck there, I'm afraid. No one saw any bodies being trundled off to the canal and tossed off the bridge. We even inquired at the Regents Park Baptist College, in the hopes that one of them might have been out and seen something." He sighed. "But no one had. The Baptists were a bit put out that we'd even asked, too."

His words had given Mrs. Jeffries an idea. Hinchley, though a small man, had been dead weight. She wondered how long it took the killer to move the body. "I expect you'll also be walking the route the killer must have taken from the victim's house to where his body was actually found. Am I right?"

"Bravo, Mrs. Jeffries," Witherspoon cried. Egads, that was a wonderful idea. He was amazed he hadn't thought of it himself. "You've done it. That's exactly what I'm going to do this morning. Frankly, I want to know precisely how long it would take to move a body. After all, the longer the killer was outside the house, the more likely it is that someone might have seen him."

* * *

Wiggins licked the last of the sticky bun off his fingers, pulled out his handkerchief and then wiped his chin. He leaned against the base of the huge, shepherd's hook–shaped lamppost and watched the front entrance of the Hayden Theatre. He'd been hanging about for an hour now and hadn't seen anyone go in or out. He was almost ready to give up.

Despite the heavy foot traffic on the Strand today, none of those feet had turned toward the theatre. "Blimey," he muttered under his breath, "this 'as been a waste of ruddy time." He straightened and crossed the road to the pedestrian island in the center. The walk in front of the theatre remained empty.

Then he saw the front door open, and a young, dark-haired girl dressed in a plain brown dress darted out. She turned and said something to a man standing in the doorway. Then she hurried off, making for the corner.

Wiggins was after her like a shot. He skidded to a halt as he came round the side of building and saw her opening the door of an opulent black carriage. A moment later, she tugged a square wicker case out, heaved it awkwardly under her arm and started right toward him.

"Can I 'elp you with that, miss?" he asked, moving quickly and blocking her path. Up close, he could see that her face was long and thin and her eyes hazel.

She stared at him suspiciously for a moment. Her gaze raked him from head to toe, taking in his neatly pressed trousers, his clean white shirt and his new boots. She smiled flirtatiously. "That's right kind of you. It is a bit heavy." She dumped the box into his outstretched arms. "I'm just taking these things round the corner to the theatre."

"My name's Wiggins," he said, falling into step next to her.

"I'm Rose," she said.

Wiggins pretended to stumble. "Sorry." He caught the box. "Cor, what's in 'ere? Feels 'eavy."

"It's just a few costumes," the girl replied. "My mistress is Theodora Vaughan."

"The actress?" Wiggins couldn't believe his luck.

"That's right. She's in a play at this very theatre," Rose said proudly. "Plays the lead. She's a star, she is."

"You're lucky to work for someone like that," Wiggins enthused. "Must be ever so excitin'."

"Oh, I am," Rose agreed. "I'm Miss Vaughan's personal maid. It's not like I scrub floors or do any heavy work."

"Is she nice then?"

"Nicest mistress I've ever had," Rose replied. "Training me proper too. I've learned to do hair and take care of all her clothes . . ."

"Like these? Are you bringin' 'em to the theatre for her?" he asked, trying desperately to keep her talking.

"Those are old costumes." Rose waved her hand in dismissal. "She doesn't need them anymore so she's giving them to the Hayden."

"Just old costumes?" He contrived to sound disappointed.

"You needn't say it like that," she snapped. "It's right kind of Miss Vaughan to be giving away these things."

"I'm sure it is," Wiggins said quickly. They were almost at the door. He couldn't lose her, not now. She worked for one of the suspects.

"Thank you ever so much for carrying this for me," Rose said as they came close to the entrance. "It was heavy."

Wiggins pretended to trip. The case flew out of his arms and landed right in front of the door. The lid popped open and a mass of black velvet and silk spilled out onto the pavement.

"Oh." Rose dropped to her knees in alarm. "Garvey'll 'ave my head if these things get dirty."

"I'm sorry." Wiggins dropped down beside her. "Tell this Garvey person it were my fault. I'm a big, clumsy oaf. My guv's right. I'm too dumb to be let out without a leash." He gave Rose his most pathetic, poor-little-me expression.

Her anger immediately evaporated and was replaced with a look of pity. "Your employer talks to you like that?"

Dumbly, wishing he could cry on cue, he nodded. "Yeah. He only keeps me on because I work real cheap."

"Why, you poor thing," Rose cried.

"Oh, it's all right." He made his lower lip tremble. "I'm used to it and my guv don't mean no 'arm. That's just the way 'e is."

"That's no excuse for treating you like dirt," Rose declared. "I'd not put up with it."

"But you work for a kind mistress." Wiggins, who was quite enjoying himself by now, pointed to the velvet trousers that Rose was folding. "Generous, she is."

"She has her moments," Rose said chattily. She put the clothes back in the case and slammed the lid down. "Mind you, she's no saint. She can be a bit . . . what's the word Mr. Delaney always uses . . . temperamental. Yes, that's it. Like all actors, she can be temperamental," she repeated, obviously proud of herself for learning such a posh word. "Came back from the country house on Saturday in a right nasty mood. Complained about the train, complained about the weather, complained about the crowds at the station. 'Course she were probably just het up because it was opening night.''

''Well, it's nice of her to be givin' away 'er costumes,'' Wiggins said.

Rose laughed. ''She's only donating these things because she doesn't want to do pantomime or trouser roles anymore. Claims those kind of parts is beneath her now.'' She jutted her chin toward the door. ''And this place can use all the help it can get.''

''What'da ya mean?'' Wiggins got up and helped Rose to her feet.

Rose flicked a glance at the front door. ''Well,'' she said softly, ''this isn't the best theatre on the Strand. They haven't had a successful show here in ages. I don't know what Miss Vaughan was thinking of, agreeing to play here. She could have her pick of parts if she wanted to. Of course, this was probably the only place that would agree to produce Mr. Delaney's play. Not that it's a bad one, mind you. But if you ask me, it is a bit dull.''

''Then why does Miss Vaughan want to be in it?''

Rose laughed gaily. ''Because she's in love with him, that's why. She'll do anything for Mr. Delaney. Anything at all. Not that I blame her . . . but still, some say it's not right.''

''What's not right,'' Wiggins asked, ''her bein' in love with Mr. Delaney?''

Rose yanked open the heavy wooden front door and stepped inside. ''Shhh . . .'' she cautioned. ''You've got to be careful what you say around here. People are always running about carrying tales. Eddie, are you about, then? Blast!'' She stamped her foot and looked around the huge foyer. ''I told that man I'd be right back. Where's he got to, then?''

''I'm right here, girl.'' Eddie Garvey, holding a hammer in his hand, frowned suspiciously as Wiggins popped out from behind a pillar. "Just leave the costumes there, girl," he instructed the maid. "I'll get them to the back."

Rose nodded and flounced out the way she'd come. "It wouldn't have hurt him to say 'thank you,' " she muttered. She stalked toward the corner. "Ruddy stage manager. Thinks he's too good to bother thanking the likes of someone like me."

Wiggins desperately wanted to get her talking about Theodora Vaughan again. But he couldn't think how to bring the subject up. Cor, he couldn't lose her. Not now. "Uh, excuse me, Miss Rose."

She whirled around. "What?"

"If I may be so bold, miss. Would you like to 'ave a cup of tea? I mean, if you're not in a great 'urry to get back. There's a Lyons just up the road."

"I'm in no rush to get back." Rose cocked her head to one side. "Tea, you say? Cakes too?"

Wiggins put his hand in his pocket. He had plenty of coins. "Cakes too," he agreed quickly. "And sticky buns as well if you want 'em."

Lilly Coltrane wasn't a very pretty girl. With her round, pudgy face; frizzy, dull brown hair and bulbous, watery blue eyes, she looked dim-witted, but Betsy had realized after only a few moments of speaking to the maid that she was as sharp as they come.

She'd deliberately cornered the girl when she'd spotted her leaving the Hinchley house, a shopping basket tucked under her arm. Getting Lilly in a conversation was as easy as snapping your fingers. "So did you like working for Mr. Hinchley?" Betsy asked. She leaned against the railing on the bridge over the canal.

Lilly shrugged. "Just as soon work for him as most.

Of course, the last three months has been dead easy, what
with him being gone to America. Quite a shock it give
Rather and me when he turned up all sudden like on Saturday afternoon.'' She laughed. ''Luckily, the house was
turned out proper, excepting for the rooms we'd closed
off.''

''I heard that Mr. Hinchley was a real nasty sort,''
Betsy ventured. Though Lilly dearly loved the sound of
her own voice, she hadn't said much that was useful.

Lilly shook her head. ''He weren't that bad. He weren't
the sort to forget a slight, I'll say that for him. But he
could be quite kind. When my mum took sick last year,
he gave me the money to make sure she had a proper
doctor and all. I was quite grateful.''

''Then how come all them actors and such hated him?''
Betsy persisted. She was going to get Lilly talking about
this if it was the last thing she did.

Lilly waved her hand. ''Oh, them. They was always
coming round and having a go at him. Silly sort, aren't
they? I mean, take that actor—Remington, his name is.
Almost came to blows with Mr. Hinchley.''

''Did this Mr. Remington actually strike Mr. Hinchley?''

''And risk being hit in the face?'' She laughed. ''Not
blooming likely. All he did was scream and carry on loud
enough to wake the dead.''

''Guess this Mr. Remington didn't like Mr. Hinchley's
review.''

''It weren't about a review,'' Lilly said eagerly. ''It
were about money. That's what was so odd about it.
Seems this actor claimed Mr. Hinchley owed him some
money and he wanted to collect it before he went off to
America. Well, they got so loud with their shoutin' and
all that Mr. Mickleshaft, our next door neighbor, he come

over and told them if they didn't quiet down so he could get some sleep, he'd have the police on them for disturbing the peace. So Mr. Remington left.''

Betsy's mind whirled with the information. ''That's not very smart, having a row in the middle of the night like that.''

''It weren't the middle of the night. Mr. Mickleshaft doesn't sleep at night. To hear him complain about it he doesn't sleep at all. He's one of them silly types that's always ailin' but hasn't really been sick a day in his life. Insomnia—who ever heard of such a thing!'' Lilly snorted derisively. Then she started toward the other side of the bridge. ''Well, I can't stand here chattin' all day. I'd best be getting back. Even with Mr. Hinchley dead there's things that need doing.''

''So you're staying on, then?'' Betsy asked as she hurried to keep up with the girl's quick steps.

Lilly smiled widely. ''This is the easiest position I've ever had. Especially now that Hinchley's dead. I'm staying until that ruddy solicitor sells the house and tosses me out. I hope it takes a long time. They're going to be selling off his house and furniture, not that they'll get much for some of that silly stuff Mr. Hinchley had about.'' She snorted again. ''Looks like something out of a picture book, the stuff in the drawing room does.''

''Oh,'' Betsy said quickly. ''Really? Strange tastes, had he?''

''Not just in furnishings, either.'' Lilly smiled slyly. ''If you know what I mean.''

Betsy could guess. ''At least you didn't have to worry about him trying to paw you,'' she said, giving the girl a knowing woman-to-woman look. ''Not like some households.''

Lilly nodded. ''Of course, the footman, he used to lead

him a merry chase. Oh, well, live and let live, that's what I always say. And like you said, it kept him from bothering me that way. Give me a bit of peace. As long as I minded myself and pretended not to notice all his silly ceremonies, he left me alone to do my work.''

''What ceremonies?'' Betsy asked. She noticed that despite Lilly's protests that she had to get back, the girl dawdled so she could continue talking.

They'd come to the other side of the bridge. Lilly stopped and gazed at Betsy thoughtfully. ''You're asking a lot of questions,'' she said.

Betsy gave her a wide, innocent smile. ''Sorry if I'm nosy. It's just that you've such an interesting way of telling things, I can't help myself.''

''I do have a way with words,'' Lilly agreed. ''Everyone says so. My mum used to say I could tell a tale better than anyone.''

''And it's dead boring where I work,'' Betsy said earnestly.

''Most houses is when you're a maid,'' she replied. ''I always liked working for Mr. Hinchley, even though sometimes he could be nasty. He left me alone as long as I minded my own business and did me work, and his house was a lot more interestin' than most places.''

''Tell me about his secret ceremonies,'' Betsy said eagerly.

Lilly looked a little sheepish. ''Well, he didn't have all that many,'' she admitted. ''Just the one, and then only on the nights when he was reviewing a new play.''

''What'd he do then?'' Betsy prompted.

''He had a complete routine,'' Lilly said. She started walking again. ''It never varied and he was right strict about it, too. First of all, he always left the house at exactly the same time, half past six. We was under instructions that once he was gone, we was to carry on, have our dinner and then go to bed. He didn't want no one waiting up for him. Right before we locked up for the night, Rather was to unlock the side door and make sure the boiler was fired so there'd be plenty of hot water for his bath."

"Is that it then?" Betsy was disappointed. "He took a bath when he came home from the theatre?"

Lilly giggled. "He took a bath all right, but he made sure he had someone there to scrub his back. That's why he insisted the side door be kept unlocked. He wanted his friend to be able to slip in without anyone seeing."

Betsy steeled herself to keep asking questions. But she had a fair idea where this was leading and it made her half sick to her stomach. She knew from her days in the poverty-stricken East End the kind of sick, ugly games the rich could buy for themselves. The fact that a side door was kept unlocked and the servants instructed to go to bed told her one thing. Whoever came to Hinchley's house wasn't a real friend; it was someone who was being paid. Probably someone who hated it and probably hated Hinchley as well.

Lilly gave Betsy a sharp look when she kept silent. "I'm not makin' this up, you know. I seen it with my own eyes. One night I had to get up and go do my business, you see, and there right in the hallway was this young man. 'Course I knew if Mr. Hinchley knew I'd spotted the fellow I'd get sacked, so I flattened meself against the shadows at the top of the stairs. A few minutes later I heard Mr. Hinchley call out that he was through writing the review and the lad could come in and help him get in the bath." Lilly broke off and stared in the distance, her giggling brightness suddenly gone. "Upset me, it did. The idea of someone being about to buy another person like that. Don't know why. God knows, us poor people don't have much choice—it's either sell your labor if you can or sell your body.''

''Are you absolutely sure it was Mr. Hinchley you saw getting in the hansom?'' Witherspoon asked the man. ''You couldn't have been mistaken, Mr. Packard?''

''Know his face as well as I know me own,'' Packard replied. ''Everyone that works in the business knew Hinchley. That man had closed more shows than a smallpox epidemic.''

''Really?'' Witherspoon found that quite odd. He could understand that actors and playwrights might know the critic, but he was quite amazed to find a limelighter who did. ''Everyone?''

Packard grinned, revealing several tobacco-blackened teeth. ''Hinchley had a lot of influence, Inspector. But even if he didn't, we would have known who he was. Mr. Swinton made sure we all knew who he was. We was under orders to make sure Hinchley didn't get backstage.''

''Goodness, Mr. Swinton gave you those instructions Saturday night?''

''Nah,'' Packard replied. ''He give us those instructions months ago. Different play here then, but that didn't make any difference to Mr. Swinton. Hated Hinchley. Didn't want him nosing about the place.''

''Did he say why?''

''Didn't say and none of us asked,'' Packard said with a casual shrug.

''But surely you've some idea?''

Packard glanced over his shoulder toward the stage. It was empty. ''Well, my guess is he didn't want Hinchley having a close look at the scenery or the props. We cut a few corners here and there, you know. Got to make ends meet.''

''The theatre is in financial difficulties?''

Packard laughed. ''That's a polite way of puttin' it. There hasn't been a money-makin' production here in five years. Part of that's due to Hinchley's bad reviews. Part of it's due to the fact that this theatre ain't what she used to be. Don't attract the top drawer anymore, the cream, so to speak.''

''That's interesting,'' Witherspoon said. ''But back to your identification of Mr. Hinchley. You're certain you saw him getting into a hansom right after the performance, is that correct?''

''Right.'' Packard pointed toward the side of the auditorium. ''It were right out in the alley. I'd gone out and gotten a hansom for Miss Vaughan and was seein' her off when all of a sudden, Hinchley comes strolling out the side door, saunters up the alley and hails a hansom. Well, blow me for a game of tin soldiers, I thought. If Mr. Swinton had seen Hinchley comin' out that door instead of the front, there'd be some heads rolling around here. I were only glad it weren't going to be mine.''

''So Hinchley must have gotten into the backstage area,'' Barnes said. ''Otherwise he couldn't have come out the side door.''

''That's right. 'Course when I asked round in here, no one would admit to seein' him.'' Packard crossed his arms over his chest. ''They might have been telling the truth too; everyone's pretty busy right after the curtain goes down. But my guess is Hinchley slipped into the back, had a good gander at the scenery and whatnot and then took himself off without so much as a by-your-leave.''

"And this was directly after the performance?" Witherspoon wanted to be absolutely, positively clear about the time.

"Not more than five minutes. Miss Vaughan asked me to get her a hansom right after she come off the stage. By the time I got him round to the side, she was waiting there to go."

"Packard, I told you to fix this ruddy door." The director's sharp voice boomed from the side of the stage. "What are you doing larking about? We've got a performance in a few hours and I don't want this thing sticking again in the first act."

Witherspoon stared at Albert Parks as he stepped into view from the side of the stage. "Mr. Packard is speaking to us," he called out. "Please don't be angry with him. He's answering a few questions."

"I'd best get back to work," Packard muttered as he edged away.

"Thank you for your assistance, sir," Witherspoon said. "You've been most helpful." He turned back toward the stage. "Mr. Parks, may I have a word with you?"

"Me?" Parks's eyes bulged. "Why on earth would you want to speak to me?"

"It's merely routine, sir," the inspector assured him. Gracious, how on earth did people think the police actually solved murders if they didn't ask questions? "We won't take too much of your time."

Parks stared at them sourly. "Oh, all right, if I must. I'll be with you in a moment."

"Too bad Mr. Swinton and Mr. Delaney aren't here," Barnes muttered softly. "This one doesn't look like he wants to tell us anything."

"Very few people do, Constable," Witherspoon said. "And I'm a tad annoyed that the other gentlemen are gone. We told them we'd be back this afternoon to ask more questions.''

Parks, pointedly looking at the watch on his waistcoat, came hurrying toward them. "Do please make this quick, sir. I've not much time."

"But it's hours before tonight's performance," Barnes pointed out.

Parks tucked his watch in. "And there's an enormous amount of work to do yet. Just because the actors aren't emoting all over the stage doesn't mean I'm not busy."

"Mr. Parks," Witherspoon began, "we'll try not to inconvenience you too much. But we've a few questions we must ask. How well did you know Mr. Hinchley?"

Parks thought about it for a moment. "I knew of him, of course. Everyone in the theatre did. But I didn't know him all that well. Not personally."

"Did you like him, sir?" Barnes asked.

"He was a critic." Parks sneered the last word. "Of course I didn't like him."

"Had he reviewed any of your previous productions?" Witherspoon asked.

Parks hesitated. "He reviewed my production of *Hamlet*. He didn't like it overly much. But Hinchley was kinder to me about it than to Remington. He actually said Remington's performance in the title role was so bad that if Shakespeare were alive to see it, he'd have died of apoplexy on the spot."

"Did you know he was in the theatre on Saturday evening?"

Again, Parks hesitated. "Well, I believe I heard someone mention they saw him out front."

That was a lie, Witherspoon thought. They'd already been told by Trevor Remington that Parks had spotted Hinchley sitting in the audience. Drat. Why did people persist in lying to the police? ''And you were unhappy that he was here?''

''He was a critic. Inspector,'' Parks drew himself up straighter. ''I'm neither pleased nor displeased to know they're in the audience. It's simply a fact of life that one has to put up with.''

''What time did you leave the theatre?'' Witherspoon asked. He remembered his discussion with his housekeeper.

''Right after the performance,'' Parks replied. ''I was in a hurry to get home. I wanted to make some notes on some changes I'm doing for the first act.''

''Did anyone see you?'' Barnes asked.

''When I got home?'' Parks lifted one shoulder in a casual shrug. ''My housekeeper might have heard me come in. It was after eleven-thirty so I didn't see her, of course. But I noticed the light on under her door when I went upstairs.''

Witherspoon asked, ''How did you get home?''

''I walked, Inspector,'' Parks said impatiently. ''I live on Pope Street. It took ten minutes to get home.''

''Did anyone see you walking home?'' Barnes prodded.

Parks shook his head. ''Not that I remember. It was quite late at night. The streets were fairly empty. I went home, let myself in, wrote up my notes and went to bed.''

''Where are they, sir?'' Barnes asked.

''Where are what?'' Parks asked irritably.

''The notes, sir? I'd like to see them.''

Parks's eyes narrowed. ''Well, you can't. I put them down backstage and now I can't find them. I don't know what you're implying. But if I were you, I wouldn't waste my time questioning innocent people. I didn't like Ogden Hinchley but I certainly didn't kill him. Ridiculous. There wouldn't be a critic left in all of England if they were murdered because they'd given a bad reviews. If I were you, I'd start talking to people who had personal reasons for hating Hinchley.''

''Who would they be, sir?'' Witherspoon asked.

''A number of people, sir.'' Parks's smile was slow and sly. ''To begin with, you might ask Edmund Delaney what he did after the performance. He hated Hinchley and his reasons were personal.''

CHAPTER 5

—⬦⬦⬦—

"I've a dreadful headache, Mrs. Jeffries." The inspector rubbed the bridge of his nose. "Absolutely dreadful. I say, is there time before dinner for us to have a glass of sherry?"

"But of course, sir," she replied as she got up and went to the sideboard. "With all this heat, it's only a light supper. Mrs. Goodge will send it up whenever we're ready. I believe a glass of Harvey's will relax you. Perhaps help your headache." She poured two small glasses of the amber liquid and, smiling sympathetically at her dear employer, handed one to him. "Oh, really, sir. It's quite awful how you exhaust yourself on these cases."

"One must do one's duty." He took a sip and sighed softly. "Today was quite trying. Theatre people are so . . . so . . ."

"Melodramatic," she finished for him. "That's what you called them this morning, sir."

"And I was right too. Not only are they a melodramatic

lot, but they're rather cavalier about the most important matters.''

''Really, sir?'' She took a sip from her own glass and waited for him to continue. As Luty would say, he'd come home with a bee in his bonnet, and she'd decided it would be best to let him unburden himself at his own pace. ''In what way?''

''Humphhh.'' He snorted delicately. ''They're not very good at keeping appointments, I can tell you that. Do you know that neither Swinton nor Delaney were at the theatre today? They knew perfectly well we were coming back to talk with them and neither of them could be bothered to show up. I say, Mrs. Jeffries, that's not good. Not good at all.''

''So you didn't learn much today, sir?'' she queried.

''I wouldn't say that,'' he replied, tossing back another mouthful. ''Actually, we had quite an interesting interview with Albert Parks. He claims he only knew Hinchley in a professional capacity. Of course, that's what all of them say.''

''Do you believe him, sir?''

''I'm not sure.'' Witherspoon thought about it for a moment. ''I think so, but then again, it's difficult to say.''

''Why is that, sir?''

''Well, I'm fairly certain he told us one lie today,'' he replied. He told her about Parks's claim that he thought he heard someone mention Hinchley's presence in the audience. ''But we know that Parks had actually seen the man out front. So I'm wondering why he'd bother to lie over a trifle like that? I mean, if he was going to lie, why not tell us that he didn't know Hinchley was in the theatre at all?'' It was most puzzling for the inspector. He hoped his housekeeper might have an idea about it.

''Does he have an alibi, sir?'' she asked.

Disappointed, Witherspoon sighed and pushed his glasses back up his nose. ''Not exactly. He claims to have gone home right after the performance to make some notes on changes he wanted in the first act. But when Constable Barnes asked to see them, he said he couldn't find them. I find that odd too, but not as odd as that silly lie.'' Really, didn't Mrs. Jeffries have any thoughts on the matter?

''I see,'' Mrs. Jeffries replied.

The inspector stared at her. ''Don't you find Parks's behaviour odd?'' he finally asked.

''I do, sir,'' she said calmly and then went back to sipping her sherry.

''Well, don't you have any thoughts on the matter?'' he asked.

Mrs. Jeffries shrugged. ''It seems to me, sir, that he wasn't really lying. He never said he didn't know that Hinchley was out front; he merely didn't mention that he'd seen the man. It could well be that in his own mind, there was no need for him to tell you the circumstances of how he came by the information.'' She could tell this point niggled the inspector, but she honestly didn't see how it could matter. ''Did you see Miss Vaughan today?''

''Not exactly,'' he replied. ''I think sending my regrets to her invitation might have offended her. She sent a note along to the theatre today saying she was indisposed.''

''Excuse me, sir,'' Mrs. Jeffries said. ''But that doesn't mean you're not going to question her again, does it?''

''Oh, no.'' He laughed. ''Of course not. I'm a policeman, Mrs. Jeffries. I must question her again. However, I do believe that it can wait until tomorrow. I know that she left the theatre right after the play ended on Saturday evening.''

He went on to tell her everything. Mrs. Jeffries listened calmly, asking questions where appropriate, clucking her tongue sympathetically and generally learning every little detail of his day. One never knew what might or might not be important.

An hour later, with dinner over and the inspector firmly ensconced in his room writing a letter to Lady Cannonberry, Mrs. Jeffries hurried down the kitchen steps.

Luty Belle and Hatchet had just arrived, Mrs. Goodge was putting the teapot on the table and Fred was jumping about, wagging his tail and generally making a nuisance of himself.

"Good, we're all 'ere, then," Smythe said. He was already seated at the table.

"Give us a minute," Betsy said as she shoved the last of the dinner plates into the cupboard. "Some of us have work to finish."

Luty, frowning thoughtfully as she watched Betsy and Mrs. Goodge bustling about the kitchen tidying up, said, "maybe I ought to send Effie over to help out when we're on a case."

"There's no need for that," Wiggins said quickly. The thought of Effie, one of Luty's homelier maids, hanging about Upper Edmonton Gardens, sent cold chills down the footman's spine. Effie was a maid whom Luty had taken in because the girl had lost her position when they were investigating an earlier case. She was sweet on the footman. Wiggins hated to hurt Effie's feelings and he was afraid that if she were here, dogging his footsteps and watching him like a lovesick calf, he just might have a slip of the tongue.

"We'd never get away with it," Betsy agreed breathlessly as she dropped into the chair next to Smythe. "The inspector would notice if there was a new maid about the place. But it's right nice of you to offer.'' She smiled at Luty.

''You look right ragged, girl.'' Luty shook her head as she took in the maid's disheveled appearance. Stray locks of hair had slipped out of Betsy's topknot, her apron was wrinkled and there was a tight, worried set to the girl's face.

''I'm just a bit rushed today,'' Betsy explained quickly. She could feel Smythe boring a hole in the side of her head with his steely stare. The man was overprotective enough as it was; she didn't want him nagging at her to take things easy. ''I was late getting back, that's all.''

''But Luty does have a point,'' Mrs. Jeffries said thoughtfully. ''The rest of us can put many of our tasks to one side when we're on a case, especially in the summer months. But you and Mrs. Goodge can't. It doesn't seem right.''

''We 'aven't been 'elpin' enough,'' Smythe said softly. ''You'll run yourself sick if you're not careful. From now on, I'll nip in early and 'elp Mrs. Goodge with the supper things.''

''You will not,'' Betsy exclaimed. ''How would we explain you washing up or setting the table if the inspector came down to get Fred for a walk?''

''But Mrs. Jeffries is right,'' Smythe protested. ''I can put off a lot of my duties and so can Wiggins.''

''I wouldn't say that,'' Wiggins interrupted. ''I've still got to see to things about the place.''

''Why don't we discuss this at another time?'' Mrs. Jeffries interrupted. ''It's getting late. We've a lot to cover tonight. Who would like to go first?''

''I believe you ought to speak,'' Hatchet said. ''It is

vitally important that we know what the inspector has learned.''

Mrs. Jeffries sighed silently as she scanned the faces at the table. They were still skittish and afraid that the inspector was going to solve this case before they could. ''As you wish.'' She spent the next fifteen minutes telling them what she'd gotten out of Witherspoon. They all listened carefully. Even Wiggins paid attention. ''That's it, then. He's going to try to talk to the rest of them tomorrow. Who'd like to go next?''

''I 'ad a bit of luck today,'' Wiggins volunteered. ''I managed to meet Theodora Vaughan's maid. I was actually right clever, got 'er to come out with me and 'ave tea. Her name's Rose, and a right nice girl she is too.''

''Get on with it, Wiggins,'' Mrs. Goodge ordered. ''You can sing this girl's praises some other time. But right now, tell us what you learned.''

Wiggins, annoyed that he wasn't going to have the chance to brag about his cleverness, frowned but did as he was told. He started at the beginning, and, as Mrs. Jeffries had taught him, mentioned every single detail of the meeting.

''But I really struck gold when we was 'avin' tea,'' he said. ''That's when I found out about Miss Vaughan and Mr. Remington. They're not divorced.''

''Divorced?'' Mrs. Jeffries repeated. ''You mean they're married?''

''Didn't I just say they was?'' Wiggins replied and frowned thoughtfully. ''Sorry, I meant to. They've been married for years. They was supposed to have gotten a divorce a couple of years back when they was tourin' in America. But they didn't. There was some kind of a legal cock-up and they're still married. But everyone in London thinks they got the divorce, ya see. For the past year, Miss Vaughan's had her solicitor tryin' to sort it out, but he can't. But that's not the important bit. The reason Miss Vaughan's been tryin' to get it all sorted out is because she's in love with Mr. Delaney. They've been together for almost a year. She wants to marry 'im, but she can't 'cause she's still married to Mr. Remington. Rose told me that Miss Vaughan is desperate to make sure no one finds out she ain't divorced from Mr. Remington.''

"Because she's living in sin with Mr. Delaney?" Mrs. Goodge asked, her face set in disapproval.

"She's not livin' with 'im," Wiggins replied. "But he's round at 'er 'ouse all the time."

"What else did Rose tell you?" Betsy asked.

"She didn't say much more than that," he admitted. "She sort of dried up. I don't think she meant to tell me as much as she did."

"That's very interesting, Wiggins," Mrs. Jeffries said thoughtfully. "Did you manage to find out if Rose could vouch for Miss Vaughan's alibi?"

He shook his head. "All Rose said when I brought it up was that she'd slept like the dead on Saturday night."

"That's too bad." Luty drummed her fingers on the table. "Seems to me if we can't find out what everyone was up to that night, we'll never solve this case."

"We'll solve it," Mrs. Jeffries said firmly. She glanced at Mrs Goodge. "Were any of your sources helpful today?"

Mrs. Goodge made a face. "Not really. The best I could do was a bit of information on Albert Parks and it weren't much. Seems he got run off from a theatre in Manchester because there was some that thought he had sticky fingers. The receipts kept disappearing when he was in charge. But it was a long time ago, and from what I could learn, that bit of indiscretion doesn't have anything to do with Hinchley's murder.''

Mrs. Jeffries wasn't so certain. But she wasn't sure she ought to ask the cook to investigate it further. She debated the matter to herself. The whole lot of them were already second-guessing their every move. It wouldn't do to imply they weren't doing the best they could. But on the other hand, on many of their other cases, things from the suspects' past had been very important.

"Excellent, Mrs. Goodge.'' she smiled brightly. "Do keep on digging. Your contributions are always so very helpful. But you know, it might be useful to find out a bit more about Parks's past,'' she ventured, watching the cook's face to see if she was offended.

"You might be right.'' Mrs. Goodge nodded eagerly. "You never know when something from someone's past turns out to be the clue that we need. We've proved that more than once. I've got people coming by tomorrow. I should find out more then and I'll get my sources diggin' up more on who was about when Parks got run off from Manchester.''

Hatchet cleared his throat. "If no one has any objection, I believe I'd like to speak next. As you all know, I've a number of connections in the theatrical world.'' Luty snorted faintly, but he ignored her. "And I must say, I do think I've learned something quite important today.'' He stopped, picked up his tea and took a sip.

"Are you goin' to tell us or do we have to guess?'' Luty snapped.

"Do be patient, madam.'' He put the cup down. "I found out that Edmund Delaney and Ogden Hinchley aren't merely professional acquaintances. They were once very good friends. Up until about a year ago, Delaney actually lived in a small house in Chelsea that Hinchley owned. The gossip was that he was paying little or no rent on the place. The two men had gone to Italy together. Hinchley was paying, of course. Delaney hasn't any money. All of a sudden, Delaney shows back up in England, packs up his stuff and moves out of the house in Chelsea.''

"I wonder what happened?" Mrs. Jeffries murmured.

Hatchet coughed. "I believe, madam, that it was a woman who caused the breach in the friendship. It was shortly after Delaney returned that he was seen squiring Miss Vaughan about. The gossip about them is equally interesting. It's being said that Miss Vaughan has provided Mr. Delaney with financial support since his return from the continent.''

There was a shocked silence. Wiggins's eyes were boggling, Mrs. Goodge was shaking her head in disapproval and even Smythe looked disgusted.

"Why's everyone so quiet?" Betsy asked.

"Because it's awful," Smythe said. "From what Hatchet's sayin', Edmund Delaney's a kept man.''

"So?" Betsy persisted. "None of you would be shocked if it was the other way around.''

"We're not shocked," Mrs. Goodge declared. "Just disgusted. A kept man, indeed. What's the world coming to?''

"Did you learn anything else?" Mrs. Jeffries asked. "Not that what you've told us isn't enough," she amended hastily. "It's excellent . . .''

Hatchet laughed. "I didn't take offense. I'll keep at it, of course, and see what else I can find out.''

"Is it my turn yet?" Luty demanded.

The housekeeper tried to hide a smile behind her teacup. Luty and Hatchet were arch rivals when it came to ferreting out clues. "Please, Luty, go right ahead."

Luty sat up straighter in her chair. "Well, I didn't have much luck findin' out who's goin' to get Hinchley's estate; Stampton wasn't available. But I'll hunt him down yet. I did find out that Willard Swinton's in hock up to his neck over that theatre."

"He's got it mortgaged?" Smythe said.

"To the hilt." Luty grinned. "And that ain't the best part. Guess who's holdin' the bulk of the note?"

"That's easy, madam," Hatchet said smoothly. "It's obviously Ogden Hinchley."

Luty glared at him. "Was you eavesdroppin' on me?"

"One wouldn't have to eavesdrop to guess that particular point of information. You were so pleased with yourself it had to be Hinchley."

"Humph."

Mrs. Jeffries decided to intervene before this got out of hand. Honestly, between worrying about keeping their confidence up and worrying about their competitiveness on gathering information, it was a wonder her wits still worked at all. "That's very interesting, Luty," she said hastily.

"And that ain't all. Supposedly, Swinton got the mortgage from some sort of middleman, he didn't have any idea until recently that it was Hinchley who held the note. My source told me that when he found out, he was so mad, he almost had a conniption fit."

"When did he find out?" Betsy asked.

"That's the best part." Luty's eyes twinkled. "Swinton found out on Saturday, the day Hinchley came back from America."

"How did he find out?" Mrs. Jeffries asked.

"From the middleman. He'd come around to the theatre

late Saturday afternoon to collect his payment, and somehow he let it slip that Hinchley held the note on the place.''

''That's most intriguing,'' Mrs. Jeffries murmured. ''Especially if he was angry.''

''Yeah,'' Luty agreed, ''but was he mad enough to kill Hinchley? That's the question. 'Cause even with Hinchley dead, his estate would still have the note on the Hayden.''

''But Hinchley wouldn't benefit from it,'' Hatchet said. ''It's too bad you haven't been able to ascertain who does benefit from Hinchley's estate.'' He smiled smugly at his employer.

''Don't you worry about that, Hatchet,'' Luty said confidently. ''By tomorrow night, I oughta know.''

''Good. We mustn't close our minds to all the possiblities in this case.'' Mrs. Jeffries looked at the only two who hadn't spoken yet. ''Who'd like to go next?''

''I will,'' Betsy said. She wanted to get it over with. Slowly, she told them about her meeting with Hinchley's maid. By the time she'd finished, she knew her cheeks were flaming and she was practically cross-eyed from staring at the same spot on the table.

Mrs. Jeffries deliberately kept her voice matter-of-fact. ''So according to Lilly, Hinchley's habit when he reviewed a new play never varied.''

''That's what she said.''

''If the side door was unlocked,'' Luty put in, ''anyone could have come in and killed him.''

''But how would they know the door was unlocked?'' Mrs. Goodge asked.

''Betsy found out easy enough,'' Wiggins said. ''Sounds to me like this Lilly told anyone who'd stand still for a few seconds anything they wanted to know.''

"Meaning that if someone wanted to find out about Hinchley's habits, they wouldn't have to work very hard at it," Mrs. Jeffries agreed.

"I think lots of people knew about his . . . er . . . habits," Betsy said. "From the way Lilly spoke, he'd been carrying on like this a good while."

"For the last year," Smythe said.

Mrs. Jeffries looked at him sharply. "What did you find out?"

"I tracked down that cabbie that took him to the Hayden," he grimaced. "You were right. Hinchley did make a stop."

"Where?"

"At a house on Lisle Street."

"Who lives there?" Wiggins asked.

"No one really *lives* there." Smythe stumbled over the words. Cor blimey, saying it out loud in front of a roomful of decent women wasn't going to be easy. "It's more like people work there, if you get my meanin'."

"A workhouse?" Betsy muttered. "On Lisle Street?"

Smythe cleared his throat. Blast, he was going to have to explain it. "It's not a workhouse."

"Then what in tarnation is it?" Luty demanded.

"I believe," Hatchet said, "that Smythe is referring to a brothel."

Luty's head jerked sharply as she looked at her butler. "How the dickens do you know that?"

"Really, madam." Hatchet clucked his tongue. "You ought to be ashamed of yourself for the ideas that are popping into your head. Surely you know me better than that? At my age and with my experience of life, there's little about London that I don't know—and certainly not because I'm a frequenter of such places. Now, if I may continue. If Smythe is referring to the place I think he is, then it's one that caters to anyone with . . . shall we say, unusual tastes.''

"Unusual tastes, huh," Luty said, shaking her head. "Well, what of it? He isn't the first man to do it and I expect he won't be the last."

"'Inchley didn't stay inside long, at least not long enough to do . . .'' Smythe broke off. There were simply no words to say what he needed to say.

"Maybe it don't take him long," Luty muttered.

Wiggins looked confused and Mrs. Jeffries deliberately kept her expression blank but the others couldn't help themselves. Betsy giggled. Mrs. Goodge snickered. Even Hatchet cracked a grin.

"He didn't stay long enough to patronize the establishment at that particular time," Mrs. Jeffries suggested quickly. "Is that what you're trying to tell us?"

Smythe nodded. "But since he didn't do anything, why'd he stop?"

Luty opened her mouth but Hatchet, fearing his mistress wouldn't bother to mince her words, spoke before she could. "Perhaps he stopped to make arrangements for later?"

"The side door," Betsy murmured. "That's it. That's why he stopped at that . . . place. He was buying someone for later. For after he wrote his review."

"Cor blimey, that's probably who killed 'im." Smythe shook his head. "This case doesn't 'ave a ruddy thing to do with the Hayden Theatre."

"I don't think so," Mrs. Jeffries said.

"Why not?" Luty demanded. "Maybe they got in an argument over the money. Maybe Hinchley didn't want to pay what he'd promised."

"Hinchley would have taken care of the business end of things when he stopped to make the arrangements," Hatchet said.

"I agree," Mrs. Jeffries said. "Besides, professional . . . uh . . ."

"Prostitutes," Luty supplied blandly.

"Right, prostitutes," Mrs. Jeffries continued, "don't generally make it a habit to murder their customers. From what Betsy has told us, Hinchley indulged in this behaviour quite often. I don't think it was a prostitute who murdered the man."

"Neither do I," Mrs. Goodge said. "I don't think this killing was done by some poor soul who was sellin' Hinchley his body. Seems to me if that were the case and they'd killed someone, they wouldn't bother wasting time getting the man dressed, dragging him to a canal and making it look like an accident. Seems to me, if it was someone like that, they'd have cleaned him out good and scarpered for the coast."

"Precisely my thoughts," Mrs. Jeffries said. She looked at Smythe. "We've got to talk to someone at that brothel before the police do."

Smythe glanced at Betsy, who was resolutely looking past his shoulder at the far wall. "Uh, you want me to do it?" he asked. "Go back to that place?"

"Well, we could send Wiggins," Mrs. Jeffries suggested dryly, knowing precisely how the overprotective coachman would react.

Wiggins shot up from his seat. "Really?"

"Down, lad." Smythe laid a restraining hand on his arm. "I'm not lettin' you go wanderin' into a place like that."

"I wouldn't mind," the footman said eagerly. "Not

that I want to go to a place like that. But this is right important. You know 'ow devoted I am to solvin' our cases.''

''That would hardly be appropriate,'' Hatchet said quickly. ''But perhaps I . . .''

''I'll go,'' Smythe interrupted bluntly. He shot a quick glance at Betsy and saw that her eyes were now flashing fire. Blast, he'd have to smooth her feathers later. But at least the lass cared enough to get good and narked at him. ''No offense meant, Hatchet,'' he said to the butler, ''but you're not likely to get anyone to loosen their tongues too quickly, and like Mrs. Jeffries says, we've got to talk to this er . . . person before the police do.''

Hatchet's eyebrows rose. ''I believe I'm quite good at getting information out of people,'' he said loftily.

''Yeah, but we need it fast,'' Luty put in. ''And we ain't got time to come up with a good story for ya. Let's face it, Hatchet. You look too much like a preacher to get any fallen angels to spill their secrets to you. Smythe is right; he's the one that ought to go.''

Smythe nodded. He did have a way to get folks to loosen their tongues. His way was quicker and more effective than any story Hatchet could come up with. He looked around the table. ''Someone's got to go there and it's goin' to 'ave to be me.''

The house on Lisle Street was easy enough to find. Smythe paused in front of the door. From inside, he could hear laughter and the faint sounds of a piano. He raised his hand to knock, lost his nerve and stepped back into the shadows of the overhanging eaves. It wasn't that he was scared. He was thirty-five years old and he'd lived hard in Australia for a good number of those years. Brothels didn't shock him. But he wasn't going to think about

his past and it wasn't his past that was keeping him from
pounding on the front door.

It was Betsy. Her face. The way she'd watched him as
he got ready to leave, her expression as shut and locked
as a bank vault. What had she been thinking? That he
wanted to go out to visit a place like this?

Oh, blast it all anyway, he thought, raising his fist and
pounding on the wood. The quicker I get in there, the
quicker I can get out.

A heavy-set, middle-aged woman with frizzy red hair
and rouged cheeks stuck her head out. She raked him with
a long, appraising glance, decided he looked like he might
have money and asked, ''What can I do for you, big
fella?''

''Ya can let me in for a start.'' He shoved at the door,
but she blocked it with her ample hips.

''This ain't a church,'' she said. ''You got any
money?''

In response, he reached into his pocket and pulled out
a roll of bills. ''Enough.''

Her eyes gleamed greedily as she stared at the bundle
between his fingers. Her painted mouth split into a wel-
coming smile. ''Then come on in, handsome. We've got
anything you want.'' She took his arm and he had to
restrain himself from shaking her off. ''And I do mean
anything.''

Smythe tried not to think about that. She tugged him
down a narrow hall and into a large room. The windows
were covered with heavy red velvet, the floor with a
gaudy Persian rug and the walls were covered with paint-
ings, most of them voluptous nudes. People, some of them
well-dressed businessmen with their collars undone and
no jackets, were sprawled on various settees and chairs.
Women, many of them wearing nothing more than diaph-

anous wraps, were entertaining their customers. Smythe was torn between pity and revulsion. The women probably had no choice. Hunger and poverty could drive a body to do just about anything to survive. So he refused to sit in judgment on these poor girls, but the men were a different matter altogether. They sickened him. Bloated, wealthy and thinking solely of their own pleasures, they sprawled about the room like little kings. But he tried to keep his feelings from showing on his face. No point in making anyone suspicious.

"See anything you like?" the madam asked. She swept her arm in a great arc. "Have a wander around and take a good look. There's more girls in the other room."

He started to tell her he didn't want a girl, caught himself, nodded and started towards the inner room, the one where he could hear the piano. Women, some of them no more than girls, smiled and preened as he walked past. He made a show of studying the "merchandise" as he went, but he was actually looking for something quite different from womanly charms. He spotted a pale-haired young woman sitting slumped in the corner, almost as though she were trying to hide. Something in her posture and the wary look in her eyes convinced him she hadn't been on the game long.

The madam, who was coming right behind him, saw where he was looking. "That's Janet. She's new here."

"She'll do." He turned to the madam and took care of the business end of things. A few minutes later, another girl, this one a maid, led him up a wide staircase and showed him into a bedroom. "Janet'll be right up," the girl said as she lit the lamp. "You want anything else? There's gin, ale or champagne; I can bring some up."

"Maybe later," he said. If cold hard cash wouldn't

loosen Janet's tongue, maybe gin would. But he'd try money first.

He sat down on the bed, wincing as the bed springs creaked dangerously under his weight. The maid went out and Janet, her eyes wide and frightened, came in. "Hello." She forced a smile, put her hands on her painfully thin hips and started towards him.

Blast, Smythe thought, up close she couldn't be more than sixteen. "What's your name?" he asked gently, even though he already knew.

"Janet." She stopped in front of him and her fingers went to the buttons on the top of her pink robe. "And I'm to do whatever you want."

"How old are you?"

She looked surprised by the question. "Nineteen." She undid the top button.

Smythe leapt to his feet and clasped his hands over her fingers. "You don't have to do this," he explained.

"You want me to keep my clothes on?"

"No. I mean, yes," he stuttered. "I mean, I just want to talk to you, lass."

Puzzled, she said, "You just want to chat?"

"Come on, lass, sit down." He eased her down on the bed and sat down beside her. "How long 'ave you been at this?"

She looked down at the floor. "I know what I'm doin', if that's what's worryin' ya."

Smythe sighed. "Look, I'm not worried about your . . . er . . . uh, whatever. I'd just like to talk, that's all."

She eyed him suspiciously. "About what?"

Smythe wondered how best to put it. "Well, I need some information."

"You're not a copper, are ya?"

"No, I promise. I'm willing to pay fer my information,'' he said quickly. "Pay ya directly, I will. You've no need to be tellin' anyone else."

She thought about if for a moment. "What do ya want to know?" she asked, glancing at the closed door.

"Was ya workin' on Saturday evenin'?"

"I work every evenin'," she sighed. "It's the only way to make a livin'."

"Around seven o'clock, did ya see a man come in?"

She laughed. "Lots of men come in 'ere."

"I mean a well-dressed man, small like and done up in evening clothes," Smythe explained. "He didn't stay long; my guess is 'e 'ad a word or two with the madam and then left."

She frowned slightly. "He's the one that come in for Rupert." She broke off and blushed. "Rupert only does the special one's like. I mean, he's a . . . ."

Smythe stopped her by raising his hand. "I think I know what 'e does. Anyways. This man who come, did 'e make arrangements for Rupert to come to 'is 'ouse later that night?"

"That's what Rupert said," Janet shrugged. "Mind you, he were right upset when he found out the whole thing 'ad been called off and 'e weren't to go. He'd been there before, you see, and knew this bloke were a big tipper. Some of the men like to give little presents on the side." She glanced quickly at the closed door again. "I mean, what she don't know won't 'urt 'er, will it? It's not like they pays us all that much."

"So Rupert was told he didn't have to go?" Smythe prodded. "How was 'e told? Did the man come back 'ere?"

"Here, what are you askin' all these questions for?"

Smythe pulled out his roll of notes, thanking his lucky stars he had more money than he'd ever spend. "I said

I'm willin' to pay for information," he said, waving the roll under the girl's nose. "And I'm not a copper, so you don't 'ave to watch what ya say."

"How much you willin' to pay?" she asked. She seemed more curious than greedy.

He pulled off three five-pound notes and handed them to her. Her eyes got as big as Mrs. Goodge's scones. It was probably more money than she made in a month. "Here, you tell me what I need to know and I'll double this."

Janet stared at the bills for a moment, almost as though she were afraid to touch them. "All this?"

"Take it, lass," Smythe encouraged. "I know you need it."

Janet grabbed the money, rolled it tightly and stuck it up her sleeve. Then she looked at Smythe and blushed. "Sorry, I didn't mean to act like such a greedy cow, but things 'as been 'ard lately. Me brother's been sick . . ."

"It's all right, lass," he said softly. "I know what it's like to be poor." He wondered if Luty could use another housemaid. "Now go on, answer my question. How did Rupert know that 'e wasn't to go to the man's house?"

"A lad came round with a note," Janet said. "Rupert almost had a go at him. Poncy little fella all tarted up in velvet and silk. Mind you, some of the others was laughin', thinkin' that Rupert 'ad lost out to a street boy, but this weren't no street boy that come 'ere with the note. He was too well fed for that. Not that 'e was fat or anythin'. But he 'ad a nice rounded backside and carried himself all nice like. Made Rupert right angry, it did."

"What time did the lad show up?"

"Right before Rupert was goin' to leave himself, around eleven forty-five. If the boy had been five minutes later, Rupert would 'ave already been gone."

CHAPTER 6

Betsy glared at the clock. What was taking him so long? He'd been gone for hours now and if he didn't come walking through that back door soon, she'd ruddy well go out after him.

She got to her feet and started to pace, thankful that Mrs. Goodge and Mrs. Jeffries had gone to bed, sparing her the need to come up with some feeble excuse as to why she was sitting here in the blooming kitchen in the middle of the night.

She stopped dead as she heard the familiar sound of the back door opening. A second later, heavy footsteps moved in the hallway and a relieved smile curved her lips.

Betsy dashed toward the back stairs. Now that she knew he was home safe, she could go to bed and get some sleep. Worrying about someone certainly was hard on the nerves, she thought as she skipped quietly up the stairs. The only thing worse would be him finding out she'd worried and waited.

*   *   *

"The inspector's just gone," Mrs. Jeffries announced as she dashed into the kitchen the next morning. "He's going to interview Theodora Vaughan, Trevor Remington and Willard Swinton again this morning."

"What about Delaney?" Mrs. Goodge asked. She picked the empty pot off the table. "Seems to me after what that Mr. Parks said, this Delaney fellow needs a bit more looking into."

"I agree," the housekeeper said as she picked up the last of the dirty breakfast plates. "But there really wasn't time to drop any hints in that direction, so we'll have to look into Delaney on our own."

"I'll get my sources working on him," Mrs. Goodge said. "I've got a few of them dropping by this morning."

Betsy, stifling a yawn, trudged into the kitchen. "I've finished up the dry larder," she said.

"Gracious, Betsy," Mrs. Jeffries exclaimed. "Are you all right? You don't look like you slept well."

"I'm fine." Betsy yawned again. "Just a bit tired is all. It was too warm to sleep much last night."

As Mrs. Jeffries knew perfectly well that Betsy had sat up waiting for Smythe until well after two A.M., she decided not to press the subject. "Try and take a rest this afternoon if you can," she advised. "Smythe and Wiggins ought to be here any moment, and then we'll have a brief meeting."

"Aren't we going to wait for Luty and Hatchet?" Mrs. Goodge asked.

"Luty was planning on ambushing one of her legal sources this morning. She's bound and determined to find out who Hinchley left his money to," Mrs. Jeffries explained, "so she wants us to go ahead without her."

"And no doubt Hatchet is so worried she'll get more

information than him, he's probably out snooping too,'' Betsy said with a grin.

Smythe came into the kitchen, followed by Wiggins. ''Mornin' all,'' he said cheerfully. ''Sorry we missed breakfast, but we 'ad to take a quick run over to the stables.''

''Are you hungry?'' Mrs. Goodge asked.

''We 'ad us some buns from the bake shop,'' Wiggins replied, ''but I could do with a cuppa.''

''So could I.'' Smythe dropped into his seat. He still didn't quite have the nerve to look Betsy in the eye, even though he knew he'd not done a ruddy thing to feel guilty about. Cor, it wasn't as if he'd *wanted* to go to that place.

Mrs. Goodge put a fresh pot on the table. ''Come on, then,'' she said, ''let's get cracking. My sources'll be here any minute and I want this kitchen to myself.''

Wiggins, who'd been trying to teach Fred to roll over, hurried to the table. Mrs. Jeffries quickly took her seat, and Betsy, without so much as a glance in the coachman's direction, sat down in her place.

''Why don't you tell us what you learned,'' Mrs. Jeffries said to Smythe. She wanted him to give his report quickly and matter-of-factly. Betsy's nose was already out of joint and it wouldn't do to torment the poor girl needlessly.

Smythe, keeping his voice casual, quickly told them what he'd learned at the brothel. ''So you see,'' he finished, ''we're no better off than we were before. We'll probably never find the lad that brung the note around.''

''Did you get a look at it?'' Mrs. Goodge asked.

Smythe shook his head. ''Janet said she'd seen the madam toss it in the stove. No reason for anyone to keep it, was there?''

''But we do know that the, er . . . person who was sup-

posed to go to Hinchley's never went,'' Mrs. Jeffries said.
''Which once again leads us right back to the Hayden
Theatre.''

''Maybe the lad that brung the note did the killing,''
Wiggins suggested.

''Don't be daft, boy,'' Mrs. Goodge said impatiently.
''Why would some lad want to kill Hinchley? It's got to
be someone from the Hayden. Seems like we've got
plenty of people right there to worry about without bringing anyone else into it.''

''Yes, indeed,'' Mrs. Jeffries interjected. ''We do have
a sufficient number of suspects and more important, Hinchley had only returned from overseas. Whatever other
enemies he may have had wouldn't have had time to
know he was back, let alone plan his murder. But we
should try to find the boy.''

''Why?'' Betsy asked. ''All he did was bring a note.''

''Because,'' Mrs. Jeffries said slowly, ''I don't think
that note was from Hinchley.''

''Then who sent it?'' Wiggins asked.

''The murderer.'' Mrs. Jeffries nodded as she spoke.
She was sure of this; she could feel it in her bones. ''It
was from the murderer.''

''How do ya figure that?'' Smythe asked softly, his
words echoing what the rest of them were thinking.
''Couldn't Hinchley 'ave sent it?''

''No. He didn't have time,'' Mrs. Jeffries replied. ''Besides, why would he? According to what Hinchley's maid
told Betsy, he was very routine in his behaviour. Nothing
we've heard about what he did that night leads me to
believe he'd changed his plans. I think the murderer sent
that note to the brothel. As a matter of fact, it's the only
thing that makes sense.''

"But how would the killer know what Hinchley had planned for his evening?" Betsy asked.

"Simple." The housekeeper clasped her hands together. "According to what Smythe said he'd learned from, the, er, young woman at the brothel, Hinchley was a regular customer who always behaved precisely in the same manner. Add that to the information that Betsy got from Hinchley's maid, that his routine never varied and was well known to everyone, and I think we may have found the way our killer managed to commit the crime. The killer knew that Hinchley had gone to the house on Lisle Street because that's what he always did. The killer also knew that the side door would be unlocked and the servants in bed. Therefore, all he had to do was send a note to the brothel telling them that Hinchley had changed his mind and his field was clear. No servants, no locked doors and a bathtub full of water."

Smythe nodded. "So if we can find that boy, 'e'll be able to tell us who gave 'im the note."

"Precisely." Mrs. Jeffries smiled confidently. She hoped she was right. Her interpretation of the facts seemed to be correct, but one part of her was quite worried. What if she was wrong? She straightened her spine, refusing to give in to self-doubt. "So I think your first task," she continued, looking at Wiggins and Smythe, "is to find the lad who brought that note."

"What are the rest of us going to do, then?" Betsy demanded.

"You must forgive me, Inspector," Theodora Vaughan gave Witherspoon a wan smile. "But I was entirely too distraught to see you yesterday. This dreadful business has put a terrible strain on my nerves."

"Of course, Miss Vaughan," the inspector replied. "I

quite understand. Do you feel up to answering a few questions today?''

She sighed and clasped one hand to her bosom. In the soft morning sunlight filtering through the gauzy curtains of the sitting room, she looked frail and vulnerable. Dressed in a pale blue-and-mauve day dress, she sat on one end of the settee, a lacy hankerchief clutched in her hand. ''One must do one's duty,'' she said.

Barnes, who thought she had a fair amount of color in her cheeks for someone whose nerves were strained, asked, ''Why did you leave the theatre so soon after your performance on Saturday evening?''

She gave him a quick, sharp look. ''Who told you that?''

''A number of people mentioned it,'' the constable replied. ''Why? Was it supposed to be a secret?''

''Of course not, Constable,'' she snapped, then caught herself and gave him a gracious smile. ''But I don't like knowing that I'm being gossiped about behind my back.''

''It was hardly gossip, Miss Vaughan,'' the inspector interjected. ''We were asking questions, you know. Please don't be angry with any of the stage workers. They were merely doing *their* duty.''

''We know you left in a hansom not five minutes after your last curtain call,'' Barnes continued. ''Wasn't that a bit odd, ma'am?''

''Not at all,'' Theodora replied smoothly. ''I was very tired. Opening night is always a bit of a strain. I wanted to get right home.''

''Did you take your stage makeup off?'' Witherspoon asked. He wasn't sure where this was leading, but the constable's query was well taken.

''No.'' She smiled brightly. ''I should have, of course. But I was so dreadfully tired and frankly, I was afraid if

I stayed too long, I'd get caught by someone.''

"Caught by someone?" Witherspoon echoed. Whatever did she mean?

She laughed. "I was afraid Trevor or Albert would get their hooks into me. Oh, Inspector, you've no idea how theatre people love discussing the performance. I knew if I went to my dressing room, one of them would come barging in insisting on going over every little detail of the night. Frankly, I just wasn't up to it so I nipped right out as soon as I could.''

"I see," Witherspoon said. "Did you happen to notice anything unusual as you left?"

"Unusual?"

"Did you see Mr. Hinchley hanging about backstage?" Barnes asked.

"No. In any case, I wasn't paying much attention. All I wanted to do was go home.''

"Did your maid see you come in?" Witherspoon asked.

Theodora smiled benignly. "I'm not a slave driver, Inspector. I don't expect my maid to wait up for me. I imagine she was sound asleep. But do feel free to ask her yourself. Shall I ring for her?''

Witherspoon nodded. Theodora gracefully got up, went to the bell pull by the door and tugged it gently. The maid, who was probably just outside, immediately appeared. "Yes, ma'am," she said, looking at her mistress.

"Rose, these gentlemen would like to ask you a few questions." Theodora gestured at the two policemen.

"The police?" Rose asked, shaking her head in their direction.

"Yes, Rose, and you must answer all their questions." Theodora smiled. "If you'll excuse me, gentlemen, I really must go and deal with my correspondence." With another beautiful smile, she swept out of the room.

Witherspoon gestured toward the settee. "Do sit down, Miss Rose. We'll not take up too much of your time, I promise."

The maid sat. She didn't look in the least nervous. "Go ahead, then, ask your questions."

"Er, uh, did you happen to notice what time Miss Vaughan came home from the theatre on Saturday evening?"

Rose shook her head. "No, sir. I was dead asleep, I was. Miss Vaughan don't like me to wait up for her."

"Then who helps her . . . uh . . . with her toilette?"

Rose frowned. "Toilette? You mean who helps her get undressed?"

"Yes." The inspector hoped he wasn't blushing. "That's what I mean."

Rose shrugged. "Not me, that's for certain. Miss Vaughan never did like me fussin' over her when she's gettin' dressed. She's right self-sufficient; she can hook up her own buttons and everything. I reckon it comes from back in the days when she was just startin' out. Actresses in the theatre have got to be able to change and undo themselves quickly. Mind you, she's got a proper dresser at the theatre now, but she didn't always have."

Witherspoon was no expert on female articles of clothing, but he did know that undoing a fancy evening dress— or for that matter, most day dresses—was a time-consuming and complicated matter. Gracious, that's one of the main reasons ladies of a certain station had maids. "So, you're not in the habit of waiting up and helping her . . . er . . . disrobe."

"Sometimes I do." Rose shrugged. "But mostly, considering the late hours she keeps, I go on to bed. Now I do her hair for her." She smiled proudly. "That's why she hired me on; I've a deft hand with hair. And I take care of her clothes and all, see that they're laundered proper and hung just so in the cupboards.''

''I see,'' the inspector tried to think of something else to ask. If the girl couldn't help confirm the time Theodora Vaughan had arrived back from the theatre, there wasn't any point in questioning her further. The maid wasn't likely to be acquainted with Ogden Hinchley. But perhaps he ought to ask anyway. ''Were you acquainted with Mr. Hinchley?''

Rose nodded eagerly. ''Not really acquainted, sir. But I knew who he was. Everybody in the theatre did. Most hated him too.''

''Was Miss Vaughan closely acquainted with him?'' Barnes asked softly.

''She knew him. Actually''—Rose glanced at the closed door—''I think she was relieved when he went off to America. They all like to pretend he wasn't worth fretting over, but the truth is, he had ever so much power.''

Witherspoon looked at her sharply. ''What do you mean by that?''

''Just what I said,'' Rose replied stubbornly. ''They was all scared of him. Mr. Remington, Mr. Parks and even that toff of a theatre owner. They was all round here a few days before Hinchlely left for America. I was bringin' in the tea and I couldn't help overhearin' what they was saying. Mr. Parks was going on and on about how he hoped one of them gunslingers blew Mr. Hinchley's brains out—''

''Excuse me,'' Witherspoon interrupted. ''I thought Hinchley had gone to New York?''

''He did.'' Rose grinned. ''I forgot to mention that they'd had several bottles of wine before I brought in the tea. Mr. Parks was drunk. But he was dead serious. He hated Hinchley.''

''And the others who were there that day, what were they saying?'' the inspector pressed. He wasn't certain this conversation had any connection whatsoever to this case, but one never knew. The girl seemed to be quite bright and obviously had a good memory.

Warming to her tale, Rose plunged straight ahead. ''Well, Mr. Delaney was trying to be casual like and pretend it didn't matter to him, but he was so excited that Hinchley would be gone when his play opened he all but danced. Mr. Remington''—Rose smiled broadly—''didn't make any bones about it, said Hinchley had single-handedly tried to ruin his career and he hoped the blighter never came back.''

''Why were they here?'' Witherspoon asked. ''This must have been several months ago. Hinchley left for New York the first week in June.''

Rose looked surprised by the question. ''They was here about Mr. Delaney's play.''

''Oh.'' Witherspoon nodded wisely. ''Yes, yes, I see. Doing the casting and that sort of thing.''

''No, sir,'' Rose contradicted. ''They didn't do that till the middle of July. They was drawing up the agreements, sir.''

Puzzled, the inspector stared at her. ''Agreements?''

''Yes, sir. Agreements. The royalties and such off the house take on receipts.''

''I would have thought that would have been between Mr. Delaney and Mr. Swinton,'' Witherspoon said slowly.

''Mr. Swinton was here that night too,'' Rose agreed. ''But they was all involved in the money end of it, sir. I mean, the business side of things.''

"I'm afraid I don't quite understand what you mean,"
Witherspoon said.

"What don't you understand, sir? Mr. Parks has a share
in the play and Mr. Remington's got a bit, but their shares
aren't very big. Of course, Mr. Swinton'll get a share of
the receipts because it's his theatre."

Witherspoon scratched his chin. "Are you saying they
all put their own money into this play?"

"Yes, sir." Rose smiled broadly.

"Is that a usual practise?" Barnes asked.

"I wouldn't rightly know, sir." Rose flicked a piece of
lint off the arm of the chair. "But I do know one thing
for certain. If Miss Vaughan and the others hadn't ponied
up the cash, Mr. Delaney wouldn't ever have had that play
of his produced."

Trevor Remington had taken rooms in a three-story townhouse on Farley Street, not far from the theatre. The house
was quite well kept; one could almost say it was opulent.
The front walkway was lined by flowering shrubs, the
stairs were freshly painted white and the brass lamp and
door knocker glittered brightly in the sunlight.

"Do you think the maid knew what she was talking
about?" Barnes asked the inspector as they reached the
front door.

Witherspoon thought about it for a moment. "I don't
think she was lying. She'd have no reason to. But I do
think it might be possible she was mistaken, confused
perhaps, about what she'd really heard that day. It was
over three months ago." He banged the knocker against
the wood. "On the other hand, she seemed quite certain."

"I thought so too," Barnes said quickly as the door
opened.

"Yes? May I help you?" A round, dark-haired woman wearing a brown bombazine dress stared at them.

"Good morning." He smiled brightly. "I'm Inspector Witherspoon and this is Constable Barnes. We'd like to see Mr. Remington if we may."

She held the door open wider and stepped back. "Of course; please come in. I'm not sure that Mr. Remington is awake yet, so if you'll go into the drawing room, I'll let him know you're here."

She nodded toward an open door down the hall and then started for the flight of stairs.

"Excuse me." Witherspoon stopped her. "But are you the landlady?"

She turned and nodded. "Mrs. McGraw. I own this house."

"Do you mind if we ask you a few questions?"

"Is it about Hinchley's murder?" she asked eagerly.

Taken aback, Witherspoon could only nod. Gracious, the woman seemed keen to talk to the police. How very refreshing. "Yes, I'm afraid it is. Did you know Mr. Hinchley?"

She laughed. "I know everyone, Inspector. I've been renting rooms to theatre people for forty years. Some of the best in the business have stayed in this house. Pinero, Irving, Ellen Terry—they've all been my guests at one time or another."

Witherspoon was rather embarrassed that the names meant nothing to him. Mrs. McGraw did seem rather proud of them. "Yes, of course. Uh, have you ever met Mr. Hinchley?"

"He's never stayed here." She grinned. "He wouldn't have to. He's rich as sin, that one."

"Yes, so I understand." Witherspoon racked his brain

to come up with another question. "Mr. Remington, uh . . . he says you were asleep when he came home on Saturday evening . . ."

"Don't be ridiculous," Mrs. McGraw replied. "Of course I wasn't asleep. I'd gone to the Hayden to see the play."

"You did?"

"Naturally. I always go and see every new play," Mrs. McGraw explained. "These people make my living for me; it's the least I can do. Besides, I adore the theatre. That's the main reason I decided to let rooms to actors. Such an interesting lot, aren't they?"

"Er, yes," Witherspoon replied.

"What time did you get home that night, Mrs. McGraw?" Barnes asked.

"Well . . ." She thought about it for a moment. "Let's see. I stopped outside the theatre and had a bit of a chat with Maisie Duncan, but we didn't talk for more than five minutes. So, by the time I flagged a hansom and got here, it must have been close to eleven-thirty."

"Did you hear Mr. Remington come in later that evening?"

"No," Mrs. McGraw's mouth flattened into a thin line. "I didn't and I was bit annoyed. My tenants know I like to be in bed by a reasonable hour. I'm quite tolerant, but there are limits. When he wasn't here by half past twelve, I woke the tweeny and told her to listen for him."

"You hadn't given Mr. Remington his own key?" Witherspoon asked.

"Certainly not," she replied. "I don't give any of them a key, Inspector."

Barnes and Witherspoon exchanged glances. Then the Inspector asked, "May we speak to the tweeny?"

Mrs. McGraw stared at them in a surprise for a moment, then turned on her heel and marched down the hall toward the back of the house. "Just a moment. I'll get her." She gestured toward an open door as she went. "Go on into the drawing room and make yourselves comfortable."

"Remington lied to us," Barnes said softly as they went into the drawing room.

"Indeed he did." Witherspoon stopped just inside, took one look at the elegant furniture and furnishings and understood why Mrs. McGraw didn't hand out keys to her tenants. "And I'm wondering why. Remington doesn't strike me as a stupid man. Surely he realized we'd check."

"You wanted to see me, sir?"

Witherspoon whirled around to see a young blonde girl wearing a maid's uniform standing in the open doorway. He introduced himself and the constable.

"I'm Elsa Chambers," the maid said. "Mrs. McGraw said you needed to ask me some questions."

"I understand you waited up on Saturday evening to let Mr. Remington in?" Witherspoon said.

"Yes, sir." Elsa replied. "I mean I let him in, but I was dozing off a bit in the chair in the hall."

"Did you notice what time it was that he came in?"

"Oh, I did, sir," Elsa said eagerly. "I mean, I didn't see the time so much as hear it." She pointed to a huge grandfather clock by the drawing room door. "The clock had just chimed three when he come home."

"How did he look?"

Elsa stared at them blankly. "Look, sir?"

Witherspoon smiled at her. "I'm sorry. I didn't phrase that correctly. I meant to ask was there anything unusual about him when he came home?"

Her thin face creased in concentration. "Well, I was

sleepy sir, but Mr. Remington seemed the same as usual to me.''

"Did he say anything to you?" Witherspoon asked.

"Just said hello and apologized for keeping me up so late."

"He didn't mention where he'd been?" Barnes pressed.

She shook her head. "Not to me. Just gave me his coat and hat and went on upstairs to his rooms."

Witherspoon tried to think of another pertinent question but couldn't. "Thank you, Elsa. We appreciate your help."

She dropped a quick curtsy, smiled and turned to leave. "Oh, excuse me, sir, I didn't see you come in," she gushed, stumbling backwards to keep from ploughing into Trevor Remington.

"It's quite all right, Elsa," Remington said, but he wasn't looking at the maid. His attention was on the policemen. She bobbed another curtsy and dashed out.

Remington said nothing for a moment. Then he sighed loudly, ran his hands through his hair and dropped onto a large ottoman at the foot of the settee. "I know what you must be thinking. But I assure you, Inspector, though I may have lied about coming straight home, I had nothing to do with Ogden Hinchley's murder."

"Where were you on Saturday evening?" Witherspoon asked. "You didn't come home right after the performance. Both Mrs. McGraw and Elsa have told us that."

Remington dropped his head into his hands. Finally, he looked up. "Would you believe me if I told you I went for a walk?"

"You went for a walk? Where?" Barnes asked.

"I walked along the embankment for a good while, then I went over to Theodora's. But I didn't go inside."

"The embankment?" Barnes repeated. "You mean you walked along the river?"

Remington nodded.

"Till three in the morning?" the constable persisted. As Delaney claimed he'd been walking along the river that night too, Barnes was beginning to think it must have been getting blooming crowded.

"No, of course not," Remington said. "I'm not a fool, Constable. With that awful murder over in Whitechapel, I realized it would be foolish to stay out there too long. But there were a few people about, and I saw a policeman or two."

"Did they see you, sir?" Barnes interrupted. That would be easy to check, and Remington, with his actor's looks and graceful carriage, would be easy to remember.

He shrugged. "I assume so. I wasn't trying to hide. But as I was saying, I walked along the embankment for a while, until it began to get quite late, and then I went over to Theodora's. But her lights were all out and I thought she'd probably gone to bed so I didn't knock or anything. I was still quite upset. Despite what the others may have told you, I don't think the play's going to be much of a success." He closed his eyes for a moment. "Add that to my seeing Hinchley in the audience and I knew I couldn't possibly get to sleep."

"So what did you do?" the inspector asked.

"By this time it was fairly late and I realized that it was foolish to be wandering around alone that time of night. I tried to find a hansom but I couldn't. I finally walked back towards the Strand and caught one close to the theatre."

"What time was this, sir?" Barnes persisted.

"About two forty-five or so." Remington flung out his

hands. "I don't know. I was upset and to be perfectly honest, very alarmed. The play wasn't perfect, but if we got lucky and had a decent review or two, we might be able to keep the house filled and turn a profit."

"And that was important, wasn't it?" Witherspoon said softly. "Your own money's invested in the play."

Remington's eyes widened. "So you know that, do you? Well, it was bound to come out."

"How much did you invest, sir?" the inspector had no idea whether it was important or not, but he thought it might be.

"Invest?" Remington laughed. "It wasn't exactly an investment. I put a thousand pounds of my own money into this play. It was the only way they'd give me the lead."

Witherspoon stared at him. "I see."

"Do you?" Remington sighed deeply. "I doubt it, Inspector. But suffice to say, I wanted to play that part. Wanted it badly enough to be hoodwinked into putting up a good portion of the production costs myself."

"Why did you lie to us?" Witherspoon asked. "Surely you must have realized we'd try to verify your statement."

"Because I was frightened you'd think I killed Hinchley if I told you the truth. I had no alibi and I hated him. Everyone knew I hated him. I'm sorry, Inspector, I wasn't trying to do anything but give myself some time."

"You knew Hinchley was in the audience that night, didn't you?" Barnes said.

Remington nodded. "Yes. I'd peeked out the side curtain and saw him take his seat. It was quite a shock. Here I'd thought I was safe from him and that wicked pen of his. When I looked out and saw him there, I almost fainted. I was so rattled I almost forgot my lines in the first act.''

''Why did you hate him so much, sir?'' Barnes asked.

''Hate isn't exactly the right word,'' Remington mused. ''Actually, I feared him more than anything else.''

''But why?'' Witherspoon pressed. ''Surely as an actor you're used to coping with critics.''

''Ah, but he wasn't just a critic.'' Remington laughed harshly. ''He was a monster. One bad performance and you were marked for life.''

Witherspoon frowned slightly. ''I'm afraid I don't understand.''

''Hinchley, odious as he was, was very influential with other critics, Inspector.'' Remington shrugged. ''I don't know why, but he was. If you got a bad review from him, you could be bloody sure that the other critics, mindless sheep that they are, wouldn't give you a decent one either. Hinchley never forgot a performance or an actor. I had the misfortune of playing in a rather shoddy production out in the provinces a while back. It was right after I'd come back from a tour of America.'' He laughed derisively. ''I only took the role to do a favor for a friend. But Hinchley came to one of our performances. I wasn't feeling well that night, but I did the best I could. Hinchley pilloried me the next day in the local newspaper. I didn't mind that; I knew I hadn't done my best. What I hated was the fact that no matter what I did after that, he never saw it.''

''Was he like that with everyone?'' Witherspoon asked.

Remington shrugged. ''More or less. Ogden Hinchley was a very strange man. I admit I hated him, but I didn't kill him.''

Witherspoon thought Remington's voice had the unmistakable ring of truth to it, but then he reminded himself that this man was an actor. Maybe a much better actor than Ogden Hinchley had ever thought. "Would you say that a bad review from Hinchley would have the power to close a production?"

"Perhaps." Remington got up and walked toward the fireplace. "Perhaps not. I do know that he had enough power to almost ruin my career, Inspector. Why do you think I was so desperate for a lead part that I was willing to put up my own money for the chance at it? My career had virtually come to a stop since Hinchley pilloried me."

"Could you give us a guess on that question, sir?" Barnes pressed. "Not that I'm doubtin' you, sir. But it's one thing to ruin an actor, and quite another to close down a play."

Remington hesitated. "Well, all right, I suppose he could. As I said a moment ago, he'd a lot of influence."

"I think I understand," Witherspoon said slowly. "So if Hinchley was in the theatre on Saturday evening, you were fairly certain he was there for the sole purpose of reviewing the play?"

"Why else would he have come?" Remington asked. "He certainly wasn't there to provide moral support for his old protégé."

"Protégé?" Barnes said. "And who would that be?"

Remington's mouth curved into a mirthless smile. "Edmund Delaney. He and Ogden were once good friends. Very good friends."

Witherspoon wasn't sure he completely understood what Remington was getting at. But he was the second person to mention animosity between Delaney and Hinchley. "So you don't think Hinchley might have come to the theatre just to see his old friend's play?"

"Hardly." Remington laughed nastily. "Ogden Hinchley hated Edmund. What's more, he hated everyone else involved in that production. Why do you think I was so depressed when I realized he was back in London? Hinchley was there for one purpose and one purpose only: to ruin us.''

''Mr. Remington,'' Witherspoon said quietly, ''you said you invested a thousand pounds. That's quite a bit of money.''

A strangled, high-pitched hysterical sound that might have been a laugh came out of the actor's mouth. ''I know how much it is, Inspector. It's virtually every penny I had in the world.''

CHAPTER 7

"It's so good to see you, Mollie," Mrs. Goodge said. She forced herself to smile at the prune-faced woman sitting like the Queen of Sheba at the head of the table. Mollie Dubay wasn't really a friend. But Mrs. Goodge thought she might be useful. The tall, gray haired woman was the housekeeper to Lord Fremont and she never for one blooming moment let you forget it.

Mrs. Goodge wouldn't even have bothered contacting the stuck-up old thing, but she was worried about making a mistake in this investigation. She'd put her pride to one side and sent Mollie an invitation to tea. Mollie might be a housekeeper for a peer of the realm now, but Mrs. Goodge could remember the days when she was scrubbing out stalls at the Lyceum Theatre.

Mollie was also the worst gossip on three continents and even better, she never forgot a face, a name or a bit of dirt.

"I was ever so pleased you decided to accept my invitation."

Mollie smiled faintly and brushed an imaginary crumb off the sleeve of her severe black bombazine dress. "Lord and Lady Fremont are in France at the moment. He's on a most delicate diplomatic mission for Her Majesty, so I'm not pressed for time. Normally, of course, I've such a large household to attend to I don't dare even take my day out." She glanced around the kitchen, her gaze sharp and calculating as she scanned the large, cozy room.

"Well," Mrs. Goodge said chattily, "then I'm very pleased Lord and Lady Fremont are gone."

"Is that Wedgwood?" Mollie jerked her chin toward the pale blue-and-white china on the dresser.

"Yes," Mrs. Goodge replied, stretching the truth a bit. One of the pieces was a Wedgwood.

Mollie's heavy eyebrows drew together in disapproval. "Really, don't you think good china ought to be locked in the china room? You do have one, don't you?"

"Of course," Mrs. Goodge replied smoothly. She was fairly sure that Mrs. Jeffries hadn't the faintest idea where the key to the china room was. As a matter of fact, the last time the cook had glanced in the tiny room off the housekeeper's bedroom, the only thing in there had been some old suitcases and other odds and ends.

"Then I don't know what can your housekeeper can be thinking, leaving it out here where it could be so easily broken."

"Mrs. Jeffries thinks that beautiful things ought to be used, not locked up."

"One must maintain proper standards." Mollie sniffed. "But perhaps this household isn't very strict. Not at all like Lord Fremont. We do things absolutely correctly in his house."

Mrs. Goodge clamped her lips together to keep from saying something rude. She took a deep breath and promised herself she wouldn't lose her temper. At least not until she got what she wanted. "Inspector Witherspoon lives quite simply, considering, of course, how very wealthy he is." She smiled in satisfaction as she saw Mollie's eyes widen.

Mollie recovered quickly. "Really? I hadn't realized Scotland Yard policemen were so well paid."

"They're not." Mrs. Goodge was careful to speak properly. "But then again, he doesn't really need his wages. Inherited wealth, you know. He only stays with Scotland Yard because he's such a brilliant detective. Why, I don't know what they'd do without him. Perhaps you've read of some of his cases in the papers."

"Murders? Hardly." Mollie stuck her chin in the air. "I've no interest in reading about such horrid things."

Mrs. Goodge decided she'd had enough of tweaking Mollie's nose. She didn't want the woman too annoyed. The whole point of putting up with the silly biddy was to get some information out of her. With that end firmly in mind, she smiled broadly. "Oh, but you really should take an interest. Murder can be quite fascinating."

She got up and bustled toward the cooling pantry. "Now, you just make yourself comfortable, Mollie. When I knew you were coming, I baked a seed cake. Oh, and I've bought us a bottle of Harvey's as well." When she got to the hall, she turned to make sure Mollie wasn't going to bolt.

Mollie was staring at her, her expression pleased and a bit puzzled. "You baked a seed cake? Why, how very nice. It's kind of you to go to so much trouble."

Mrs. Goodge felt a flash of guilt. Some of the starch had gone out of her guest. As a matter of fact, the woman looked almost pathetically pleased that someone had done something special for her. Perhaps Mollie wasn't such a snob. Maybe she was just one of those lonely women who spend their lives in the service of others and forget that they have a right to want something for themselves.

"It's no trouble at all," the cook lied graciously. Baking that seed cake had taken hours, and the only reason she'd splurged and bought the sherry was because if she remembered correctly, Mollie couldn't hold more than a glass or two before she lost control of her tongue. "I've a tray made up in the pantry. I'll just go get it and we can have a nice, long chat."

Wiggins reached down and pretended to wipe a bit of dust off his shoe. The girl was just ahead of him and twice now, he'd caught her looking back at him, like she knew she was being followed.

A second later, his worst fear was confirmed. She turned away from the shop window and charged toward him. "'Ere, are you followin' me?"

For a moment, he was struck dumb. He hadn't had a good look at her face when he'd seen her coming out of the Parks house; he'd only dashed after her as she set off down the road toward the shops. But even with an accusing frown on her face, she was the prettiest girl he'd ever seen. Her eyes were widely spaced, deep brown in color and framed with the longest lashes in the world. A small, turned-up nose, skin the color of pale cream, an adorable rosebud of a mouth and perfectly shaped winged brows came together to form a perfect face. Her hair was tucked under a maid's cap, but it was the color of dark honey and curling tendrils escaped to dance around her long, slender neck.

Without thinking, Wiggins blurted out the truth. "Uh, yes. I was."

For a few seconds, she eyed him suspiciously. Then her mouth curved in a slow, satisfied smile. "So, you admit it then?"

He could feel the blood rushing to his cheeks. "I'm sorry, miss. I didn't mean no 'arm. It's just that . . . that . . ." What? His mind was completely blank.

"You're not the first to follow me." She laughed. "And you look harmless enough."

"Thank you," he mumbled, not sure if being called "harmless" was a compliment or an insult. "May I carry your shopping basket?"

"What? You're wantin' to follow me about and carry my shopping? Is that it, then?"

"Well, I've nothing else to do today," he replied truthfully. "It wouldn't be any trouble and I do 'ate to see a delicate lady like yourself 'aving to trundle this great basket around."

"You've a glib tongue on you." She laughed again and shoved it into his hands. "This thing does get heavy. I accept. Come on, then." Turning on her heel, she started toward the butcher shop on the corner. Wiggins grimaced at the sight of the hanging carcasses in the open air front. But the girl stalked on past the butchers, turned the corner and went toward the grocer's. "Come on," she called over her shoulder. "Hurry up. I've not got all day."

"Sorry." He dashed up to her and reached for the handle of the door. "Didn't mean to dawdle."

She gave him a dazzling smile. "That's all right. I shouldn't have snapped. But I've got a lot to do today and I want to get this ruddy shopping done. It's not even my job. But the housekeeper quit all sudden like, and if we're going to eat, I've got to get some food in. If I waited for Mr. Parks to remember to buy it, we'd starve to death.''

Wiggins opened the door for her. "Is that who you work for, Mr. and Mrs. Parks?"

"Just Mr. Parks," the girl said in a low voice as they went toward the back of the shop. A stern-faced woman wearing an apron stood behind the counter, watching them.

"Have you got your list, Annie?" the woman asked, holding out her hand.

"Right here." She handed it to the shopkeeper.

The proprietress scanned the list with a frown. "Quite a bit, here, Annie."

"It's not all that much," Annie said. Wiggins could hear a note of desperation in her voice. "Only a few things to get us through till the end of the week."

"And will Mr. Parks be coming in to pay last month's bill?" the woman asked.

"He said he would. He said he'd be in to settle up sometime this week."

She tapped the paper against the top of the counter. "All right, then. But you tell Mr. Parks that if he doesn't come in and pay up by Saturday, there won't be any more credit. Do you understand?"

"Oh, yes," Annie said quickly. "I'll make sure I tell him." She grabbed the basket out of Wiggins's hand and shoved it on the counter. "Just put the things in this. I've got to go to the fishmongers and then I'll be back for it." With that, she turned and flew towards the front door, a puzzled Wiggins right on her heels.

"I hate going in that place," she said as soon as they were outside.

Wiggins could understand why. "Then how come you shop there?"

"Because it's the only shop that'll give Mr. Parks credit," she said. "Oh, I shouldn't have said that, and I shouldn't have let you carry my basket. Mr. Parks will have a fit if everyone in town knew he weren't payin' his bills." She bit her lower lip and Wiggins watched in horror as her beautiful eyes filled with tears.

"Here now." He stepped closer, using his body to shield her from the interested stares of pedestrians. "Don't cry."

"I'm sorry." Annie covered her face with her hands and sobbed. "But I can't seem to stop. You saw what happened in there," she choked out. "It's like that everywhere and it's so ruddy embarrassin'."

Panic hit him. What should he do? He couldn't stand to see a woman cry. Suddenly, he remembered Mrs. Jeffries and the sensible, kind way she always dealt with weeping and wailing. Wiggins straightened his spine and glared at an elderly woman who was openly trying to peek around him at the sobbing girl. "Look, Miss Annie. You'll make yourself ill if you carry on like this. Things is never as bad as ya think."

"Yes, they are," she wailed. "And they're gettin' worse too. What's goin' to happen when Mr. Parks doesn't pay the bill? We'll bloomin' starve to death, that's what."

"There's a tea house just up the road," Wiggins said. "Let's nip up and 'ave a nice cuppa."

"I don't have any money." She sniffled. "Mr. Parks hasn't paid me this quarter."

"I do." Taking her arm, he led her toward the corner. Wiggins thanked his lucky stars that he'd had the good sense to put some coins in his pocket before he left this morning. Mind you, he thought, without their mysterious benefactor he probably wouldn't have had any coins. But for the past year, someone in the household at Upper Edmonton Gardens had been buying them all useful presents. Nice things like note paper and shoe polish and even brand new shirts. So much so that when he got his quarterly wages, he put most of it in the post office account the inspector had opened for him. Consequently, he always had a few coins to jingle in his pocket. He was pretty sure he knew who their benefactor was; after all, he was getting pretty good at investigating. But Wiggins wouldn't say a word to anyone. Not one word.

"This is very nice of you." Annie hiccupped gently.

"I'm right pleased to do it," he replied. "I 'ate seein' a nice girl like you so upset." He held her arm protectively as they reached the tearoom. Guiding her inside, he led her to a table and pulled out a chair for her. "You sit down and 'ave a rest. I'll go get us some tea and cakes. Would you like that?"

She nodded mutely and then looked up and gave him an adoring smile. "I haven't had proper tea cakes in ages."

"You're goin' to 'ave some now," he boasted. "As many as you like. What's your favorite?"

"I think you're the nicest man I've ever met," she said softly.

Wiggins's heart melted.

"Madam," Hatchet hissed at Luty Belle, "you cannot go in there. It's the St. James. Women aren't allowed." He shuddered as he thought of his employer hurtling through the doors of the most exclusive men's club in London.

"Then how the dickens am I gonna git my information?" Luty started towards the stately club. "Stupid goldarned rules anyway. No women allowed. Humph! What woman worth her salt wants to go in and watch a bunch of fat geezers sittin' around tiddling whiskey and flapping their lips? But that old fool's been in there for hours and I need to talk to him.''

"Madam.'' Hatchet grabbed her arm. "Please go wait in the carriage. I'll go in and tell Mr. Stampton you wish to speak to him.''

Luty's eyes narrowed suspiciously. "That's all you'll say? You wouldn't try pumpin' the old goat yourself?''

Hatchet glared at her. That was precisely what he'd planned on doing. Now, of course, he couldn't. "Certainly not,'' he replied huffily. "I wouldn't dream of doing something so crass.''

She snorted. "Pull the other one, Hatchet. You know danged good and well you ain't found out diddly about this case. I can see you chompin' at the bit to get your hooks into my source.''

"I'll have you know, madam,'' Hatchet said pompously, "I've found out a great deal more than you have about this murder.''

"Oh, yeah?''

"Yeah . . . I mean yes,'' he snapped. "However, I'm waiting until our meeting tonight at Upper Edmonton Gardens before I share any of it. Now, if you'll stop making a spectacle of yourself and go wait in the carriage, I'll ask Mr. Stampton to step outside.''

Luty weighed her choices. She could either try charging the St. James and get tossed out on her ear or she could send Hatchet in to fetch the man. The third choice was to wait out here till the old buzzard stumbled out himself. That wasn't much good either. If someone else was buying the drinks, Stampton might be in there till the cows come home. And she had to see him. Blast it! Much as she hated to, she'd just have to rely on Hatchet. In any other situation, she'd trust Hatchet with her life. She had trusted him with it on more than one occasion. But when it came to digging up clues and investigating murders, Hatchet was as sneaky as a polecat creeping up to the chicken coop. Especially when he wasn't getting anywhere with his own sources. Still, she really didn't have much choice here.

"Okay, Hatchet," she said reluctantly, "you go get him. I'll be in the carriage. But if you're not back in ten minutes, I'm coming in."

"You do realize what this means," Witherspoon said to Barnes. He grabbed the door of the hansom as the cab hit a particularly large pothole and almost jolted him off his seat.

"Well, sir, I reckon it means that all of them had a reason for wishing Hinchley had stayed in New York," Barnes replied. "From what Remington said, they all had put up money in the production, and if Hinchley closed it, they'd get worse than just a bad review. They'd be ruined financially. At least Remington, Parks and Swinton would."

"Precisely, Barnes." Witherspoon nodded. He wasn't sure himself what to think about the information they'd received. It was reassuring to hear that the constable had come to the same conclusion. "But what worries me is whether or not one review from a critic could have such a devastating effect."

"I don't reckon the truth of that matters all that much, sir. They believed it could," Barnes pointed out. "That's what's important, and one of them believed it enough to kill him." He cleared his throat. It wasn't his place to be telling Inspector Witherspoon what to do, but in light of what they'd gotten out of Trevor Remington, he thought he ought to point something out. "Inspector, I think we ought to have another look at everyone's alibis, sir. We know that Mr. Remington didn't go straight home like he said before. It seems to me the others might be lying as well.''

Witherspoon nodded. ''I've had the same thought. Really, Barnes, I don't know what's come over me. I ought to have checked the alibis more thoroughly right away.''

But the inspector did know what was wrong. It was that wretched last case. The one he'd solved by listening to his instincts and his ''inner voice.'' He'd been waiting for his ''inner voice'' to start talking to him on this case too. But so far, the wretched thing had been stubbornly mute. He sighed inwardly and resolved to talk to Mrs. Jeffries more frequently. There was something about his chats with her that helped clarify his thoughts. He wished now he'd taken the time to have a longer conversation with her at breakfast. But he hadn't and now he felt totally lost and at sea. Drat. Perhaps he'd go home early today for tea. ''Why don't we start with the cabbies at the Hayden? We know that one of them took Miss Vaughan home right after the performance, so let's find out if Parks, Swinton or Delaney got one as well.''

''Delaney claimed he'd gone for a walk by the river and Swinton was supposed to have been in counting the receipts until after one in the morning,'' Barnes mused. ''But they might be lyin'.''

''That's what I'm afraid of,'' Witherspoon said slowly. ''But if one of them is lying, we'll find out. Whoever killed Hinchley would have had to have left the theatre district sometime that night. Hopefully, in a hansom.''

''Unless they walked there, sir,'' Barnes pointed out. ''It's not quite three miles.''

''I hadn't realized it was quite that far.'' Witherspoon stared out at the heavy traffic on the Strand. Drat, that was another point he should have checked immediately. Gracious, he must get a hold of himself; he was forgetting to take care of even the most elementary aspects of good policing. Perhaps it would be best if he retired his 'inner voice' altogether. It certainly wasn't doing him any good on this case. "However the killer got to Hinchley's house, I think we can safely assume that he probably went there quite soon after the performance ended."

"He might have gone home first," Barnes said.

"True. We don't know exactly when Hinchley was murdered. But I'm betting that whoever killed him did it as quickly as possible and then hurried home himself. After all, you're far more likely to be noticed by a policeman or a night watchman or even someone who can't sleep and is looking out their window if you're wandering the streets or catching hansoms at three in the morning rather than at midnight."

Barnes nodded. "That's true, sir. Back when I was on the streets, I always took care to notice them that was out in the middle of the night. So you're pretty sure Hinchley was murdered, say, before two in the morning?"

Witherspoon pursed his lips. "Not absolutely, Constable. It's just, you see, these people strike me as being so . . . excitable, so dramatic. I've a feeling that if one of them did it, they did it quickly and without thinking. I could be wrong, of course, but somehow, I don't think I am."

Barnes scratched his nose. "And all of them probably knew about Hinchley's private . . . er . . . habits."

"You mean about the door being unlocked"—the inspector hesitated, then reminded himself this was a murder case—"and a male prostitute being expected?" He looked away, sure he was beet red.

"Everyone knew about Hinchley and his habits, and

according to Remington, it wasn't a secret. The way he tells it, everyone in the theatre district laughed at the man behind his back.''

"We've only Remington's word for that," Witherspoon reminded the constable. "But it's certainly something we can easily check."

"Let's say Remington was tellin' the truth and everyone did know about Hinchley's little habit on the nights he reviewed a play," Barnes continued. "Wouldn't the killer have expected Hinchley to have company?"

"That's why I think he acted quickly. Remington also said that Hinchley wrote his review before the person arrived. He was most strict about that"—again Witherspoon could feel his cheeks flaming—"so I'm quite sure that the murderer got there right after Hinchley got into his bath. As a matter of fact, that would explain why we didn't find a copy of the review when we searched the victim's house. The killer took it."

"Then why didn't the prostitute"—Barnes didn't even stumble over the word—"raise the alarm when he arrived and found the place empty?"

"Come now, Constable, someone in that profession must be discreet," Witherspoon explained. "I expect when this person got there and found the place empty, he turned and left, assuming that the customer had changed his mind." He coughed. "After we finish at the Hayden, we'll have to go to Lisle Street."

"I know the place, sir." Barnes's mouth curved in distaste. "High-class brothel. Caters to men with lots of money and some with unusual habits."

Witherspoon sighed. "Let's hope we can get them to talk with us, Barnes. I don't think places of that sort are all that keen on the police."

"I'd say not, sir." Barnes turned his head so Witherspoon wouldn't see his smile. Sometimes he forgot that for all the inspector's brillance at solving homicides, he'd spent most of his years at the Yard working in the records room. For a copper, he was amazingly innocent about some aspects of life.

"Let's hope we can make some progress on this case, Barnes."

"You'll suss it out in the end, sir," Barnes said cheerfully.

The hansom pulled to a stop and they got out. Barnes paid the driver and then followed Witherspoon to the front door of the Hayden Theatre.

Inside the theatre, Witherspoon stopped a limelighter and asked, "Is Mr. Swinton here?"

"The guv's in the office," the man replied, yanking his head toward the auditorium. "You want me to show the way?"

"We know our way, thank you," the inspector replied. They went into the darkened theatre and down the aisle.

Two men were on the empty stage and from the sound of their raised voices, Edmund Delaney and Willard Swinton were having a heated argument.

Barnes and Witherspoon stopped. They were far enough back that neither man had seen them.

"I tell you, just because he's dead doesn't mean we're out of the woods," Swinton snarled. "He wasn't the only critic in town. If you don't change that first scene in the second act and put a bit more life in it, we'll be shut down by the end of the month."

"I'm not changing a bloody thing." Delaney threw out his arms. "I didn't write a music hall review . . ."

"More's the pity," Swinton cried. "If you had, we might actually be making some money."

"You told us we were sold out for the next three

weeks," Delaney charged. "Or was that just a lie you told for the convenience of the police?"

Swinton's hands rolled into fists, but he didn't raise them. "It wasn't a lie, you idiot. We are sold out. But that's only because of Theodora. She's a star. People come to see her, not your play. But even her drawing power won't keep them coming in if the play gets panned by every critic in England."

"The critic from the *Gazette* loved it," Delaney cried passionately.

"He was the only one," Swinton yelled. "And if you don't make some changes in this ruddy bunch of rubbish I got hoodwinked into producing, we're going to all be stone broke in two months. And that, my friend, includes our illustrious star and your patron." Swinton stepped back, a satisfied smile on his face. "I think you'll find that Theodora won't be quite as amenable to your charms once she's bankrupt."

"You despicable cur." Delaney took a step closer, his face contorting with rage. "How dare you imply . . ."

"Gentlemen, gentlemen," Witherspoon called. He would have liked to have heard more, but he couldn't in good conscience let a situation become violent. From the look on Edmund Delaney's face, the inspector was sure he was only seconds away from throttling Swinton.

Startled, both men reacted. Delaney's whole body jerked. Swinton stumbled backwards. The playwright recovered first. "Who's there?" he called, squinting into the darkened auditorium.

"Inspector Witherspoon and Constable Barnes." They moved closer to the stage. "And if you don't mind, we'd like to have a word with both of you."

*   *   *

Smythe desperately wanted to talk to Betsy alone. Things hadn't been right between them since they'd rowed about her mysterious errand to the East End a few days ago. Matters hadn't improved any when he'd gone to the house on Lisle Street, either. But he wasn't one to let a wound fester. Better to have a frank talk with the lass and get everything cleared up and out in the open.

He stopped at the head of the back stairs and listened to the hubbub from the kitchen. Mrs. Goodge, Betsy and Mrs. Jeffries were below, getting things ready for an early tea. Everyone was due back for a quick meeting, and after that he'd probably be back out at the pubs doing more digging.

But if Betsy did what she often did, she'd pop up to her room to tidy her hair before tea. He'd have a chance to talk to her in private. He waited a few more minutes and then his patience was rewarded as he heard Betsy say, "I'll be right back. I just want to tidy myself up a bit."

Smythe turned and raced for the back stairs. By the time Betsy got to the third floor, he was leaning against her door. "I'd like to have a word with ya."

"Now?" She stared at him like he'd gone daft. "But the others will be here any minute. Can't it wait?"

"No," he said patiently. He was always patient when something important was at stake. "It can't. And Luty and Hatchet aren't due for another fifteen minutes. Besides, this won't take long."

"Oh, all right," she said peevishly. "But I don't see what's so important it can't wait until after supper." She crossed her arms over her chest. She wasn't going to invite him into her room. The inspector and Mrs. Jeffries ran a very liberal household, but even they would look askance at her entertaining men in her bedroom. "What is it?"

Smythe cleared his throat. "It's about us."

"Us?" She raised her eyebrows.

His heart plummeted to his toes. Then he decided she was just being contrary. She did that when she was annoyed. "Yes, us," he insisted, "so don't go pretendin' you don't know what I'm on about. You and I 'ave been keepin' company."

"All right," she capitulated, "so what if we have?"

"Things ain't been right between us," he stated, his expression daring her to argue that point. "Ever since we 'ad that little tiff about you flouncin' off the East End on yer own . . ."

"Little tiff," she yelped, outraged. "You were tryin' to boss me about. Tell me what to do. I'll not have that, Smythe."

He raised his hand in a placating gesture. "I weren't tryin' to boss you about," he said. "I was worried because there's a murderin' maniac on the loose and I didn't want you to get 'urt."

Betsy relaxed a little. Blast the man, anyway, he did make it hard to stay annoyed with him. "I know that," she said bluntly. "But I do have some sense. I know how to take care of myself."

"Never said you didn't," he replied. "But that street woman that got 'erself butchered thought she could take care of 'erself too."

"She was out in the middle of the night," Betsy protested. "I went to Whitechapel in broad daylight."

Smythe decided he'd better change tactics. This was old ground they were covering. Best to move on. He touched her arm. "I don't think I could stand it if anythin' 'appened to you, Betsy," he said sincerely. "You're right important to me."

Her heart melted. She couldn't think of what to say.

He was important to her too. "Oh, Smythe," she murmured.

"And I didn't like goin' to that brothel, either," he continued as he watched her soften. "I could tell that put your nose out some . . ."

"It didn't bother me at all," she snapped, wanting to box his ears for bringing that subject up. It was one she preferred to forget. "But you certainly stayed there long enough that night."

"How do you know how long I was?" he asked. "You were asleep. Besides, I had to find out . . ."

"Betsy, Smythe," Wiggins yelled up the staircase. "Are ya comin'? The others is already 'ere and Mrs. Jeffries wants to get things started."

"We'd better get downstairs," Betsy mumbled. She started for the staircase, but he grabbed her elbow and stopped her.

"We'll finish our talk later," he promised. "There's still a few things we need to clear up."

"All right," she agreed quickly, annoyed with herself for letting it slip that she knew what time he'd come in. She hoped that he wouldn't press her about why she'd gone to the East End. She didn't like the way things were between them now, either. It wasn't that she didn't believe him; she was female enough to realize that he was telling the truth. He had been worried about her. But he was also very adept at whittling away some of the walls she'd erected between her past and her present. Betsy had shared much of her past with him, but she wasn't sure she could share all of it. One part of her was still afraid that if he knew exactly where she'd come from, exactly how bad it had been, maybe he wouldn't hold her in such high esteem.

She couldn't stand that thought. Smythe, in truth, had become very important to her as well.

As soon as they were all seated at their usual places, Mrs. Jeffries plunged right in. She'd spent most of the day fruitlessly tracking down clues that hadn't led anywhere, talking to people who knew nothing and trying to think of each and every possible solution to this murder. She sincerely hoped the others had had a better day than she had.

"I'll start," Mrs. Goodge announced in a tone that brooked no argument. "I had an old acquaintance of mine around this afternoon . . ."

"Is she the one that ate all the seed cake?" Wiggins demanded.

"I'll thank you not to interrupt," the cook said tartly. "And she didn't eat it *all*."

"Then why aren't we 'avin' some now?" Wiggins persisted. He'd been looking forward to that cake all day. Ever since he'd spotted Mrs. Goodge baking it that morning.

"For goodness' sake, don't you ever think of anything but your stomach?" Mrs. Goodge glared at him. "I'm savin' the cake for some more sources I've got comin' by tomorrow."

Wiggins opened his mouth to protest, but Mrs. Jeffries, seeing another tempest in a teapot, quickly intervened. "Please, Wiggins, do let Mrs. Goodge have her say. We haven't much time today; the inspector might be home early for supper."

"Yeah, and I want to go next," Luty said. She was busting to tell them what she'd found out. "Go on, Mrs. Goodge," she encouraged, knowing full well that none of the others had a patch on her today.

"Thank you." The cook nodded regally to Luty. "As I was saying, an old acquaintance of mine came around for tea today. This person doesn't have any theatre connections now, but she did at one time. I found out the most extraordinary thing from her. It seems that when Edmund Delaney suddenly left Hinchley and more or less took up with Miss Vaughan, Hinchley was so upset that he publicly vowed vengeance on Delaney."

"Publicly? How?" Mrs. Jeffries asked.

Mrs. Goodge smiled. Normally, repeating what she was about to say would have made her blush, but Mollie Dubay wasn't the only one who'd had a couple of glasses of sherry that afternoon. "Hinchley accosted the couple right outside the Empire Theatre on Leicester Square. Silly man made a fool of himself in front of dozens of people. He told Delaney he'd make him sorry he left him for, as he put it, 'a has-been actress like Theodora Vaughan.' Delaney was furious with Hinchley, and from what my source told me, they had more than a few words. It ended with Delaney yelling that if Hinchley came near Miss Vaughan, he'd kill him." Satisfied, Mrs. Goodge sat back.

"A death threat," Mrs. Jeffries murmured. "Exactly when was this?"

"It would have been a little over a year ago, just after Hinchley came back from Italy."

"So Delaney could well have thought that Hinchley was going to have his vengeance against Miss Vaughan by giving her a terrible review," Mrs. Jeffries said. "I wonder if that's motive enough for murder?"

"It wouldn't be the first time a man's killed to protect 'is woman," Smythe added.

"Well, fiddlesticks," Luty cried. "That don't make any sense at all."

"Excuse me." Mrs. Goodge straightened up in her chair. "It makes perfect sense to me."

"Not in light of what I found out today," Luty charged.

"Really, madam," Hatchet said quickly. "Mr. Stampton's information might not be true. The man was in his cups when we talked to him this afternoon."

"It is true," Luty snapped. "Drunk or sober, Harold don't have the imagination to make up tales."

"Make what up, Luty?" Mrs. Jeffries asked.

Luty, her face set in a frown, shook her head. "That Edmund Delaney is Ogden Hinchley's heir."

"His heir?" the cook repeated.

"He inherits?" Betsy said. "But Hinchley hated him."

Luty nodded and a slow grin broke across her face. "Hate him or not, Edmund Delaney is now a rich man. He stands to inherit over a hundred thousand pounds."

Mrs. Jeffries looked from Luty to Hatchet and then back. She didn't wish to offend Luty, but this was one point they had to be absolutely sure about. "Was your source absolutely certain of this?"

"Harold might have been drunk as a skunk," Luty said, "but he don't get things like that wrong. Hinchley redid his will right before he left for New York. Edmund Delaney gets the whole kit and caboodle. The estate, the house and all Hinchley's money."

CHAPTER 8

"This case is getting very confusing," Mrs. Jeffries admitted. She didn't doubt that Luty was telling the truth, but she wondered if Luty's drunken solicitor could be trusted. "Why would Ogden Hinchley leave a fortune to a man he'd come to hate? A man he'd threatened to ruin?"

"Stampton didn't know." Luty shrugged. "But he was sure about it. His firm has handled Hinchley's affairs for years. It wasn't the first time Hinchley'd changed his will."

"But he changed it after Delaney left him for Miss Vaughan?" Mrs. Goodge murmured. "The man must be daft. Sounds like he's got a few ingredients missin' from his cupboard."

"Cor blimey," Smythe interjected. "I wonder if Edmund Delaney knew he was goin' to inherit a ruddy fortune?"

"Stampton didn't know that either," Luty replied.

"Useful fellow is Stampton—pour a couple of drinks down his throat and he'll tell you anything."

"For a solicitor he certainly isn't very discreet," Hatchet agreed. "It's a wonder he hasn't been tossed out of the legal profession on his ear."

"You're just bellyachin' cause I found out somethin' important." Luty grinned.

"Oh, really?" He arched an eyebrow. "For your information, madam, I too have something to report."

"So do I," Wiggins added.

Mrs. Jeffries glanced at the clock and saw that it was getting late. "Please, Hatchet, tell us what you found out. Then Wiggins can go. As interesting as Luty's information is, we must get on. The Inspector will probably be home soon."

Hatchet put down the teacup he'd been holding. "Willard Swinton lied about his alibi the night of the murder. He wasn't at the theatre counting receipts. He waited until everyone had left and then left himself. Furthermore, according to my information, he didn't get home until after three in the morning."

"So he doesn't have an alibi either," Betsy said eagerly. "I wonder why he lied?"

"Most people lie 'cause they don't want to tell the truth," Wiggins said somberly.

"Well, of course that's why they do it," Mrs. Goodge said impatiently. She was rather annoyed that all the information she'd worked so hard to drag out of Mollie Dubay was being overshadowed by everyone else.

Wiggins shook his head. "That's not what I meant. I mean, I know people lie 'cause they don't want to tell the truth, but there's lots of different reasons for not wantin' to tell the truth, if you see what I mean. Take Annie, fer instance, she's been fibbin' a bit, but it's not because she's done something wrong.''

"Who's Annie?" Smythe asked.

"Albert Parks's maid," Wiggins replied. He leaned forward eagerly. "I had a nice long chat with 'er today. Mind you, I did 'ave to take 'er fer tea." He glanced quickly at the cook. "You're right, you know. People do tell you ever so much more when you're feedin' 'em.''

Mrs. Goodge "humphed" softly. She wasn't all that sure she wanted the others to be using her methods. But she could hardly complain about it now. "Well, get on with it, boy. What did this Annie tell you?"

"She told me plenty." He grinned. "Seems Albert Parks is in a bad way with money. He don't 'ave none. His housekeeper quit yesterday 'cause 'e ain't paid this quarter's wages and 'e was late payin' last quarter's. Poor Annie's been 'avin' to go round to the shops and all and get credit just to buy food. She's ever so embarrassed about it too. It's right 'umiliatin' for the poor girl. It's digustin' the way people get treated just because they've got to 'ave a bit of 'elp. Sometimes I think the radicals are right . . .''

"Get on with it, lad," Smythe said sharply. "We don't 'ave time for one of yer political speeches.''

"Yes, Wiggins." Mrs. Jeffries intervened quickly. "Do go on and finish telling us what you got out of Annie." She didn't want to let him digress. Wiggins had a very soft heart. He could spend ages harping on how badly the working classes were treated in this country. Mrs. Jeffries had noticed that his political opinions had sharpened somewhat since their neighbor, Lady Cannonberry, had taken to spending so much time visiting. Underneath her upper-class facade, Lady Cannonberry was a bit of a rad-

ical. Not that Mrs. Jeffries didn't agree with most of her
attitudes—she did. The poor in this country were treated
abominably. But Smythe was right; they didn't have time
for the luxury of a political polemic right now. Unless
one guided Wiggins firmly, he was very likely to stray
off the point.

Unabashed, Wiggins took a quick gulp of tea. ''Well,
Annie told me that Albert Parks 'as been skint ever since
he invested in Edmund Delaney's play.''

''If Parks were broke, why'd he invest in the first
place?'' Smythe demanded. ''Did ya find that out?''

'''Course I found out.'' Wiggins looked offended.
''Parks didn't 'ave no choice. 'E wanted to direct the play
and the only way the others would take a chance on 'im
was to make 'im put up some money. 'E took a loan out
on 'is 'ouse.''

''From a bank?'' Luty asked eagerly. She knew lots of
bankers and she was pretty darned good at getting them
to talk too.

Wiggin's face fell. ''I, uh, didn't ask that.''

Disappointed, Luty said, ''Find out, will ya?''

''I'm seein' Annie again tomorrow,'' Wiggins said,
looking doubtful. ''But she might not know 'ow Parks got
the loan.''

''Why didn't the others want to take a chance on
Parks?'' Luty asked curiously.

Wiggins made a face. ''I didn't think to ask.''

''Why is this Annie staying on with Parks if he's not
paying her?'' Betsy asked.

Wiggins brightened. He did know the answer to that
one. ''She don't have anywhere else to go,'' he explained.
''And at least it's a roof over her head. Besides, the play's
doin' well. She's pretty sure Mr. Parks is goin' to be able
to pay her next week. She's just hopin' there'll be enough

money for 'im to pay off the grocers. If he don't settle up with them, they're goin' to stop givin' him credit.''

''Did you learn anything else from her?'' Mrs. Jeffries prompted. ''What about Albert Parks's alibi? Did he come right home on the night of the murder?''

Wiggins nodded eagerly. ''I asked Annie that and she didn't know. She were asleep. But I'll see what else I can get out of 'er tomorrow.''

''Good, Wiggins; you do that,'' Mrs. Jeffries said. She looked at Betsy and Smythe. ''Who wants to go next?''

Betsy shrugged. ''I didn't learn anything useful today. I talked to a footman from Theodora Vaughan's household, but he didn't know anything.'' The lad had been more interested in trying to get to know her better than in answering questions. After listening to him complain about the mountain of luggage that the actress traveled with, and dodging his quick hands, Betsy had decided to try elsewhere for information.

Mrs. Jeffries smiled kindly. ''There's always tomorrow, my dear. You mustn't let one bad day dampen your spirits.''

Betsy gave her a strained smile. Truth was, not only hadn't she learned anything worthwhile, but her conscience was bothering her too. Even putting the money in the collection plate at St. Jude's hadn't completely washed away her guilt. Every time she looked at the coachman, she just knew he was hurt to the bone because she wouldn't tell him the truth.

Smythe said, ''Don't take it so 'ard, lass; I didn't 'ave much luck today either.'' But he fully intended to have plenty tomorrow. It was time to make contact with one of his sources, Blimpey Groggins. Someone had to know something about this ruddy murder. And if there was any information about the city, Blimpey was sure to find it.

"The only thing I learned was that except for the 'ansoms that Hinchley took back to his 'ouse and the one Theodora Vaughan took that night to go 'ome, no one else took one. Least of all, none of the drivers I talked to could remember pickin' up a fare and takin' 'em to Hinchley's neighborhood."

"Maybe the killer didn't take a hanson," Hatchet suggested.

"I thought of that," Smythe said, "but unless they walked, 'ow else would they get there? All the suspects live close to the Hayden. Hinchley lived almost three miles away. That's a fair walk."

"Maybe the killer took the Underground," Wiggins said.

Smythe shook his head. "There's not an Underground station close to Hinchley's and even if there were, the trains don't run that time of night."

Mrs. Jeffries thought about it for a moment. Smythe did have a point. How did the killer get there? She had a feeling he wouldn't have walked; that was too risky. People tended to be noticed when the streets were deserted. The killer wouldn't have wanted that. Also, with that awful murder in the East End, she knew the police had doubled their street patrols all over the city. The killer would have known that as well. That fact had been in every newspaper. "Do any of them have private carriages?"

"Theodora Vaughan has one," Betsy said. She'd forgotten she'd found that out. "But it's at her cottage in the country. Oliver was ever so put out because they had to come up to Victoria by train on Saturday because the carriage had a bad wheel."

"Who's Oliver?" Smythe asked quickly.

"The footman," Betsy replied.

"So the carriage definitely wasn't here on Saturday evening?" Mrs. Jeffries asked.

"It still isn't." Betsy reached for a slice of bread. "Oliver told me that too." More like he'd bent her ear for ten minutes complaining about the fact that without the carriage, he had to accompany Miss Vaughan all over London to carry her ruddy packages. She smiled at the memory. She couldn't really blame the lad for being put out. Theodora Vaughan liked to shop. The only day she didn't head for Regent Street was Sunday.

"So once again, we're back to our original question," Mrs. Jeffries mused. "How did the killer get there that night?"

There were dozens more questions that needed to be answered, but focusing on this one at least gave her a place to start. She knew she needed to think about this case more thoroughly. But if the truth were told, she was almost as nervous about her abilities as the rest of them were. Quickly, she squashed that notion. She refused to think they were finished. They'd had far too much success in the past to be completely wrong now.

"What do we do next?" Betsy asked, her words echoing everyone else's thoughts. "I mean, do we keep on as we are or try somethin' a bit different?"

"I think we ought to keep on as we are," Wiggins declared. "I'll 'ave another go at Annie tomorrow and the rest of ya can keep right on doin' what you've been doin'. We're learnin' lots of things."

"But are we learnin' anything that's goin' to lead us to the killer?" Luty asked bluntly. "Or are we just chasin' our tails?"

No one said anything for a moment. Mrs. Jeffries looked at the others. Mrs. Goodge was eyeing the plate of bread on the table as if she expected it to talk to her. Smythe was staring off into space; Luty's mouth was set in a flat, thin line. Hatchet's eyes were worried and Betsy was biting her lower lip. The only one who didn't look concerned was Wiggins. He was leaning back in his chair, a dreamy expression on his young face.

"We're not chasing our tails," Mrs. Jeffries said firmly. "We're solving a heinous and horrible murder. We are serving justice, and I, for one, am going to keep at it till the killer is caught. If any of you feel that you can't, or that it's too difficult, you've a perfect right to bow out now."

That got their attention.

"But what if we're wrong?" Betsy said. "What if it's like the last time . . ."

"It won't be," the housekeeper declared. "We're far too good at this to be wrong again. Now, we've got to get cracking. As I see it, someone slipped into Hinchley's house sometime after midnight on Saturday night, found him in the bathtub, drowned him and put his body in the Regents Canal." She paused for a moment to gather her thoughts. The others were watching her carefully, their expressions a mixture of hope and fear. "We know who our suspects are and we know that one of them is probably the killer. So here's what I propose we do now."

Mrs. Jeffries, her mind working furiously, began issuing orders like a general. She had no idea whether she was on the right track or not, but she knew that activity, any activity, would be better for them the constant doubts about their own abilities.

"As soon as the inspector gets home this evening," she finished, "I'm going to relay the information you've all gathered to him."

''Be careful, Mrs. J.,'' Smythe warned. ''We don't want the Inspector gettin' suspicious.''

''I intend to be,'' she promised, getting to her feet. ''I won't tell him everything this evening—that would be a bit too much. But I've breakfast tomorrow to work on him. Now, I want all of you back here tomorrow for lunch.''

''But that's in the middle of our day,'' Wiggins whined.

''I know, but it's important. I've got to pass on to you what I get out of the inspector tonight and tomorrow morning. Don't worry; you'll have plenty of time for gathering information. If any of you are right in the middle of something, then, naturally, you'll be excused from attending. But do try to be here.''

True to her word, Mrs. Jeffries pumped the inspector ruthlessly before he went in to dinner that evening. She also kept him well supplied with sherry. ''Have a bit more, sir,'' she urged, topping up his glass for the third time. ''It's been a very warm day and you could do with a bit of relaxation. Mrs. Goodge is making something special this evening, so there's no hurry.''

''Thank you, Mrs. Jeffries,'' he said with a grateful sigh. ''This is so very nice. I will admit it's been rather a tiring day.''

''You work too hard, sir,'' she replied sympathetically. ''I must say, you were particularly clever today.'' She laughed delightedly. ''But then, you always are.''

Witherspoon, who'd already unburdened himself and felt much better for it, straightened his spine. ''Oh, thank you, Mrs. Jeffries. It's good of you to say so. Er . . . uh, I'm interested in which of my methods you thought clever.''

"Really, sir"—she poured herself a glass—"now do stop teasing. You know very well what I mean. It was uncanny how you managed to get Remington to 'spill the beans,' as Luty would say about the others."

As Remington had spilt quite a few beans, Witherspoon wondered which ones she meant. "Could you be a bit more specific?"

She contrived to look surprised. "Why, the information about how virtually everyone involved in the play had to put up money. That's most important, don't you think?"

Witherspoon sincerely hoped it was, but the truth was, this case was so muddled it was difficult to understand what was important and what wasn't. That was why he was so glad he had his housekeeper to talk with. She was rather good at helping him clarify his ideas. "Yes," he agreed eagerly. "I believe it is. Then you don't think the information about Remington not having an alibi is important?"

"But of course I do, sir," she exclaimed. "It's vitally important. I'm so glad you're going to be checking into the others' alibis as well." She hesitated. This part was going to be tricky. "Take Mr. Swinton, for instance."

"What about him?" Witherspoon looked at her expectantly.

"Well, he claimed he was in the theatre, counting the receipts. But from what you said about that dreadful row he was having with Mr. Delaney today, I think it's very possible he might have had more than a passing interest in making sure that Hinchley didn't have a chance to give the play a bad review. From what you overheard, Swinton doesn't think much of the production in the best of circumstances. Wouldn't you agree?"

"That's true," Witherspoon said. He wondered what

she was getting at. ''But that doesn't mean Swinton killed him. Besides''—he sighed—''Swinton's alibi will be very difficult to verify.''

''Perhaps for an ordinary detective, sir,'' she enthused, ''but not for you.''

''Really?''

''Really, sir. Why, of course you know how to verify it.'' She smiled serenely. ''You're going to check with all the watchmen and constables on patrol in the area. If Swinton was indeed sitting in his office adding up receipts, someone will have seen the lights.'' It was weak and she knew it, but after thinking about the matter, it was the best she could come up with.

Witherspoon brightened. ''Yes, yes, of course, that's exactly what I'm going to do.'' He'd already decided to check with the police constables, but it had never occurred to him to question the night watchmen in the area. It was a commercial area too, so many of the businesses and buildings in the neighborhood had both watchmen and porters.

''And you'll do the same for Delaney, I'm sure.'' She hoped he would take the hint. She didn't want to have to go into too much detail. But honestly, with half of the London police on foot patrols because of that wretched East End murder, it had finally occurred to her that if Edmund Delaney had indeed been walking by the river, someone—probably a police constable—would not only have seen him, but would have remembered him. She'd bet her housekeeping money that every face a constable passed was etched in his memory. ''Goodness, sir, I almost forgot.''

''Forgot what?''

''Oh, I know I shouldn't bother you with such trifles,

but I did promise the old dear I'd pass it along . . .'' She broke off and gazed at him anxiously, waiting for him to take the bait.

Witherspoon, who was still trying to determine how many porters or watchmen might have been awake that night in the vicinity of the Hayden, realized that his housekeeper had said something. "Trifles? You never bother me with trifles. What is it?"

She looked embarrassed. "This is so awkward, but Mollie so insisted we mention it."

"Mention what?"

"Well, sir''—her face flushed slightly, an effect she'd achieved by holding her breath for several seconds—"one of Mrs. Goodge's old acquaintances dropped by yesterday. It seems you're quite famous, sir. This person, a Miss Mollie Dubay, had some information about one of your suspects. Naturally, Mrs. Goodge told her we couldn't possibly interfere in one of your cases, but Miss Dubay was quite insistent we tell you."

Flattered, Witherspoon's chest puffed out a bit. "I'm hardly famous, Mrs. Jeffries. But please, do go on and tell me what Mrs. Goodge's friend said."

Mrs. Jeffries took a deep breath and plunged right in. In the course of the conversation she not only told him everything Mrs. Goodge had gotten out of Mollie Dubay, but she also managed to mention the rumor that Edmund Delaney was Hinchley's heir.

Spellbound, Witherspoon listened. From the expression on his face, Mrs. Jeffries could see that he was taking in every single word.

Mrs. Jeffries sat staring out at the London night. A wispy fog drifted in off the river, softening the glow of the gas lamp across the road. She liked sitting in the dark when she was trying to think.

Sitting back, she let her mind drift for a moment. Sometimes, putting the puzzle together began with nothing more than letting the bits and pieces float about aimlessly until, all of a sudden, a piece or two would fit together.

The inspector was fairly certain that Hinchley had been murdered soon after the play ended. That piece might be important. Mrs. Jeffries was inclined to agree with Witherspoon's reasoning. Whoever did it wouldn't have wanted to be found roaming the streets at three or four in the morning. With the police out in full force all over London, the killer wouldn't have risked being stopped by a constable.

Then there was the argument the inspector had overheard. She frowned because it really didn't make sense. If Swinton thought Delaney's play was that bad, why had he agreed to produce it in the first place? Even with Theodora Vaughan as a draw, it was obvious that the owner had realized that wouldn't keep the show open long if the play was awful. Yet he'd not only produced the play; he'd invested his own money in it as well. Why? Then she remembered the inspector telling her that the theatre was in a bad way, that they hadn't had a success there in years. She nodded to herself. Perhaps Swinton hadn't had a choice. Perhaps even producing a bad play with a big star was better than letting the theatre sit empty.

For a long time, she sat in the darkened room, her mind going over and over all the pieces of information. Had Hinchley come back early from America for a reason? Could he have come back for the express purpose of destroying Delaney's play with a bad review? Where was the review? The police hadn't found it when they searched his house; Mrs. Jeffries had asked the inspector that this morning at breakfast. She thought not finding it might be important. If what they'd heard of the victim's habits were true, then that meant the killer must have either destroyed it (she made another mental note to ask Witherspoon if there'd been a fire in the grate) or taken the review with him.

Finally, unable to come to any conclusion except that she needed more facts and information, Mrs. Jeffries got up and went to bed.

The next morning at breakfast, Mrs. Jeffries managed to feed the inspector the remainder of the information. It was hard work; she couldn't use Mollie Dubay this time. In the end, she couched everything in terms of "possible" and "maybe" and "didn't the Inspector think." By the time Witherspoon left with Constable Barnes, Mrs. Jeffries felt she'd spent the morning walking on egg shells.

As soon as the door closed behind the two policemen, she hurried upstairs and put on her hat. The others had already gone out. Pausing only to tell Mrs. Goodge that she would be back before lunch, she dashed out the front door and down to the end of the road. Going out to Uxbridge Road she debated a moment, wondering if it would be faster to take an omnibus or a hansom to St. John's Wood. But her mind was made up when a hansom pulled up just then. She smiled at the elderly woman alighting from the cab, waited till the fare was paid and then hopped in herself. "Avenue Road, St. John's Wood, please," she called to the driver.

She had the hansom drop her at the North Gate of Regents Park. The day had dimmed, and a layer of yellowish fog had crept in to cover the sun. Mrs. Jeffries glanced across the intersection of Avenue Road. Time enough to get a good look at the victim's house later. She turned and walked slowly into the park, towards the canal. Towards Macclesfield Bridge.

When she got to the edge of the bridge, she took a moment to study her surroundings. Down the path to her left was the entrance to the Zoological Gardens. The water in the canal was a dark wine color. Cool looking and deep, it reeked slightly of damp and rotting vegetation. Stepping onto the bridge, she walked until she came to the middle and then peeked over the side.

The drop wasn't very far. Only a few feet. Leaning further, Mrs. Jeffries craned her neck until she could see under the bridge. But all she saw was the dark water lapping against the sides of the supports. The carriage wheel that the body had landed on was gone. Taken away, probably, by the police.

Mrs. Jeffries turned and walked back the way she'd come. Crossing Albert Road to Avenue Road, she found herself in front of Hinchley's house. His was the last one at this end of the street. She edged closer to the house, her eyes darting from the front door to the side. A cobblestone walkway veered off from the walkway and led round the side of the tall building. It took only a second to realize that the killer must have used the side door, which was flat against the pavement, or been as strong as an ox. There were six steps leading up to the front door. Carrying a body down them wouldn't have been easy. She studied the side of the house for a few more minutes, trying in her mind's eye to imagine what the area would have been like in the dark of the night. Glancing over her shoulder, she noted that on the corner there was a gas lamp. Across the intersection, just outside the North Gate entrance, was another one. The were small gaslamps, not like the huge ones on Oxford Street or the Strand, but they would have been lighted. The killer could have avoided the lamp on the corner by veering out into the darkened street. But he would have had to pass the one by the park entrance.

Then she turned and slowly began to measure just how far it was to the bridge. She pretended she was carrying a dead weight over her shoulder and slowed her steps accordingly.

Then she did it again.

And again.

Each time, she mentally ticked off the passing seconds in her head. By her estimation, the killer must have been visible, out where people could see him, for at least a minute and a half.

"'Ow much you willin' to pay, mate?" Blimpey lifted the pint of beer Smythe had just paid for and took a long, greedy sip.

"That's what I like about you, Blimpey," Smythe replied, taking a sip from his own glass, "you don't waste time askin' a lot of questions."

"Just takin' care of business, mate. No offense meant. After all, snoopin' about in a murder could be dangerous."

"All you've got to do is ask a few questions, Blimpey. You're not riskin' life or limb. Besides, don't I always pay a good price?" Smythe replied. "You can trust me on that."

Blimpey wiped his mouth with the cuff of his dirty, checkered sleeve. He grinned and slapped the glass on the counter. "Yer good fer it, mate. Just tryin' to rattle ya a bit. Now, what's them names again?"

They were standing at the bar of the Baying Hound Pub on Wapping High Street. The place was old and dark and smelled of rotting wood, stale beer and unwashed bodies. It was Blimpey's favorite pub and the one place he could ususally be found during the daylight hours. During the night hours he worked. His job was an odd one, and Smythe had found it useful on several occasions.

Blimpey bought and sold information. He also did other things. Things that occasionally skirted the law a fraction, but as long as Smythe didn't know the details, he didn't ask questions. But for all Blimpey's criminal associations, and Smythe knew he had plenty, he was a good sort. Once you paid him, he got what you needed and then kept his mouth shut. He wasn't one to sell out a friend, either. Not for any amount of money.

"You want me to write 'em down for ya?" Smythe asked.

Blimpey shook his head. "What'd be the point? Can't read now, can I?" He laughed heartily at his own wit. "Is there anythin' in particular you want me to find out?"

Smythe thought about it for a moment. He didn't doubt that Blimpey could find out most anything. But he wasn't sure himself just what it was that he was looking for. Blast a Spaniard, he felt a bit of a fool, not even able to say what it was he wanted to know. "No, just general stuff. Anythin' about the night of the killin' and anythin' about them names I give ya."

Blimpey's eyebrows rose so far they almost disappeared under the brim of his filthy pork pie hat. "What da ya mean, general stuff? Come on now, mate, I'm good, but I can't get blood out of a bleedin' turnip. These people ain't crooks. It's not like I'm goin' to be able to tap my usual sources."

Irritated with himself more than Blimpey, Smythe answered harshly. "Look, I've given you the bloomin' names. Just find out if any of 'em 'as come into a bit of money or is plannin' on leavin' town or . . . or . . .''

"Or anythin' else," Blimpey finished. He took another swallow of beer. "This is gonna cost you. Thems a lot of names, I'll 'ave to spread the lolly about a bit to cover 'em all."

"Spread as much as ya 'ave to," Smythe retorted, then caught himself and quickly picked up his own beer. Bloomin' Ada, he'd forgotten for a moment that Blimpey only thought of him as a coachman. When he glanced at the other man over the rim of his tankard, Blimpey was staring at him with a long, speculative gleam in his eye. "What are you lookin' at?"

Blimpey smiled slowly. "Nuthin'. Just wonderin' where a coachman gets that kind of lolly."

"I told ya before, I play the 'orses."

"Then we'll 'ave to go to the races together some-time," Blimpey said amiably. "The way you spread the stuff about, you must be bloomin' good at pickin' win-ners."

"So what if I am?"

"You was out in Australia a while back, wasn't ya?"

Smythe blinked, surprised by the abrupt change of sub-ject. "Yeah, what of it?"

"Nuthin', just chattin'." Blimpey pointedly looked down at his now-empty glass. "I could use another."

Smythe nodded at the barman, who hustled over with another glass of beer and slapped it down in front of Blim-pey.

"Seems to me, even if ya play the ponies a bit, you're always ready with the cash," Blimpey said softly. "Not that I'm askin' any questions, mind ya. Just curious like."

"Good, 'cause I'm not answerin'." Smythe wondered if Blimpey was going to raise his price now.

"The price is the same," Blimpey said, as though he

could read the coachman's mind. "But ya know, if I 'ad the kind of money I think you 'ave, I wouldn't be 'angin' about drivin' someone else's 'orses. I'd be buyin' my own."

"You're talkin' daft, man," Smythe retorted. But he knew then that Blimpey knew the truth. Cor blimey, he'd been a fool to think the likes of Blimpey Groggins wouldn't get curious about him. Especially considering the kind of money he'd tossed Blimpey's way for information—and in one case for a little more than information.

He'd no doubt that Blimpey knew to the penny exactly how much money Smythe had.

"I'm daft?" Blimpey laughed. "Look, Smythe, you're a good sort and I owe you one. So don't think I'm goin' to be spreadin' any stories about you. If someone as rich as you wants to go on livin' in a policeman's 'ouse and drivin' a team of ruddy 'orses, that's yer business."

Puzzled, Smythe stared at him. He didn't remember doing Blimpey Groggins any favors. "You owe me one?"

"Forget I said that," he said quickly, slamming his glass on the counter. "I'd best get crackin'." Blimpey was obviously flustered; he hadn't even finished his beer. "I'll get back to you in a day or two." He turned and started for the door. Smythe grabbed his arm. "Come on, Blimp, what'd ya mean?"

Blimpey blushed.

Smythe gaped at him as a red flush climbed Blimpey's cheeks and spread all the way up to his dirty forehead. "I didn't mean nuthin' by it," he protested. "Now leave off and let me git to work."

But Smythe had to have his curiosity satisfied. "Oh, no, ya don't. Tell me what ya meant."

Blimpey glared at the hand on his sleeve for a moment

and the shrugged. "Oh, well, if you must know. There was a woman . . . a friend of mine, like."

"Yeah?" Smythe encouraged. For a talker, Blimpey had sure got tongue-tied quick enough.

"Ya 'elped 'er, that's all."

"What woman?" Smythe asked. He couldn't remember helping any friends of Blimpey's. "What's 'er name?"

"Abby," Blimpey replied.

"Abby?" Smythe looked at him blankly.

"Sometimes she uses 'Abigail.' "

Then he remembered. It had been back at the beginning of the case in which the inspector had been a suspect in those businessmen's murders. Oh, yes, he remembered all right.

"Ya 'elped 'er out a few months back," Blimpey continued. "She wouldn't come to me."

"Why?" Smythe asked. "Why wouldn't she come to ya?" As he recalled, his helping sweet Abigail had caused a few problems between him and Betsy. It didn't do to let a woman see another woman throw her arms about your neck. Even when it didn't mean anything but a bit of gratitude. Betsy's nose had really been out of joint when she'd seen Abigail's hug of thanks.

"'Cause we'd 'ad words over some triflin' matter," Blimpey said irritably. He wished he'd never brought the bloomin' subject up, but he owed Smythe. "And she weren't speakin' to me. Silly woman, rather go 'ungry than give in to 'er pride. She come to you at the stables and you lent 'er a few quid. It were enough to keep her off the streets. I'm grateful for that. She means somethin' to me. Now leave off and let me go. I've got work to do."

Amazed, Smythe watched as Blimpey stalked off. He couldn't believe it! Blimpey Groggins was in love.

CHAPTER 9

"Did we have any luck on the brothel?" Witherspoon asked as he and Constable Barnes waited at the pedestrian island for a dray to pass. He felt a flash of guilt when he thought of the house on Lisle Street. He really should have gone there himself, but he simply hadn't had time.

Barnes brightened. "We did, sir. It seems that Hinchley had been there that night, before he went to the theatre. He'd made arrangements for later in the evening. But then he cancelled and the . . . er . . . person never went."

"Cancelled?" Witherspoon queried. "How'd he do that?"

"He sent a lad round with a note." Barnes checked the traffic and started across the road. "The message said that he'd changed his mind and no one was to come to his house that night."

"Was the police constable sure they were telling him the truth?" Realizing how awkward that sounded, the inspector quickly amended his words, "I mean, is he sure the people at the brothel aren't lying to protect a member of their establishment?''

''Oh, yes, sir. Constable Giffith questioned everyone at the brothel himself. He's sure no one's lying. The maid and half a dozen other people swear that Rupert Bowker never left the premises that night.'' Barnes chuckled. ''Bowker was the one scheduled to go to Hinchley's. Seems this Bowker was quite put out about the whole thing. I gather the madam kept the money and as he'd not gone to the client, she wouldn't pay him.''

''I don't suppose the message was in writing?'' Witherspoon turned the corner.

''Yes, but the madam burned it.''

''Burned it?''

''She tossed it in the stove with the rest of the waste-paper the next morning.''

''Drat.'' Witherspoon would have liked to have had a look at that note. ''What time did the messenger get there?''

''About eleven forty-five, sir,'' Barnes replied. ''Just a few minutes before Bowker was set to leave.''

''Eleven forty-five, huh?'' Witherspoon mused. ''Barnes, remind me to have another chat with Rather.''

''The Hinchley butler? Why?''

Witherspoon really didn't know. But he had to say something. ''Well, the note had to be written some-where,'' he said. Aware of the constable's quizzical gaze, he hastily asked, ''Did we get a description of the lad who brought the message around?''

Barnes grimaced. ''Not much. But the madam told Griffith he was small, dressed well, had black hair and wore a cap pulled low over his face.''

''So it wasn't a street arab?''

''The madam thought it was Hinchley's footman.''

Witherspoon sighed. Drat. Now they'd have to try and track down this footman. "But all Hinchley's staff had been let go, so it couldn't have been one of his footmen."

"It could have been someone from the theatre district," Barnes ventured. "An actor or someone like that. Hinchley could have hired someone to take the message round for him."

"Yes, I suppose that's what must have happened. Have you had any reports back on the hansoms?" Witherspoon asked Barnes as they stopped in front of Theodora Vaughan's town house.

Barnes held open the wrought iron gate for the inspector. "According to the reports, the only two of the suspects they can determine actually took a cab that night were Miss Vaughan and the victim."

"Let's keep at it, Barnes," Witherspoon said bracingly. He might still be a tad confused about a few aspects of this case, but all in all, he felt ever so much better. It had been a most enlightening morning.

First, he'd gone to the Yard and sent out the word to the constables on patrol. Then he and Barnes had gone to pay a visit to Mr. Hinchley's solicitor. That conversation had been quite enlightening.

"Excuse me, sir," Barnes said as they reached the front door, "but why are we comin' here to see Edmund Delaney? Won't he be at his own home?"

Witherspoon banged the brass door knocker. "I believe"—the inspector dropped his voice to a whisper—"he spends rather more time with Miss Vaughan than he does in his rooms. If you'll remember, his landlady said he's rarely ever there."

The door opened, and a few minutes later Witherspoon and Barnes were ensconced in Theodora Vaughan's delightfully feminine drawing room.

The walls were a pale ivory and the carpet a deep, rich red. A crystal chandelier hung from an intricately patterned ceiling. Delicate rose velvet settees and wing chairs were scattered artfully around the room. But it was the painting hanging over the mantel that caught one's eye.

Drawn to the picture, Witherspoon wandered toward the fireplace, his gaze fixed on the portrait of Theodora Vaughan.

Her hair was loose and flowed like a deep auburn cloak over her shoulders, spilling over a deep blue gown. Her hands were clasped demurely together, and her head angled slightly to one side.

"Beautiful," Witherspoon murmured.

"Juliet," Edmund Delaney said from behind them.

"Juliet?" the inspector repeated. "Oh, you mean the play. Shakespeare. *Romeo and Juliet.*"

Delaney smiled and crossed the room to join them. "She was twenty-six when she played that part. This portrait was done at that time. She was superb. All of London was at her feet. She went from being a poor, struggling actress stealing apples for supper and sneaking lifts off the backs of cabs to being the toast of the town."

"She is a remarkable actress," Witherspoon agreed. "I'm privileged to have met her."

"Goodness, Inspector, you make it sound as though I'm retiring," Theodora said from the doorway. She was dressed in a pale yellow day gown, her hair was elegantly arranged in a mass of brilliant curls and her face wreathed in a charming smile as she advanced into the room.

"Forgive me, dear Miss Vaughan." Witherspoon felt like he ought to kiss her hand or bow, but wasn't quite certain how one did that sort of thing. "It will be a great tragedy for the stage when that dreadful moment comes."

"How very kind you are, Inspector." She gestured

gracefully toward the settee. "Please sit down. Shall I ring for tea?"

"No, thank you." Witherspoon sat down. Barnes took one of the wing chairs and Delaney, all the friendliness gone from his face, sat down on the love seat next to Theodora.

"Why have you come, Inspector?" Delaney asked bluntly.

Witherspoon silently debated the wisdom of asking his questions with both of them present, then he decided it really didn't matter. No matter how delicate or diplomatic he was, the next few moments were going to be rather painful and embarrassing for both of them. "I've a few more questions to ask," he said.

"But we've answered all your questions." Delaney got up and began to pace. "Really, sir, this is beginning to be annoying."

"It's all right, Edmund," Theodora said soothingly. "The inspector is only doing his duty. Please, ask me anything you like."

Witherspoon took a deep breath. He was surprised at how difficult it was to form the words properly. "How well did you know Ogden Hinchley?"

"He was a critic," she said, looking surprised. "I've known him for years, but I didn't really *know* him, if you understand my meaning. Not socially."

"So you would say you have merely a professional relationship with him?" Barnes asked.

Theodora glanced at Delaney. "For the most part," she replied.

Witherspoon watched her carefully, reminding himself that this woman was an actress. "Are you aware that Hinchley had threatened to ruin you?"

"Yes," she replied, her expresssion hardening just a

bit. "I am." She kept her gaze on the inspector, not on Delaney, who had stopped by the mantel. "I didn't take it seriously."

"But he had the power to do it," Barnes put in. "Weren't you worried?"

"Not at all," she said, folding her hands in her lap. "He's only one person, Constable. Admittedly, Ogden Hinchley was the most powerful critic in London, but his word was hardly law."

"I see." The inspector thought her attitude most sensible. He waited a moment, hoping that Barnes would carry on and ask the next question. But the constable was busy scribbling in his notebook.

So Witherspoon cleared his throat and tried and failed to make himself look at Theodora Vaughan. "Were you aware of why Ogden Hinchley wanted to ruin you?" he asked gently as he stared at the carpet. His head jerked up when he heard Delaney's exclamation of disgust.

"For God's sake, Inspector," Delaney snapped.

"It's all right, Edmund." She smiled slightly, as though she were amused by the inspector's obvious discomfort. "Of course I knew why Hinchley wanted to ruin me. Half of London knew. He was ridiculously jealous of my relationship with Edmund," she said calmly, "but I naturally assumed he'd get over it."

Witherspoon looked at Delaney. This one wasn't an actor. His face was showing strain. He'd gone pale around the mouth. "Mr. Delaney, forgive me for bringing up such a delicate matter, but . . . er . . . would you mind telling us what your relationship with Hinchley was? I mean, before the two of you quarreled."

Delaney's lips tightened. "We were once good friends. At least, it was friendship on my part."

"You weren't"—Barnes coughed—"more intimately involved?"

"No," Delaney said fiercely. "I'd heard the rumors about Ogden, of course. But he never approached me in that way." He began to pace back and forth across the room. "Try and understand. I was a poor, struggling playwright when we first met. I was flattered that he took an interest in me, that he wanted to be my friend."

"When did he start paying your rent on the house in Chelsea?" Barnes asked bluntly. He didn't much like this kind of questioning, but he figured he'd do better than the inspector at getting at the truth.

Delaney sighed. "You make it sound so ugly, Constable. It wasn't like that at all. I paid Hinchley rent on the Chelsea house."

"That's not what we've heard, sir."

"I know what all the rumor mongers said," Delaney replied wearily, "but it simply isn't true. I've got rent receipts. You can see them if you like."

Barnes glanced at Witherspoon, who nodded encouragingly. "I would like to see them, sir," the constable said. "You can bring them by the station."

"Fine," Delaney agreed grudgingly. "I will. Ogden didn't charge me very much, but nonetheless, I did pay rent. He knew I didn't have much money, just a small income that had been left to me by my father, and that I was trying to write. So he lowered the rent because we were friends. It was only later, when he invited me to Italy, that I realized his feelings for me were much deeper than mine for him. By that time, I'd met Miss Vaughan and we'd . . . we'd . . ."

"Fallen in love," Theodora finished. "As a matter of fact, Inspector, congratulations are in order."

"Really, Theodora," Edmund said quickly. "I don't
believe this is the time . . .''

"Oh, nonsense." She laughed gaily. "I'm too happy
to keep this all to myself. Edmund and I are going to be
married."

Witherspoon was totally at a loss. Questioning people
who'd just announced wedding plans seemed a tad churl-
ish. "Er, congratulations—to both of you. When is the
happy event taking place?"

"As soon as possible, Inspector," Theodora replied,
smiling broadly. "We've waited long enough. But I've
just had word that the difficulties surrounding my divorce
from Trevor Remington have been resolved. By the time
Edmund and I can get a license and make the arrangements, I'll be free to marry him."

"All the very best to both of you," Barnes muttered.
He cleared his throat and looked pointedly at the inspector, who was staring at Theodora Vaughan.

"Excuse me, Miss Vaughan, did I just hear you say
you're married to Mr. Remington?" Witherspoon asked
incredulously.

"*Was* married to Mr. Remington," she replied. "I received word from my American lawyers while I was at
my country house that our divorce had finally been obtained." She got up, walked over to Delaney and linked
her arm with his. "We've waited a long time, Inspector."

Barnes's head was spinning, but spinning or not, he had
a few more questions to ask. Especially since it looked as
if the inspector was too shocked to do anything but stand
there gaping at the happy couple. "Mr. Delaney," he said
quietly, "is it true you threatened to kill Hinchley?"

Delaney gasped. "For God's sake, that was over a year
ago."

"Nevertheless, you admit you did it?"

"I lost my temper, Inspector," Delaney cried. "He accosted us in public. I tell you, he was out of his mind with rage and jealousy. He went on and on about how he was going to ruin us. Kept screaming that I'd never see one of my plays on the boards and that he'd make Theodora a laughingstock. I didn't mind so much him having a go at me, but when he turned his venom on her, I lost my temper and told him if he came near her, I'd kill him. But I hardly think you ought to put any credence in something that happened so long ago. If I was going to kill the man, I'd have done it then, when I was good and angry."

As they'd planned, Wiggins met Mrs. Jeffries by the Serpentine in Hyde Park. "How did it go?" she asked.

"I found out the name of Parks's 'ousekeeper," Wiggins replied. "Mind you, it weren't easy. Annie was lookin' at me funny when I started in askin' all them questions again."

"It's never easy, Wiggins." Mrs. Jeffries patted his arm. "But you are very good at it. Now, what's the housekeeper's name and where does she live?"

Wiggins grinned broadly, delighted by the praise. "Her name is Roberta Seldon and she lives with her sister in Clapham. Number six, Bester Road."

"Excellent." Mrs. Jeffries already had an idea about how to approach the woman. "And did Annie know where Parks had gotten the loan on his house?"

"No," he said. "She said Parks never told her and she never asked. So what do I do now?" After his success with Annie today, he was raring to have at it again.

The housekeeper thought for a moment. She still had no real idea about the solution of this case, but she felt that keeping everyone busy was very important. "I think you ought to have another snoop around the victim's

neighborhood," she said. She didn't think there was much
more to learn there. The police had questioned the neigh-
bors thoroughly and no one had seen anything that night.
But it was something for the boy to do and one never
knew—sometimes the police overlooked things.

"Sounds fair enough." Wiggins grinned. "You takin'
off for Clapham now?"

"Yes, I want to find out precisely why this Mrs. Seldon
left Parks's employment."

"But Annie said it was because they 'adn't been paid."

"I know, but sometimes there's more to a situation than
meets the eye."

Betsy couldn't believe her eyes. What was Smythe doing
with someone like that? She dodged behind the oak tree
in the center of the communal gardens behind the inspector's house and peeked out. Smythe, his back to her, was
standing at the far end of the garden talking to a short,
chubby man in a checkered coat and a porkpie hat.

She wondered if she ought to call out, to let him know
that she was here. But there was something about the way
the two men stood close together in the shadows of the
wall, almost like they were hiding, that kept her silent.

Besides, she told herself firmly, it wasn't like she was
spying on him deliberately. Could she help it if just when
she'd followed him out here to tell him the truth about
her trip to the East End, he'd decided to have a visitor?

Guilt pierced through her like an arrow. She ought to
call out and let him know that she was here. Or better yet,
she ought to nip out from behind this tree and go back
into the house. Smythe had a right to his privacy. Goodness knows, she'd harped on that subject herself to know
enough to respect it for others.

But she couldn't bring herself to move.

As she watched, she saw the fat man's mouth moving a mile a minute, his hands punctuating the air as he talked. Smythe was leaning towards him, like he was listening with his whole body.

From his vantage point at the other end of the garden, Blimpey Groggins had seen the girl slip behind the tree. He grinned.

"You took a chance on comin' 'ere," Smythe said. "Cor blimey, I only give ya the job this mornin'."

"I 'appened to be passin' this way," Blimpey said conversationally. "And as I'd learned a thing or two, I thought I'd stop round. You said you needed this information right quick. Make up yer mind, man. Do you want it or not?"

"'Course I want it." Smythe cast a quick glance over his shoulder. "I just didn't expect to open the back door and find you standin' there like a ruddy statue. What'd ya find out?"

"A couple of things." Blimpey decided to wait until after he'd finished and gotten some of his pay before telling Smythe about the girl spying on them from behind the tree. No point in making the big man angry over trifles that couldn't be helped. "First of all, the servants left at the Hinchley 'ouse is doin' fine now that the old geezer's gone to his reward. Hinchley's solicitors ain't inventoried the estate yet, so the two of 'em are 'aving a fine old time sellin' off some of his smaller treasures."

"They're stealin' from the dead man's 'ouse?" Smythe asked incredulously. "Cor blimey, that takes a bit of nerve." But it was hardly a motive for murder.

"Not really." Blimpey figured the dead man was probably getting what he deserved. Not that it mattered now. "If there's no family about to see to things, you'd be surprised how often things like that 'appen."

"But won't the solicitors notice that things is missin'?"

"So what if they do?" Blimpey shrugged. "By then the maid and the butler will be gone. The solicitor went round there yesterday and told them to start lookin' for other positions. The maid was right annoyed about that too. Ranted and raved about what bastards lawyers are to every shopkeeper on the ruddy 'igh street." He chuckled. "Mind you, she were also narked that they weren't gettin' anythin' from the dear departed, the solicitor made that clear enough. She's started lookin' for another place. God knows where she'll end up. And the butler's already booked passage on a steamer for America."

Smythe's brows drew together in a fierce frown. Stealing from the dead just didn't seem right.

Blimpey, correctly interpreting the coachman's expression, quickly said, "Look, don't you be gettin' on yer 'igh 'orse because two servants is 'elpin' themselves to a few bits from the old bastards 'ouse. From what I 'eard about Hinchley, 'e's gettin' what 'e earned in life. As ye sow, so shall ye reap; that's what my old gran used to say."

"Don't worry, I'm not goin' to be blatherin' to the police about what you've told me," Smythe said. "Anythin' else?"

"I found out where that Swinton fella was on last Saturday night," Blimpey said. "Fella's got a nasty 'abit."

"How nasty?"

"Likes to smoke opium." Blimpey scratched his nose. "Showed up at a den down by the river at around midnight and stayed until almost three in the morning."

"Swinton was in an opium den?" Smythe knew such places existed, but he'd never actually known of anyone who frequented them.

"That's right. Accordin' to my sources, Swinton's a real regular. That's why 'is business 'as gone to pot, so to speak. Spends what money 'is theatre brings in on blowin' smoke up 'is nose."

No wonder Willard Swinton claimed to be in the office, counting receipts on his own, Smythe thought. That was a better alibi than admitting you were in an opium den. "Anything else?" Smythe pressed. He was beginning to get nervous about being out here with Blimpey. Mrs. Jeffries or Wiggins or even, God forbid, Betsy might come home any minute and come looking for him.

"Not much. I'll keep workin' on them other names you give me," Blimpey said.

"What about the theatre?" Smythe pressed. He'd asked Blimpey to see if anyone had seen anything suspicious at or around the Hayden on Saturday evening. "Did any of yer sources 'ave any luck there?"

Blimpey made a face. "Nah. Most of 'em was pickin' pockets that night, not watchin' the crowd."

"So that's it, then?" Smythe started to reach in his pocket for his roll of bills.

"'Ang on a minute," Blimpey warned, his gaze fixed on a point over Smythe's shoulder. "I wouldn't be flashin' that wad of yours unlessin' you want people to see it."

Smythe dropped his hand. "Are we bein' watched, then?"

Blimpey grinned broadly. "Right, mate. And she's a pretty little snoop, she is. Blond 'air, slim, got a right graceful way of dodgin' behind a tree, she 'as. Been there ever since you come out. Matter of fact, I'd say she followed ya out 'ere."

Blast, Smythe thought. Betsy. "All right, then, Blim-

pey. You go on and keep yer ears open. I'll meet ya at
the pub tonight around ten to see what else you've got
for me and to pay ya.''

Blimpey tugged nattily on his filthy porkpie hat and,
whistling a merry tune, sauntered off toward the gate.

Smythe whirled around. From the side of the tree he
could see a bit of light blue fabric sticking out.

Betsy froze. She hadn't had the wits to make a run for
the house when she had the chance and now she didn't
dare move. Smythe was charging toward her hiding place.
Lifting her chin, she stepped out from behind the tree
before he got there and caught her hiding like a thief in
the night.

''I've been waiting for you,'' she said boldly. ''And
who was that funny man you were talking to?'' She'd
decided it would be best just to brazen it out.

Surprised, he stopped. Then he put his hands on his
hips. ''Seems to me that you're askin' a lot of questions,''
he said, remembering how she'd refused to tell him about
her mysterious errand the other day. ''Aren't you the one
that's always goin' on about 'ow everyone has some
things that are private?''

''It couldn't be too private with you and him out here
in broad daylight,'' she sputtered. ''Besides, I was just
asking. It's none of my business. I was only bein'
friendly.''

''Friendly? You was hidin' behind a ruddy tree and
spyin' on me,'' he yelped.

Embarrassed, she took refuge in anger. ''I wasn't hiding, I was waiting for you,'' she snapped. ''I wanted to
talk to you, but if you're too busy, I won't bother.'' She
started to stomp past him but he caught her arm.

''Betsy,'' he said. ''Let's stop this. We've been pickin'

at each other for days now and I can't stand it.''

"I don't like it either," she admitted, relieved that he wasn't going to be angry over her watching him. "And that's why I followed you out here. I wanted to tell you about why I had to go to Whitechapel."

"Go on," he urged.

She glanced back at the inspector's house. "This might take a few minutes, and I don't want the others coming back and interrupting us."

"They're not due for a bit yet," he said soothingly. "We've got time." It was ten minutes until one o'clock. Smythe hoped that, for once, everyone would be late.

"Let's sit down." She nodded toward a wooden bench under one of the other trees. "I'd feel better talkin' about this if I was sitting down."

Taking her arm, Smythe led her to the bench, waited till she was seated and then dropped down next to her. He wanted to reach for her hand, but she was holding herself as stiff as one of them mummies at the British Museum, so he merely waited.

Betsy swallowed heavily. There was only one way to do this. "I went over to Whitechapel because I wanted to put some money in the collection plate at St. Jude's," she said. "Five pounds. I gave them five pounds."

Smythe waited for her to continue. But she was staring straight ahead, her gaze blank and unfocused. He was going to have to coax the story out of her. "Why'd ya give 'em so much?" he asked gently.

"I owed it."

"Owed it?"

She nodded stiffly. "Yes. Would five pounds pay for a broken window?" That had been worrying her. She hoped she'd put in enough.

''Depends on how big the window was,'' he admitted honestly. ''But unless you smashed a great painted-glass one, I'd say you give 'em enough.''

She looked relieved. ''Well, that's why I went to Whitechapel.'' She started to get up, but he put out his arm and gently pushed her back down. ''That's not all of it, lass, is it?''

''No.'' She sighed. ''But it's such an ugly story. I'm ashamed, Smythe. I want you to think well of me, and once you hear what I did, I don't think you will.''

''There's nothin' you could 'ave done that would make me think less of you,'' he said honestly. And he meant every word too. ''I know what it must 'ave been like for you tryin' to survive in the East End.''

She looked up at him, her eyes shimmering with unshed tears. ''Survival's one thing. Bein' deliberately wrong is something else. What I did was wrong, and even worse, I did it to the house of God.''

''Tell me about it,'' he urged softly. ''I don't want there to be any secrets between us, lass.'' Maybe if she shared all of her past with him, he'd find the courage to tell her about his secret.

''It was years ago,'' she began. ''I told you, I had two sisters.''

''Yeah, I remember.''

''And I told you that one of them got sick and died of a fever—do you remember that as well?''

''I remember everything you told me,'' he assured her.

''Well, when my sister got sick, we knew she was real bad off. Mum wanted to take her to the doctor, but she was only workin' as a barmaid and it took every penny we had just to pay the rent and buy a bit of food.'' She drew in a deep breath as the memories came flooding back. ''So Mum went over to the parish church, St.

Jude's. The vicar that was there had been known to lend a hand every now and again. But they had a new one, a Reverend Barnett and his wife. He didn't believe in givin' the poor money, said it only made the problem worse. So he turned her away with nothin'. Ann died two days later.'' She swiped at a tear. ''We was heartbroken. A few weeks after that, a crowd had gathered in front of the church. I don't know why they was there; I expect I knew at the time but I don't remember. But it wasn't the first time crowds had come round there and caused trouble. A scuffle broke out and before you knew it, people was pickin' up stones and bricks and hurling them at the church.'' She closed her eyes. ''I don't know what come over me; maybe I was half out of my mind with grief. But I picked up the biggest brick I could find and I hurled it right at one of the windows. Broke it too.''

''Then what 'appened?''

''About that time someone called out that the police were coming, so I ran off.''

''How old were you, Betsy?''

''Thirteen, maybe fourteen.'' She shrugged. ''Old enough to know better. But I was so angry . . . they wouldn't help my mum. They wouldn't part with a few pennies to buy medicine or get a doctor for a dying child. And we'd not done anything wrong. We were just poor.''

Smythe reached for her hand. ''Betsy, why didn't you tell me this?''

She looked at him, her expression incredulous. ''Don't you understand? I broke a church window. Deliberately. I sinned against the house of God. I was part of a mob . . .''

''You were a child still 'urtin' over losin' your baby sister,'' Smythe said angrily. He couldn't believe she'd risked herself goin' all the way to bloomin' Whitechapel to make up for something she'd done years ago. She'd spent her hard-earned money to boot. "And all you did was break a window in a buildin'. If it'd really been God's 'ouse, that old preacher would 'ave 'elped your mum. I can't believe you went all the way back there to give 'em the money. Cor blimey, it's not like the Church of England is poor, lass. They've got more ruddy money than the Queen."

Mrs. Jeffries stood in front of the last house on a row of terraces near Clapham High Street. She wondered for a moment precisely what approach to take and then decided that she'd make up her mind when she had a look at Roberta Seldon.

She walked up the walkway to the front door, noting that though there were cracks in the paving stones, the small lawn was neatly tended and someone had planted several rose bushes under the front window. The house was neatly painted too.

Taking a deep breath, Mrs. Jeffries climbed the two steps and knocked.

A moment later, she heard footsteps coming down the hall.

A short, dark-haired woman who appeared to be in her mid to late thirties stuck her head out. "Yes?"

"Mrs. Seldon?" Mrs. Jeffries smiled brightly.

"I'm Roberta Seldon. Have we met?"

"No, but I do hope you'll be able to help me." She wanted to get inside and talk to the woman. What she needed to know about Albert Parks couldn't be obtained by standing on a door stoop.

"Help you how?" Roberta Seldon replied. "Are you collecting for a charity?"

"No, no," Mrs. Jeffries said quickly. "I'm actually

seeking some information for my employer. I'm sure you'll understand when I tell you it's most confidential, most confidential indeed.''

''What kind of information?'' The woman was still wary, but Mrs. Jeffries could see that she was interested too.

''About Albert Parks,'' Mrs. Jeffries replied, deciding to go for the direct approach. ''I believe you used to be in his employ.''

Roberta Seldon said nothing; she simply stared at her. Mrs. Jeffries was afraid her bold approach had failed.

Finally, she said, ''You'd better come inside, then. I've got quite a bit to say about Albert Parks.''

CHAPTER 10

Wiggins couldn't make up his mind what to do. If he went back to meet the others at Upper Edmonton Gardens, he'd lose her. He hesitated at the corner, keeping one eye out for the omnibus and the other on the clock over the bank. Across the street, he could see the girl from Hinchley's house tapping her foot impatiently as she waited at the bus stop.

The omnibus came around the corner. Wiggins made up his mind and sprinted across the street. The girl's head swiveled as she heard his footsteps pounding towards her.

''Didn't want to miss it,'' he explained, jerking his chin toward the omnibus and giving her his most charming smile.

She wasn't impressed. She turned her head and went to pick up her case.

''Let me,'' he said quickly as the vehicle drew up and stopped.

Startled, she drew back, raked him with a swift, calculating gaze. Apparently finding him harmless, she said, "Go ahead, then."

They climbed aboard and Wiggins, though he dearly loved riding up top, dutifully followed her inside the bus. She took a seat by the window. Wiggins put the suitcase down in the aisle and dropped down next to her. "You don't mind, do ya?" he asked.

She shrugged. "It's all the same to me where ya sit. Thanks for carryin' my case. Thing's heavy."

The conductor came and they paid their fares. Wiggins noted the girl paid all the way to Victoria Station. He cursed himself for not letting her pay first, as he'd only paid to Hyde Park.

"Goin' on a trip?" he asked.

"Wish I was." She snorted delicately. "It's all right for some. But the rest of us has got a livin' to earn."

"My name's Wiggins." He tried again. If this girl was Lilly, the one Betsy had talked to, then she'd changed in the last couple of days. Betsy had claimed that girl would talk a fence post deaf. "What's yours?"

She kept her gaze straight ahead. "That's not your concern now, is it?"

"Sorry." He cringed. "I wasn't tryin' to be bold, miss. Just friendly."

The girl turned, looked at him for a moment and then gave an apologetic shrug. "My name's Lilly. I'm not in a very good frame of mind, if you know what I mean."

"Is there somethin' wrong?"

"Well, I've had better days, I can tell ya that." She turned and gazed out the window again.

Wiggins wondered what to do. Something had happened at the Hinchley house—he was sure of it. But he sensed that Lilly's mood was as changeable as the weather. Women were funny creatures. You never knew when you'd say the wrong thing and they'd shut up tighter than a biscuit tin. He didn't want that. Then he remembered how Mrs. Jeffries often got people to talk. He dropped his voice slightly. "I 'ate to see a pretty lass like yourself lookin' so sad," he said sympathetically.

"You'd look sad too if you'd put up with what I've 'ad to lately," she retorted. "Bloomin' solicitors."

"You've 'ad a bit of a rough time." He patted her arm. "Maybe it would 'elp to talk about it some? Make you feel better."

She sighed. "Don't see what good talkin' about it will do; won't change things none. But as I'm stuck on this ruddy omnibus all the way to Victoria, I might as well."

By one-fifteen, Inspector Witherspoon had finished his lunch and gone to meet Constable Barnes at the Yard. As soon as the door had closed behind him, Mrs. Jeffries hurried down to the kitchen.

The others were already seated around the table. Mrs. Goodge had put out plates of bread, cold roast beef, buns and turnovers for the household's meal.

"If you don't mind, Mrs. Jeffries, we'll eat as we talk," she said as the housekeeper took her seat. "I'd like to get this kitchen cleared as quickly as possible," Mrs. Goodge explained. "I've got more people droppin' by this afternoon."

"That's a splendid idea," Mrs. Jeffries agreed. "We are a bit pressed for time and I, for one, have quite a bit of information to share."

"So do I," Luty said, helping herself to a turnover. "Are we goin' to wait for Wiggins?"

"I wouldn't," Smythe said. He helped himself to a slice of brown bread. "'E were goin' back over to the

Hinchley neighborhood to snoop about. As 'e's not back yet, 'e's probably on to something.''

Mrs. Jeffries nodded and reached for the teapot. ''Then I'll start.'' She told them everything she'd gotten out of the inspector at lunch. ''He was quite shocked, poor man. I don't think he'd ever met a woman quite like Theodora Vaughan. As he put it, 'in one breath she announced she's divorced and a moment later, she's announcing her engagement.' Poor man. He was quite taken with the woman too—until this afternoon.''

''Actresses,'' Mrs. Goodge muttered darkly. ''And her older than him by a good ten years!''

''But Rose told Wiggins that the divorce was off,'' Betsy exclaimed. ''There was some sort of legal muck-up.''

''Apparently, Miss Vaughan's American lawyers straightened it out.''

Betsy shook her head. ''But why wouldn't her personal maid know that?''

''From what I gather,'' Mrs. Jeffries said, ''Theodora Vaughan only found out herself last week. Maybe the maid didn't know.''

''And now the woman's fixin' to marry Delaney,'' Luty said incredulously. ''Some women just don't learn. She finally sheds one husband and now she wants another one.''

''Really, madam.'' Hatchet clucked his tongue. ''That's rather a cynical point of view. Marriage is an honorable estate . . .''

''If it's so honorable, how come you ain't ever got hitched?'' she shot back.

''Or maybe she was keepin' it a secret,'' Betsy murmured, then flushed when she glanced up and saw Smythe grinning knowingly at her. She resisted the impulse to stick her tongue out at him. Cheeky devil. But she felt ever so much better now that they'd cleared the air.

"Was that all you got out of the inspector?" Mrs. Goodge prodded. She really did want the lot of them to get a move on. None of her sources would say a word if they walked in and found half of London sitting at the kitchen table.

Mrs. Jeffries added a few more details about the inspector's morning and then plunged in with her own tale. "I managed to get Roberta Seldon, Albert Parks's former housekeeper, to tell me quite a bit," she continued. "Apparently, she did quit. As Wiggins said, she hadn't been paid. But, and this is the important part, she also told me that Parks didn't come home right after the performance on Saturday evening. She was still awake at half past eleven. As a matter of fact, she heard him come in at around two A.M."

"Don't tell me 'e was out walkin' along the ruddy river too," Smythe said disgustedly. "Cor blimey, there's more bloomin' foot traffic on that embankment than there is on Oxford Street."

Mrs. Jeffries shook her head. "Mrs. Seldon had no idea where he was, only that he didn't come home that night when he claimed. There's something else too. I'm not sure if it's important or not. Mrs. Seldon said that when she went into his study to tell him she was leaving, he was locking something in his desk."

"What was it?" Hatchet asked.

"She wasn't sure; she only got a glimpse of it," Mrs. Jeffries explained. "But she thinks it might have been a note of some kind. All she saw was a flash of white. It struck her as odd because Parks jumped ten feet when she walked into the room. Furthermore, he'd never locked that desk before. Mrs. Seldon said he kept the keys right out on his desk all the time, so she was quite surprised when she suddenly found him locking it up tighter than the Bank of England. When Parks saw that she'd seen him, he gave her specific instructions not to touch it. Not that it mattered to her; she'd come in to tell him she was leaving his household.''

"Did he leave the keys out?'' Hatchet asked.

"No,'' Mrs. Jeffries replied. "He put them in his pocket. Mrs. Seldon was rather annoyed. She thought he might have been locking up an envelope of money and he did owe her her wages.''

"So he was lockin' somethin' up and he ain't got an alibi,'' Luty muttered.

"None of them have an alibi,'' Betsy pointed out.

"One of 'em does,'' Smythe said. He passed on the information Blimpey had given him about Willard Swinton.

"An opium den!'' Mrs. Goodge's eyes were as round as saucers behind her spectacles. "I can't believe it. A respectable businessman like that.''

"It's true,'' Smythe said. "My source was sure of it. That's one of the reasons the Hayden's been doin' so poorly the last few years. Swinton's addicted. Every bit of money that comes in goes right up his nose. And I learned something else too,'' he said, reaching for a another bun. In between bites, he told them about Hinchley's servants. "Stealin' from a dead man, they are,'' he concluded.

"Shocking,'' Mrs. Goodge said indignantly. She hadn't enjoyed herself so much in days. "Absolutely shocking.''

Mrs. Jeffries cleared her throat. "Actually,'' she said, "I've got more to tell you about Parks.''

"Sorry, Mrs. J.," Smythe said hastily. "Didn't mean to steal yer thunder."

"That's quite all right; your comments were pertinent to the subject at hand," she said. "But as I was saying, Mrs. Seldon asked Parks when she could expect to be paid her wages. She claims he got a 'funny little smile' on his face and then told her he fully expected to come into money very soon. Enough to pay her and the rest of his debts."

"I don't suppose he told the Seldon woman how or why he was comin' into this money?" Luty asked.

"No," Mrs. Jeffries replied. "He didn't."

"I think I know," Betsy said. "From the theatre. The inspector said the play is sold out for a number of weeks."

"I asked Mrs. Seldon that," Mrs. Jeffries said. "And she was positive that wasn't it. The day after opening night, Theodora Vaughan, Trevor Remington and Swinton had a meeting at Parks's house. Mrs. Seldon overheard them talking. They were discussing what they were going to do if the play failed. They were fairly certain it would too."

"Delaney wasn't there?" Smythe asked.

"No, he wasn't," Mrs. Jeffries answered. "I find that most signficant."

"They was sure that Ogden Hinchley was goin' to give the play a bad review and kill it," Luty murmured.

"But Hinchley didn't give it a bad review," Betsy pointed out. "At least not that any of them knew about. He was already dead by then. No one ever saw the review."

"Oh, I believe someone did, Betsy," Mrs. Jeffries replied. "The killer saw it."

Mrs. Goodge cast a quick, frantic glance at the clock. "I've got a bit to say too, and as we're still talking about

Albert Parks, I'd like to get on with it." She forged right ahead. "Remember how I told you that Parks had been run off from a theatre in Manchester? Well, guess who it was that was behind gettin' rid of him."

"Ogden Hinchley," Smythe said.

She nodded. "That's right. Hinchley was only an actor back then, but he was a rich one. He put up most of the money to produce the play. Accordin' to what I heard, he was so bad at it, that's the only way Hinchley could ever get a part. But as he'd put up the money, he took quite an interest in the business end of things. When the money from the receipts didn't match the head count at the door, Hinchley got suspicious. Parks was only a stage manager at the time, but he was the one that got the blame for the shortfall between the receipts and the head count. Hinchley run him off and what's worse, every time the man tried to get another stage manager's position, Hinchley would make sure whoever was fixing to hire Parks knew that he'd been accused of theft. As you can imagine, Parks's reputation wasn't worth much after that. That's how he came to be a director. He couldn't get work here in England, so he went to Germany and fell in with a theatre there. That's where he learned this directin' business. He was there for a goodly number of years."

"Pardon me, Mrs. Goodge," Hatchet interrupted smoothly. "But how did Parks end up owning a home and having a staff? From what you've told us, he was unemployed and broke."

"That's why he come back to England," she replied. "His granny died and left him the house and a bit of an income. Not really enough to live on—he still needed to work. Especially as he'd taken a loan on his home and put cash in Delaney's play. He was hoping this play would be his . . . his . . ." She hesitated, trying to think of the right word. "Entry back into the British theatre."

"Looks instead like it might be 'is entry to the Old Bailey," Smythe mumbled.

"Yes, it's beginning to look that way," Mrs. Jeffries agreed. Some of the puzzle pieces were starting to fit together. Or were they? From the back of her mind, something niggled her, but she firmly ignored it. This time, she wasn't going to think the situation to death.

"You think he might be our killer?" Luty asked eagerly.

Mrs. Jeffries didn't want to commit herself, but on the other hand, not committing herself might make the others believe she lacked confidence in them and her own powers of deduction. "I think we can assume that Hinchley was killed because he was a critic. He had the power of life or death over a play. The evidence against Parks is quite substantial. He, more than the others, appears to have had more to lose if Hinchley gave the play a bad review, and consequently, the play failed. It wasn't just his reputation that was at stake anymore, it was his entire future."

"But what about Mr. Delaney?" Betsy challenged. "He'd got a lot to lose."

"Yes, but he wouldn't be ruined financially," Mrs. Jeffries pointed out. "He is marrying Miss Vaughan. She's quite a wealthy woman. Furthermore, there's a long and honorable tradition in the theatre of playwrights having both successes and failures. In other words, one failed play wouldn't necessarily mean he'd never write another, more successful play. Especially if he was married to Theodora Vaughan."

"And Willard Swinton's got to know that no matter 'ow much money 'e gets, as long as 'e's addicted to opium, it'll never be enough," Smythe said thoughtfully.

"Remington's a pretty successful actor," Luty added.
"One bad play wouldn't kill him. Even though he'd invested all his money, it wasn't like he'd never be able to
work again."

"He could always tour the American West again,"
Hatchet put in, just to annoy Luty. "I believe that in many
of the more barbarian and desolate villages, the population
is desperate enough to watch anything."

"What d'ya mean, 'again'?" Luty asked. She'd take
him to task for that barbarian remark when she got him
back in the carriage.

Hatchet smiled. "One of the bits of information I
wanted to share today was that I learned that Miss
Vaughan and Mr. Remington had toured the western part
of the United States eighteen months or so ago. According
to what I heard, they quarreled publicly through six states,
two territories and several major cities. Apparently, by the
time they reached San Francisco, they hated each other
so much that Miss Vaughan, in a fit of rage, shot Mr.
Remington. Luckily, she's a better actress than she is a
marksman, and she only wounded him slightly in the
shoulder." He shrugged. "A nice bit of gossip, I'm afraid,
but hardly pertinent to the problem at hand."

"Do you really think Parks might be the one?" Betsy
asked Mrs. Jeffries.

"I'm not sure. But if the inspector manages to find a
constable or a watchman that saw Delaney and Remington
walking along the river on the night of the murder, then
I don't think there's anyone else it could be." She honestly didn't know what to think. On the last case, she'd
ignored the obvious and run herself in circles without
coming up with the right answer. She didn't want that to
happen again. "But sure or not"—she got to her feet—
"we've got to keep at it."

They all looked at her expectantly. For a moment, her mind went blank. But she recovered quickly. "Betsy, why don't you have another go at Rose and find out why Theodora Vaughan kept her divorce a secret." She looked at Smythe, but he was getting to his feet as well. "I've got a few things to chase up," he said. "There's still a few pubs I need to do over near the 'ayden."

"I've got a banker or two I need to pester," Luty added. "I'm determined to find out about that loan Parks got on his house."

"I'll help you, madam," Hatchet said.

Mrs. Goodge breathed a heartfelt sigh of relief as they all got up. Then the back door opened and pounding footsteps sounded in the hall.

"Sorry, I'm late," Wiggins yelled breathlessly, "but I was on to somethin'."

"What is it?" Mrs. Jeffries asked.

"Is there any tea left?" Wiggins dashed toward the table. "I'm parched."

"Listen, boy," Mrs. Goodge snapped. "You pour yourself a cup and then clear out. I've got people comin' and I don't want you hangin' about puttin' your oar in."

"But I'm hungry," he protested. "I didn't 'ave time to eat."

"Here, then." The cook slapped a slab of beef between two slices of bread and handed it to him. "Now, get off."

"But I want to tell ya want I learned." Unable to help himself, he jammed a bite of the sandwich in his mouth. "It's about Hinchley's servants. I think they've been robbin' the man blind, or they would be if 'e wasn't already dead . . ."

"We already know about that," Smythe said kindly.

"But . . . but . . ."

"It's all right, Wiggins." Mrs. Jeffries wanted to go

out to the garden to have a good think. "You've done quite well, but we are in a bit of a hurry. Mrs. Goodge needs the kitchen."

"But what about . . ."

"Go up and have a rest," Betsy advised. "We'll fill you in later on what all we've learned."

Mrs. Jeffries sat on the bench and gazed blankly at the grass. Her conscience was bothering her. She wondered if the others had observed what she'd done on this case. So far, none of them had said anything, but then again, perhaps they wouldn't even if they'd noticed.

It hadn't been intentional. Had it? Had she deliberately kept information from the inspector so that she could solve the case first? She honestly didn't know. She hadn't realized she'd even done it until today at lunch when he'd told her about how shocked he was to learn that Remington and Theodora Vaughan had been husband and wife.

She'd known about the marriage. She hadn't passed that bit on to him. She'd meant to, she really had. But somehow the time hadn't been right.

She forced herself to think back to the beginning, to try to remember what she'd told the inspector and, more important, what she hadn't.

But it was no use. She was in such a muddle, she simply couldn't remember. She thought she was getting worse too. Just a few minutes ago she'd forgotten to tell the others something else she'd done today. She'd talked Roberta Seldon into going to Scotland Yard to see Inspector Witherspoon. Why hadn't she told the others that? Was it because she was afraid that if she told everyone everything and then didn't solve this case, she'd be humiliated?

But surely she wasn't that smallminded. That petty.

Surely she was more interested in justice than in gratifying her own sense of importance. Or was she? She pushed the idea out of her mind. She hadn't deliberately kept anything from the others. They'd been in a dreadful hurry today and she'd simply forgotten. She'd tell them tonight.

She'd also have a nice, long chat with the inspector. If there was something else she'd forgotten to tell him, he'd learn it right after supper.

"Hepzibah." Lady Cannonberry's voice jolted her out of her reverie. "How nice to find you out here."

"Gracious, Ruth, I didn't expect you back until next week." Mrs. Jeffries smiled at the fair-haired, slender middle-aged woman walking toward her.

"I came back early." Ruth Cannonberry sat down next to her and gazed out at the peaceful garden. "This is so lovely, so quiet. The train station was an absolute madhouse today."

"You came back by train?"

"Yes. I'd forgotten how crowded the trains are this time of year. The crush was awful. But it still amazes me that even in such a huge crowd, one always manages to run into someone one knows." She laughed.

"That does happen."

"I did something terrible, Hepzibah," she confided. "Jane Riddleton was at the station too. She must have come up on the same train as I did. But naturally, she'd have ridden in first class. No mixing with the masses for Jane. God forbid the woman actually speak to someone who might work for a living. I ducked behind a pillar so she wouldn't see me."

"Is she not a nice woman, then?" Mrs. Jeffries asked politely. Lady Cannonberry's late husband had been a peer of the realm, but Ruth Cannonberry was a vicar's daughter with a social conscience and political opinions that bordered on the radical. But she rarely said anything nasty about someone. She was simply too nice a person. If she made negative comments at all, she generally reserved them for the government, the church, or a variety of other institutions that she believed oppressed people, especially the poor.

"She's a terrible gossip," Ruth replied bluntly. "I knew if she caught me, I'd have to listen to her make catty remarks about my sister-in-law, Muriel. Muriel is behaving like an idiot, but I didn't particularly want to listen to Jane go on about it."

"Oh, dear."

Ruth sighed. "That doesn't make any sense, does it? I'm annoyed with Muriel too. More than annoyed, actually. I'm furious."

"What on earth has she done?" Mrs. Jeffries queried.

"Muriel is making a complete fool of herself over some young man and the whole county is talking about it," Ruth replied. She crossed her arms over her chest. "That's one of the reasons I came home early. My tolerance for the intrigues and excitements of picnics, balls and dinner parties just isn't what it used to be."

Mrs. Jeffries gazed at her curiously. "Gracious, you do sound like you've had an interesting visit."

"More tiring than interesting, I assure you. Because I'm a widow, Muriel decided I could act as chaperone for her. She apparently exhausted her mother some time ago. The silly girl dragged me to every social event in Sussex. Besides, if I hadn't left, I'm afraid I'd have done something unforgiveable."

Surprised, Mrs. Jeffries said, "You?"

"Yes, me." Ruth grimaced. "Muriel's following the poor young man about everywhere, pestering him mercilessly and even going so far as to try to discredit the young lady Thomas is in love with. Isn't that despicable? She's telling terrible tales about a perfectly nice young woman just so Catherine will be humiliated and come back to London. I was very much afraid I was going to lose my temper and box Muriel's ears. Goodness knows, she certainly deserved it. Honestly, what some people will do to win back a suitor.''

"Win back?"

"Oh, yes, Muriel and Thomas were engaged. But he broke it off when he met Catherine. Muriel, instead of acting with any dignity about the whole affair, has instead behaved like a shrew. Thomas absolutely loathes the sight of her. Even if Catherine came back to London, he certainly wouldn't have a thing to do with Muriel.'' She paused to take a breath, then closed her eyes briefly. "Oh, forgive me, Hepzibah, I'm wittering on like a magpie. It's terribly rude. I haven't even asked how you are.''

But Mrs. Jeffries didn't hear her; she was too busy thinking.

"Hepzibah?" Ruth prodded as the housekeeper stared straight ahead. "Is everything all right?''

A dozen puzzle pieces clicked together in Mrs. Jeffries's mind.
She leapt to her feet. "Ruth, you're a genius. Thank goodness you came back. Thank goodness. I've got it now. I'm sure of it.''

"Got what?"

"You must forgive me," Mrs. Jeffries cried as she dashed toward the house, "but I've got to get Betsy before she goes out. Do come by later on and I'll tell you all about it.''

"Is it a murder?" Ruth asked excitedly.

"Yes.''

"Can I help?"

Mrs. Jeffries laughed. "You already have."

"You want me to what?" Betsy asked.

"I want you to find this Oliver person who told you about Theodora Vaughan's broken carriage." Mrs. Jeffries explained. "And I want you to find out several very specific things."

She gave Betsy detailed instructions. When she was finished, Betsy said, "I understand, but what if I can't get to him? He's likely to be in the house."

Mrs. Jeffries thought about that problem for a moment. "Go to the back door and tell the cook you've a message from Oliver's mother. If you have to, lie. Make up a sad tale of some sort and get that boy outside so you can question him away from the house. It's imperative that no one, especially Mr. Delaney or Miss Vaughan, overhears you talking to him."

"I'll do my best," Betsy said doubtfully.

"You're a very intelligent woman, Betsy," Mrs. Jeffries said honestly, "and if I had time, I'd explain everything to you. But the truth is, I don't have any idea how much time we do have. If I'm right, Inspector Witherspoon may be on the verge of arresting the wrong person."

Betsy straightened up and lifted her chin. "I'll get the answers, Mrs. Jeffries. You can count on me."

"Good. I knew I could. Off you go, now."

As soon as Betsy had gone, Mrs. Jeffries hurried upstairs to find Wiggins. By the time she reached his room on the third floor, she was breathless. She knocked and then shoved the door open.

Wiggins was sound asleep. Fred was curled up at his

feet. The dog woke first, spotted the housekeeper and thumped his tail in apology for being caught on the bed. But Mrs. Jeffries had far more important matters to worry about than a bit of dog hair. "Wiggins." She shook him by the shoulder. "Wake up this instant."

"Huh?" Wiggins mumbled groggily. "What's wrong?"

"Nothing's wrong," Mrs. Jeffries said. "But I need you to do something right away. It's urgent."

"Urgent? All right," he mumbled. It always took him a moment or two to wake up.

Mrs. Jeffries waited patiently for his eyes to focus. "Are you awake yet?"

"I think so."

"Good. I need you to go out and find Smythe."

"Where do I look?"

"Try the area around the Hayden Theatre, but find him and tell him to get back here as soon as he can." She wondered if she was going to make a fool of herself in front of everyone and then decided that it didn't matter. She'd take her chances. "As soon as you find him, go over to Luty's and tell her and Hatchet to get here right away."

Wiggins stumbled to his feet. "What do I tell 'em?"

"Just tell them to get here as quickly as they can. I think I may have figured out who killed Ogden Hinchley."

The later it got, the more Mrs. Jeffries's nerves tightened. She'd no idea why she had such a sense of urgency, but she did. As afternoon faded into evening, she almost wore a hole in the drawing room carpet. Mrs. Goodge's sources were in the kitchen and she didn't want to disturb the cook.

Finally, though, she heard footsteps on the back stairs. Betsy popped her head around the corner. She grinned. "I did it. I found out just what you wanted."

"Excellent, Betsy. Does Mrs. Goodge still have guests downstairs?"

"The butcher's boy was just leaving when I came in," Betsy replied. "Should we go down?"

"Yes," Mrs. Jeffries said. "With any luck, the others will be here soon."

Mrs. Goodge gazed at them curiously when they came into the room. "Is everything all right?"

"No, Mrs. Goodge," Mrs. Jeffries replied. "It isn't. But hopefully, when the others get here, it will be."

"Should I make us a pot of tea?"

"That would be a wonderful idea," the housekeeper replied.

Despite the curious looks from Betsy and Mrs. Goodge, Mrs. Jeffries refused to say anything more until the others arrived. It wouldn't be fair. She'd no idea whether or not Wiggins would be able to track down Smythe, but considering how guilty she felt about the way she'd conducted herself on this case, she'd wait till they were all here to say what was on her mind. It was the least she could do.

Smythe came in first. "Wiggins'll be here soon with Luty and Hatchet," he announced. "What's up? The lad said it was urgent."

"Why don't we wait till the others are here?" Mrs. Jeffries said as she sat a pot of tea on the table. "I'll explain everything then."

Smythe nodded and, as soon as the housekeeper's back was turned, glanced at Betsy. She shrugged to indicate she didn't know what was going on either. But they only had to wait a few moments before they heard the back door open. "I've got 'em," Wiggins called out from the hall.

Luty and Hatchet hurried into the room. "What's goin' on, Hepzibah?" Luty demanded. "I was on my way out to corner old Mickleshaft when Wiggins come flyin' in sayin' ya needed us."

"Sit down everyone," Mrs. Jeffries commanded. "And I'll explain everything."

Something in her tone brooked no argument or questions, and without another word, everyone took their seats.

Mrs. Jeffries looked at Betsy. "Tell me what you learned from Oliver."

"Who's Oliver?" Smythe asked.

"Theodora Vaughan's footman," Betsy said quickly. "He told me that he'd accompanied Miss Vaughan from her country house up to Victoria Station last Saturday. You were right, Mrs. Jeffries. She did run into someone she knew. It was a man."

The knot of tension in Mrs. Jeffries's stomach began to ease. "Did Oliver remember what he looked like?"

"He was small and well dressed," Betsy continued "He and Miss Vaughan talked for a good fifteen minutes. Oliver said the man must've said something to upset her because she was in a real rage by the time she hailed a hansom and got her in it."

Mrs. Jeffries closed her eyes as relief flooded her whole body. She was right. She had to be. It was the only answer. "Thank you, Betsy. You did very well, my dear."

"Hepzibah, what in tarnation is goin' on?" Luty demanded.

"I'm sorry. Do forgive me for being so mysterious. But you see, I had to be sure."

"Sure of what?" Hatchet asked.

"The identity of the killer."

"But I thought you said it was Albert Parks," Mrs. Goodge complained.

"Until I spoke to Lady Cannonberry this afternoon, I was sure it was Parks," she admitted honestly. "But she said something to me that made me suddenly realize that we—that I," she hastily amended, "was making a big mistake. You see, I'd assumed that Hinchley was killed because he was a critic. But his being a critic had nothing to do with his death."

"Then why was he killed?" Wiggins asked.

"For love, Wiggins. Love and money." She realized that time was getting on and she had to get busy. Witherspoon might be getting ready to arrest Parks. "I don't have a lot of time to go into it right now. If we don't act quickly, the inspector will be at the Hayden Theatre soon, probably arresting the wrong man."

"The inspector'll 'ave to find 'im at 'ome, then," Smythe said. "Theatre's dark tonight. Closed."

"Are you sure?" Mrs. Jeffries asked him.

"Positive. I was just over there."

She frowned. This was a problem that hadn't occurred to her. But before she could think of what to do next, Wiggins spoke up.

"Seein' as yer all 'ere, can I tell ya what I learned today?"

"I'd rather know who the killer is," Mrs. Goodge said testily. "If it's not Albert Parks, then who is it?"

Mrs. Jeffries took a deep breath. If she was wrong, she'd give up snooping about in the inspector's cases. "Theodora Vaughan," she said firmly. "She killed Hinchley to keep from losing Edmund Delaney."

No one said anything for a moment, then Hatchet

cleared his throat. "Mrs. Jeffries, how did she get the body to the canal? Hinchley was small, but as you yourself pointed out, he was dead weight."

"She had an accomplice," Mrs. Jeffries replied. "Rather. Hinchley's butler."

CHAPTER 11

There was an ominous silence from the others. Mrs. Jeffries began to understand what an actor felt like when the play ended and the audience booed and hissed. Not that any of them would do that; they were far too polite. But from the incredulous expressions on their faces, she was going to have talk hard and fast to convince them.

"Rather?" Hatchet finally said. "May we ask why?"

Mrs. Jeffries wasn't sure how to persuade them she was on to something, but at least no one's life was at stake at the moment, so she had time to make her case. "Because he lied to the inspector. Rather told him that both he and the housemaid had planned on being gone well before Hinchley came back from America. But Lilly, Hinchley's maid, told Betsy that working at the Hinchley house was the easiest position she'd ever had and she'd had no plans to leave."

"But that was after the murder, Mrs. Jeffries," Betsy

said softly. "When she knew he definitely wasn't coming back."

"I know, Betsy." Mrs. Jeffries couldn't think of how to express what was really more a feeling than a fact, but she was sure she was on to something. "But I got the impression from you that the girl had never had plans to go anywhere. Isn't that what you thought?"

"Well, yes," Betsy agreed, somewhat reluctantly. "But I don't see how Rather telling one fib to Inspector Witherspoon makes the man a murderer."

"Not a murderer, an accomplice," she corrected. "All he did was carry Hinchley's body to the canal." They were still staring at her like she'd lost her mind, so she plunged straight on, telling them some of the other reasons that led to her conclusions about the killing.

"So you see," she concluded, "we've got to get the inspector to keep a watch on Rather. I suspect that before he leaves London, he'll be contacting Theodora Vaughan. He'll want money for his silence."

"How sure are you about this?" Luty asked.

Mrs. Jeffries glanced around the table. Luty's doubts were mirrored on several other faces. For a moment, she wasn't sure at all about it. What if it was like the last case and she was completely and utterly wrong about everything?

"We'd best get crackin', then," Wiggins said as he stood up. "The butler's plannin' on leavin' tonight."

"Tonight?" Smythe exclaimed. "Well, why didn't ya tell us?"

"I tried to this afternoon," Wiggins cried defensively, "but everyone told me to get out of the kitchen and go 'ave a rest. I didn't know the man was an accomplice, did I? Rather's plannin' on takin' a night train to the coast tonight—that's what Lilly told me when we was on the omnibus today.''

"You spoke to Lilly?" Betsy said.

Wiggins nodded excitedly. "It were 'ard work too, gettin' her to talk. Lilly was right upset about the solicitor tossin' 'er out on 'er ear. Would 'ave been really narked only she's got another position. You'll never guess where she's goin'." He paused dramatically. "Theodora Vaughan's country house. Lilly said the offer come right out of the blue. Miss Vaughan sent 'er a note this mornin', tellin' her to go down there and see 'er 'ousekeeper if she were interested in a position. Well, Lilly 'adn't been, but then Rather and the solicitor put their 'eads together and before Lilly knew it, she was out of work and Rather was packin' his trunks. He's goin' to America on a ship.''

Smythe flicked a glance at the clock as he got up. "What time's 'is train?"

Wiggins shrugged. "She didn't say."

"Should I go find the inspector?" Smythe asked Mrs. Jeffries.

"Yes, but give me a moment." Her doubts about the case had vanished. She knew she was right. But she didn't understand why Theodora Vaughan would offer Hinchley's housemaid a position. "Wiggins," she asked, "why did you say you thought Hinchley's servants were robbing him blind?"

"Because when I was carryin' Lilly's case out to the platform, the latch sprung open on one end. When I put it down to try and shove it back in, she got all nasty and pushed me away. Told me she'd fix it 'erself. I got suspicious about the way she was actin', so I 'ad a good look inside." He grinned at his own cleverness. "She couldn't put the latch back in without poppin' open the other end, and when the lid tipped open a bit, I saw all sorts of bits and pieces in 'er case. There was a silver candlestick and a bit of crystal inside. You know, things no 'ousemaid would own. Why? Is it important?''

''I'm not sure,'' she said, frowning slightly. ''But I did wonder.''

''So Rather's got the place to himself,'' Mrs. Goodge said derisively. ''He's probably filling his cases with Hinchley's belongings right this very minute.''

As soon as the words left the cook's mouth, Mrs. Jeffries understood. She couldn't believe she'd been such a fool as not to see it sooner. ''Rather's there alone. Oh, my goodness, we've got to hurry,'' she exclaimed. ''Gracious, I've been so stupid about this. I only hope we're in time.''

''What's the rush?'' Luty asked. ''Theodora Vaughan ain't goin' nowhere. Just this butler feller. The inspector can send a wire to have him picked up before he boards his ship.''

''He won't be boarding that ship,'' Mrs. Jeffries said. ''If what I suspect is true, Rather won't be going anywhere.'' She turned to the footman. ''Wiggins, go and get me some of your notepaper and then I want you to go and find the inspector. But you must listen carefully. It's imperative that you follow my instructions to the letter. Otherwise, someone else is going to die tonight.''

''Too bad Parks wasn't at home,'' Barnes said to Witherspoon. He grabbed onto the strap hanging from the ceiling of the hansom as the cab suddenly dipped. ''After hearing what that Mrs. Seldon had to tell us, if I was a bettin' man, I'd say Parks has a lot of questions to answer.''

''He most certainly does,'' Witherspoon replied. ''It

was good of Mrs. Seldon to come forward. Er . . . Constable, you don't think we're on a wild goose chase, do you?" He was a bit concerned that the note that Wiggins had brought around to the Yard had been written by a crank. "I mean, there were spelling errors in the note. It suddenly occurred to me that it might be some prankster having a bit of fun with the police."

"I don't think so, sir," Barnes assured him. "Young Wiggins said a girl brought it round to Upper Edmonton Gardens herself. A prankster would've sent it by post, not shown up on your doorstep and risk bein' identifed later."

"But this girl didn't give Wiggins her name," Witherspoon protested. "She simply shoved the note in his hand and ran off. That's most odd."

"Not really, sir," Barnes replied kindly. Sometimes the inspector was so innocent. It was as plain as the nose on his face why the girl hadn't wanted to come to the police station and make a statement. "The lass didn't want to risk being questioned, but her conscience was botherin' her because she'd seen Rather on the night of the murder."

"But why wouldn't she want to be questioned?" Witherspoon said.

"Because she'd probably slipped out to be with her young man in the park, Inspector," the constable explained patiently. "You know, to be alone . . ." he looked at Witherspoon meaningfully.

It took a moment for him to get it. "Oh," he exclaimed. "You mean they were . . ."

"Most likely, sir," Barnes grinned. "Now, the girl couldn't come forward with what she'd seen, not if she'd been playin' about with a man in the middle of the night, could she? She'd lose her position."

"Yes, yes, I see." Satisfied with the explanation, Witherspoon sat back and patted the pocket containing the grubby, wrinkled message. He glanced out the window and saw the North Gate entrance to the park up ahead. "Driver," he yelled. "Pull over in front of the park entrance, please."

The hansom bounced one last time, then pulled up and stopped. They got out, paid the cabbie and then waited until it pulled away. Witherspoon pulled the note out of his pocket, unfolded the paper and held it close to the lamplight. Squinting, he read it through one more time.

Inspector. You should ask Mr. Hinchley's butler why he was in Regents Park at two in the mornin on Saturday night. I'd ask him quick if I was you, the blighter's gettin reidy to scraper off to America.

"Ready, sir?" Barnes asked.

"Yes. Let's see what Rather has to say for himself." They started across toward Avenue Road. There wasn't much pedestrian or vehicle traffic on Albert Road and none at all that Witherspoon could see on Avenue Road. As they crossed the intersection, their footsteps echoed heavily in the silent evening. Witherspoon felt the back of his neck tingle, as though he was being watched. He whipped his head around, but saw nothing but an empty street.

"Something wrong, sir?" Barnes asked as saw the inspector looking behind him.

The inspector felt a tad foolish. Gracious, he was getting silly. Of course he wasn't being followed. "No, Constable."

They turned up the walkway leading to Hinchley's house. Barnes stopped. Witherspoon, thinking something

was amiss, stumbled to a halt next to him. "Look, sir"—
the constable pointed at the house—"the door's ajar."

"And not many lights on," Witherspoon mused. He
could only see the faintest of glows from inside the house.
"Let's hope that Rather hasn't already scarpered off and
left the place wide open . . ." He broke off as a loud, ear-
splitting bang filled the air.

"That sounds like a gunshot, sir. It came from inside."
Barnes leapt toward the front stairs and took them two at
a time. Witherspoon was right behind him.

They bounded into the house and slid to a halt. Inside,
it was eerily quiet. The front hall was dark but there was
a dim light from the far end. "The butler's pantry," Witherspoon yelled, hurrying in that direction.

They raced down the hall. From the pantry, they heard
a soft groan and the sound of scrapping. The inspector
thought he heard the front door slam behind him, but he
didn't stop to look. Flying into the room, Witherspoon
stumbled over a large object on the floor. Barnes, seeing
the inspector stumble, jumped over it.

"Egads," Witherspoon cried. "It's Rather."

Rather moaned softly.

Simultaneously, both men dropped to their knees. Even
in the poor light, they could see blood seeping out of the
butler's shoulder. Barnes pulled the man's coat away from
him. "He's bleeding, sir. But it doesn't look too bad."

Rather lifted his hand and gestured toward the door.
"Go after her. I'll be all right. Hurry. In the park. Go,
go. I'll be fine."

Barnes and Witherspoon looked at each other for a split
second and then raced out. They flew back the way they'd
come. Witherspoon was behind the constable by a nose
as they sprinted down the steps and leapt onto the pave-

ment. Their prey had reached the entrance to the park by
the time they cleared the walkway and dashed into the
road.

"Halt in the name of the law," Witherspoon cried. But
the figure kept on running, hurtling through the gate and
heading straight for the bridge.

"Stop, I tell you," the inspector cried. His breath was
coming in short, hard gasps and beside him, he could hear
the constable wheezing as they gave chase.

She was fast, so fast that Witherspoon was afraid they'd
never catch up and the suspect would make it across the
canal bridge and into the park, disappearing into the night.

All of a sudden, another figure leapt out from the shadows of the bridge and hurled itself at the fleeing criminal.

There was a scream of rage and pain as the two shapes
merged for an istant before crashing against the pavement
with a loud thud.

Witherspoon and Barnes skidded to a halt beside the
struggling bodies. "Ow . . ." one of them cried just as the
constable waded in and grabbed him by the scruff of his
neck. With surprising strength, he flung him toward the
inspector, who surprised himself by getting a grip on the
fellow's arm. Then the constable yanked other one to his
feet.

"Egads," Witherspoon cried as he drug his captive
closer to the lamplight. "Wiggins?"

"Blow your whistle, sir," Barnes cried as he lugged
his struggling prisoner toward the lamp. "We need help.
There's coppers on patrol in the park."

"Yes, right." The inspector pulled his whistle out of
his pocket and blew hard on it several times. Immediately,
the answering call of another whistle rent the air and the
faint sound of pounding footsteps echoed in the night.

Barnes finally managed to manuever his captive into

the small circle of light cast by the lamp. Witherspoon
gasped. "Good gracious. It's Theodora Vaughan."

Dressed in an ill-fitting pair of trousers and a man's
jacket, she glared at him coldly from beneath the porkpie
cap pulled low over her head.

"This is an outrage, Inspector," she said haughtily.
"Can't one take a walk in a park without being set upon
by ruffians?" She jerked her head toward Wiggins and
then slapped at the constable's hands as he reached into
her jacket pocket. "Stop that, you idiot . . ."

"I'm not a ruffian," Wiggins yelped. "And you was
runnin' from the law."

"Here's the gun, sir," Barnes said, holding up a derringer he pulled out of her jacket. "It's still warm."

They heard footsteps pounding across the bridge. Two
police constables were coming towards them at a fast run.

Witherspoon didn't quite understand what was going
on, but he did know that this woman whom he'd so admired had tried to murder a man tonight. "Theodora
Vaughan," he said somberly, "you're under arrest for the
attempted murder of Mr. Rather."

"I bet she killed Mr. 'inchley too," Wiggins added.

Theodora Vaughan said nothing for a moment. Then
she smiled slowly, triumphantly. "Try to prove it, Inspector."

"I don't think that will be very hard, Miss Vaughan,"
he said. "Your bullet hasn't killed the man. I'm sure he'll
be quite able to testify against you."

She laughed. "Then it will be his word against mine,
won't it? Remember this, Inspector: I'm Theodora
Vaughan, one of the greatest actresses of the English theatre, and I can assure you, when I'm in the dock at the
Old Bailey, I'll make you look a fool. I shall give a performance of a lifetime."

*   *   *

"All this waitin' is goin' to drive me plum loco," Luty snapped. "It's been hours since them three left. What the dickens is takin' so long?"

"I don't know," Mrs. Jeffries said, her expression worried. She prayed she hadn't been wrong. But as the clock hands moved, she was beginning to think she'd made a terrible mistake.

Betsy leapt to her feet as they heard the back door opening. "That's them now," she cried, dashing to the stove and putting the kettle on to boil.

Smythe and Hatchet hurried into the room. Fred jumped up, wagged his tail a few times and tried to butt Smythe on the knees. "Down, boy," the coachman said, giving him a quick pat.

"What happened?" Mrs. Jeffries cried.

"Where's Wiggins?" Mrs. Goodge yelped.

"About time someone got back here," Luty grumbled.

"Are you all right?" Betsy asked anxiously, her gaze fixed on Smythe. "I've got the kettle on for tea."

"We're fine," Hatchet assured them as he sat down. "So is Wiggins"—he grinned—"but I expect the young man will have to do some fast talking when he gets to the station."

"You mean the inspector spotted him?" Luty snapped.

Hatchet grinned broadly. "You could say that. He was instrumental in capturing Theodora Vaughan. One could also say, had it not been for Wiggins, she might have made her escape."

"Oh, dear." Mrs. Jeffries frowned. "Tell us what happened. Were we in time?"

"Almost," Smythe said. "She did shoot the butler, but like Luty said, she's not a good shot and she only wounded him. The coppers were takin' 'im to 'ospital when I left to come back 'ere. I overheard one of 'em say it was only a flesh wound. 'E'll be all right. He'll be able to testify against Theodora Vaughan.''

Mrs. Jeffries sagged in relief. "Thank God." She'd never have forgiven herself if that man had been killed.

"I did like ya said, Mrs. J.," Smythe continued, "and we was lucky you sussed it out when ya did. I got to the Vaughan 'ouse just in time to see her nippin' out the back door. She was dressed in boy's clothes." He paused to toss a quick smile of thanks at Betsy as she set a mug of tea in front of him. "I followed 'er to 'inchley's house, saw her go inside and then a minute later, I 'eard the shot. Bloomin' Ada, I didn't know what to do! But just then, the inspector and Constable Barnes showed up. They 'eard the shot too and went barrelin' inside. Then, just a few seconds after they'd gone in, she comes flyin' out and takes off across the road toward the park.''

"I, too, didn't know what to do at that point," Hatchet added. "As Mrs. Jeffries had instructed, I was keeping watch on the Hinchley house from across the street. I saw her go in, and before I could gather my wits about me, I saw a hansom draw up and the inspector and Constable Barnes got out." His brows drew together. "At that point, I'd no idea what was going to happen. About then, the shot rang out and everything moved so quickly after that I didn't have time to do anything.''

"But she was arrested?" Mrs. Goodge asked.

"She were nicked, all right." Smythe grinned. "You'da been right proud of Wiggins. If 'e 'adn't come flyin' out of the shadows and brought 'er down before she crossed that bridge and disappeared into the park, there's a good chance she'd have gotten away.''

"Good fer Wiggins," Luty cried. Then a worried frown crossed her face. "I hope he's got enough sense to spin some kind of yarn for the inspector. Otherwise, we're all in trouble.''

Mrs. Jeffries had the same concern. "He's a very bright young man," she said. "I'm sure he'll think of something.''

Mrs. Goodge leaned toward the housekeeper. "Before the inspector gets back, are you goin' to tell us how you figured it out?''

"There may not be time," Mrs. Jeffries said uneasily.

"You've plenty of time. The inspector will be tied up for hours," Hatchet interjected.

"All right." She took a deep breath and tried to force herself to relax. Thank goodness she had been right about this case. "As I said," she began, "it was when Lady Cannonberry made those remarks about her sister-in-law this afternoon that I realized the truth. We'd all assumed the motive for Hinchley's murder was to stop him from publicly reviewing Edmund Delaney's play. Yet as Ruth talked, I realized that there was another motive that had been apparent all along.''

"Doesn't seem that apparent to me," the cook complained.

"Nor to me until today," Mrs. Jeffries agreed. "But as Ruth told me about the outrageous things her sister-in-law had done to try to get her young man back, I saw the similarities between that young woman's behaviour and the way Hinchley acted. Then I realized the truth. Hinchley was still infatuated with Delaney. That's why he changed his will naming Delaney as heir before he left for the United States. He might have hated Delaney for rejecting him, but the sad truth was he had no one else. Hinchley still loved Delaney enough so that he wanted him to have his property in the event something happened to him while he was away. Once I looked at the case from that point of view, it was quite simple.''

''I still don't get it,'' Betsy said, echoing the confusion the rest of them felt. ''Even if Hinchley was in love with Delaney, why would that make Theodora Vaughan hate him enough to kill him? Delaney had left Hinchley over a year ago.''

''I know,'' Mrs. Jeffries replied. ''That's one of the reasons I didn't see it until it was almost too late. Theodora Vaughan didn't kill Hinchley because she hated him, though I expect she did. She murdered him for money. The money Edmund Delaney was going to inherit when Hinchley died. Remember, she planned to be Delaney's wife. I expect she realized that once she and Delaney were actually man and wife, Hinchley would finally give up and disinherit Delaney. She didn't want to lose over a hundred thousand pounds.''

''Money?'' Luty exclaimed. ''But how did she know that Hinchley had left his fortune to Delaney?''

''Hinchley told her,'' Mrs. Jeffries explained. ''According to what Oliver told Betsy, Theodora Vaughan was in a rage after talking to a small man at the train station on Saturday. That man was Ogden Hinchley. He wasn't a subtle person; I expect he told Theodora Vaughan quite plainly that he'd made Delaney his heir and that he was going to do everything in his power to win Delaney back. More important, I suspect he tormented her about Delaney's play. You see, I'm quite sure he'd come back for the sole purpose of reviewing it and I'm equally certain he knew it wasn't very good. But most important, Theodora Vaughan had invested a goodly amount of money in that play. If Hinchley managed to close it down, not only would her lover be disgraced, but she'd be quite poor.

Perhaps even bankrupt. Beautiful as she is, she's a number of years older than Delaney. With no money of her own, I expect she was worried that she wouldn't be able to keep Delaney.''

''But how would Hinchley know that the play was so awful if he was in New York?'' Hatchet asked.

''From Trevor Remington. Remember, supposedly Remington and Hinchley had a quarrel about money before Hinchley left for America,'' Mrs. Jeffries clarified. ''Lilly told Betsy that. I'd quite forgotten it until yesterday.''

''Ah, I see.'' Hatchet nodded in understanding. ''You think that Hinchley's been paying Remington all along.''

''Correct. I also think the reason there was a problem with Theodora Vaughan obtaining her divorce from Remington might have also been Hinchley's doing.''

''How could 'e do that?'' Smythe asked. ''They got the divorce in America.''

''He coulda done it,'' Luty interjected. ''We don't know what state issued the divorce decree. All Remington woulda had to do was claim he lost the papers or not signed something. Some states have a waitin' period between goin' to court and gettin' the divorce.''

''But what was Remington gettin' paid for?'' Mrs. Goodge wailed. ''I still don't understand.''

''For keeping Hinchley informed,'' Mrs. Jeffries said. ''As long as Delaney and Theodora Vaughan weren't married, Hinchley had hopes of winning him back. But when her American lawyers managed to get the decree despite Remington's lack of cooperation, Hinchley took the first ship back from America. By this time, Hinchley had probably learned from Remington that Delaney's play was being produced and that it wasn't very good. As luck would have it, Hinchley ran into Theodora Vaughan at the train station. Actually, I'm not so sure that meeting was accidental or whether he arranged to run into her. We don't know for certain precisely what day he arrived back from New York, but it's not particularly important whether he met her accidentally or on purpose—he accomplished what he'd set out to do. He couldn't stop himself from taunting the woman, thereby sealing his own death warrant.''

"But 'ow did you suss out the way she'd done it?" Smythe asked.

Mrs. Jeffries smiled. "I didn't, not until it was almost too late. But the evidence was right there. Remember when Wiggins told us about Rose, Theodora's maid, taking that case of clothes to the theatre? There were boys' clothes inside. Velvet and silk, the same kind of clothes the lad who'd brought the note to the brothel on Lisle street wore. Rose also told Wiggins that Theodora didn't do 'trouser parts' anymore.''

"What's that?" Mrs. Goodge asked grumpily. She was a bit put out that she hadn't figured any of it out and she still wasn't sure she understood it.

"It's a woman playing a boy's role in a play," the housekeeper explained. "Theodora Vaughan got rid of those clothes because they were evidence. She'd worn them the night of the murder. She'd dressed as a boy to take that note to the brothel . . .''

"But how did she get to the Hinchley house?" Luty interrupted.

"She took a hansom.''

"But Smythe talked to all the cabbies and none of them remembers pickin' up a boy that night.''

"I know 'ow she did it." Smythe grinned. "The same

way she did it tonight. she hitched a ride by 'angin' on the back. Bloomin' good at it she was too—hopped right on like she'd been doin' it all 'er life.''

"Precisely," Mrs. Jeffries agreed. "Anyway, she knew all about Hinchley's . . . uh . . . habits, so when she realized he was determined to ruin the play and in turn, ruin her, she decided to kill him." She shook her head in disgust. "I should have realized it when the inspector told us she'd left the theatre right after the performance that night. She hadn't even taken off her makeup. Instead, she went home, put on boys' clothes and a dark-haired wig. Dressed as a boy, she went to Lisle Street. The last thing she wanted was for a male prostitute to show up while she was committing murder. Then she went to Hinchley's and let herself in the side door, which she knew would be unlocked. I expect his being in the bathtub was sheer luck.''

"You don't think she planned on drowning him?" Betsy queried.

"No, I think she was going to shoot him. But unluckily for him, he was in the bath. She walked up, grabbed his ankles and pulled him under. Unfortunately for her, Rather hadn't gone to bed. Instead, he came in and caught her red-handed."

"But why did he carry the body to the canal?" Hatchet asked. "Why didn't he call the police?"

Mrs. Jeffries shrugged. "From what the inspector told me, Rather wasn't particularly fond of his employer. I expect Theodora Vaughan offered him money. Probably the money to go to America and start a new life."

"I wonder whose idea it was to toss the body in the canal?" Luty asked.

"Probably Theodora Vaughan's," Mrs. Jeffries guessed. "Once Rather did that, once he willingly participated, he was then an accomplice. I think she was hoping that act would buy his silence.''

''But if she'd paid him,'' Betsy asked, ''why did she try to kill him tonight?''

''Because I expect he wanted more. By this time, she'd realized that accomplice or not, Rather could blackmail her for the rest of her life.''

''So she did it for money,'' Luty muttered. ''Greed.''

''And for love,'' Mrs. Jeffries added. ''I think she really did love Edmund Delaney. Even knowing his play wasn't very good, she helped him get it produced on the stage.''

From outside, they heard the rattle of a hansom pull up in front of the house. Fred leapt to his feet and ran for the stairs. ''That'll be the inspector and Wiggins,'' Mrs. Jeffries said.

Luty and Hatchet were already up and scurrying toward the back door. ''We'll be back tomorrow for the rest of the details,'' Luty called over her shoulder.

Smythe, Betsy, and Mrs. Goodge started to get up too, but Mrs. Jeffries waved them back into their chairs. ''No, stay here. Wiggins might need a bit of moral support. It'll look better if the inspector sees we were all concerned for him.''

The inspector and Wiggins came into the kitchen just as the back door shut behind Luty and Hatchet. Fred, who'd followed them into the back hall to say goodbye, trotted in, spotted the newcomers and bounded over to greet them, his tail wagging frantically as he bounced between his two favorite people.

''Gracious,'' Witherspoon said as he took in everyone sitting at the table, ''you shouldn't have waited up for me.''

''We were concerned, sir,'' Mrs. Jeffries said. ''When

226 Emily Brightwell

that girl arrived here with the note and then Wiggins didn't come right back from taking it to you, we feared something was amiss.''

''Well, I'm very touched,'' the inspector said. He spotted the teapot. ''I say, is there more of that?''

The housekeeper quickly poured him a cup and put it in front of the chair that Luty had just vacated. ''Do sit down and tell us what happened, sir.''

''Thank you, Mrs. Jeffries.'' Witherspoon sat down. ''Now, sit down, Wiggins, and stop your sulking. I didn't mean to be sharp with you earlier, but you could have been hurt tonight. You were very, very brave and I'm quite proud of you, but still it was a foolish thing to do. I'd never forgive myself if something happened to you.''

''What happened?'' Mrs. Jeffries asked, though she knew perfectly well exactly what had happened.

''Well.'' Witherspoon told them what they already knew. But all of them played their parts perfectly as he spun his tale.

Mrs. Goodge clucked her tongue, Betsy shook her head in disbelief, Smythe occasionally mumbled something under his breath and Mrs. Jeffries vacillated between sympathetic glances and stern frowns.

When he'd finished, Mrs. Jeffries asked, ''Does she really think she'll convince a jury she's innocent?''

Witherspoon shrugged. ''She'll try. But with the physical evidence against her and Rather's testimony, I don't think she'll succeed.''

''What about Rather, then?'' Betsy asked. ''Is he bein' charged?''

''No, he's agreed to turn Queen's Evidence,'' Witherspoon explained. ''In exchange for testifying against her, he won't be charged as an accomplice.''

After a few more questions, Betsy, Smythe and Mrs.

Goodge excused themselves. Wiggins took Fred out for a brief visit to the gardens. As the boy and the dog disappeared down the hall, the inspector turned to Mrs. Jeffries, a concerned frown on his face. "Honestly, Mrs. Jeffries, I don't know what to do. I didn't like to be sharp with Wiggins, but he took a terrible risk tonight."

"He only wanted to help you, sir," she replied hesitantly. As she didn't quite know what story Wiggins had cooked up to explain his presence at the Hinchley house, she wasn't sure what to say.

"That's why I feel so responsible." Witherspoon clucked his tongue. "Gracious, the lad jumped on the back of our hansom, followed me all the way there and then leapt upon an armed killer. It was very brave of the boy, but I'd never have forgiven myself if he'd been shot. Gracious, what if she'd been holding that wretched derringer instead of carrying it in her jacket? Egads, it could even have gone off in the struggle."

"Did he tell you why he'd followed you, sir?"

"That's what I wanted to talk to you about." Witherspoon glanced toward the back hall to make sure Wiggins was still out. "I really must ask you to be more careful about loaning him books, Mrs. Jeffries."

"Books, sir?"

"I think it's wonderful the way you're encouraging him to read. He is, after all, quite a bright lad. But some of them have the most dreadful effect on him. He told me he'd been reading some poem by that American fellow, Mr. Edgar Allan Poe."

"Edgar Allan Poe?"

"Yes, some poem about a blackbird . . . no, no, I tell a lie, it's not about a blackbird, it's a raven. Anyway"— Witherspoon waved impatiently—"the point is, I gather it's quite a gloomy piece with this bird carping on and on

about 'nevermore' or some such thing. There's a dead
woman in it as well and the bird's going on and on and
on about this 'nevermore.' " He shrugged helplessly.
"Poor Wiggins told me this poem so upset him that when
he brought that note around to the Yard this evening, he
was quite sure he'd never see me again. That's why he
followed me. Honestly, Mrs. Jeffries, I've no idea what
to do. I'm touched by his devotion, but he mustn't ever,
ever, take such risks. You will speak to him, won't you?
Tell him not to take poetry so seriously." He yawned and
rose slowly to his feet.

"I'll have a word with him in the morning, sir," she
promised. She'd fix him a special breakfast too, she told
herself. "By the way, sir, Lady Cannonberry's back from
the country."

Tired as he was, Witherspoon positively beamed.
"That's wonderful. Shall we invite her round for tea tomorrow?"

"I expect she'll be happy to drop by," Mrs. Jeffries
said as she got to her feet and picked up the teapot. Ruth
would probably be here before breakfast demanding to
know everything. "You'd better get some rest, sir."

"Good night, Mrs. Jeffries, and do see that Wiggins is
all right, will you?"

"Of course, sir," she called as he headed for the stairs.

Wiggins and Fred came in a few minutes later. He
stopped by the door and grinned at her.

She arched an eyebrow. "Edgar Allan Poe?"

"I was right pleased with myself for thinkin' of that so
quick. Good thing I'd read that poem."

"Wiggins," she replied, "you missed your true calling.
You should have been an actor. You convinced him completely."

"Nah, wouldn't want to be one of them," he said.

"Too borin' by 'alf. But I do think maybe I'll try my 'and at spinnin' tales. I think I might be right good at it."

"I think," she replied sincerely, "you'll be excellent at it. As a matter of fact, you'll do us proud."